THE BUSIEST PLACE YOU KNOW

A GREEN BRANCH NOVEL

ALLISON DEROSIA

ISBN 979-8-218-73257-8 (Paperback)

Cover design by Austin Drake | Bottle Cap Creative

Printed in the United States of America

allisonderosia.com

For my mom and dad.
Thank you for believing in me — especially when I didn't.

CONTENT WARNING

This story mentions anxiety, parental and spousal infidelity, cancer, Alzheimer's, suicide, and loss of a parent. Read with caution.

Though we bury ourselves in the dirt now, come spring, we will have roots in what once covered us, and a view from much higher up.
—Wells Stevens, *Honeycomb*

1

NOW

The rain whips against my windows, begging me to stay inside, but I'm already sliding on my shoes and cursing myself for ever joining a book club that requires me to leave the apartment. Chicago in the fall is exactly what anyone expects out of a Midwest city. Wet. Damp. Gray.

I flip out the light and grab the book we were supposed to be reading off the counter.

The rain continues to pelt off the windows as the driver zips through the city and all but kicks me to the curb when we get to the bookstore. I hurry inside with my jacket over my head, forcing myself to not look up at the apartment above the bookstore, knowing it would make me even more late. And even more sad.

Ford's Books is the first bookstore I wandered into when I moved here a year ago. Back then, the only sign of a friend was my agent. So when I saw the sign in Ford's window advertising a book club, I was desperate enough for human connection that I joined.

"Lauren, are you good? We almost started without you." The head of the book club and owner of the bookstore itself, Elyse

Ford, is standing with a fresh bottle of wine under her arm and big glasses in her hand. She reaches over, flips the sign to "Closed," and locks the door behind me.

"Sorry. You know. Traffic and the weather." I shrug and take in the smells of the paper and whatever earthy candle is burning. Traffic and weather are always excuses to blame in the city. If not the traffic, then the weather. If it's sunny, there are extra people outside. If it's storming, people don't watch where they're going. It's a safe bet. And it's Friday. You can always blame Friday.

In front of the shop's big front window is where Elyse and her husband have a couple of leather couches and antique chairs turned toward a fake fireplace. The bookshelves are a mismatched collection of sizes and woods.

With the thunder beginning to roar outside and the flickering candle on the side table, I'm glad I came.

Elyse said the shop has been nothing but a bookstore for generations. Different names and different owners, but somehow, always a bookstore. The dark, towering shelves make it feel more like an Ivy League dean's office, with drooping plants cascading down the shelves. Books from now and long ago fill every open space the eye can find. Picture frames of unknown faces Elyse claims to have rescued from flea markets hang on the few bare spots of the walls.

"Well, come in! Don't just stand there. We have wine, and Faye brought pie." Elyse waves me over.

Her smile is quickly followed by a wink so brief I almost miss it. I always thought she was meant to be a teacher with that gift of helping anyone know they're seen. A gift I didn't have when I was a teacher. I hang my jacket on the old brass coatrack, dry my shoes on the rug, and join them.

Faye, the tall, stick-straight fairy of a girl, cuts into her pie, demanding for me to come try a piece. Nikki, Faye's sister, with the same slick hair but darker eyes, is curled up with a cup of coffee on the far side of the couch.

"So." Elyse sits. "What did we think of the book?"

"Can we talk about the girl's brother?" Faye says as she hands me a piece. "I mean, I want a book about *him*. He's so hot."

Nikki sputters a laugh from her quiet little corner. "You're joking. Right?"

"I'm serious. Listen to this." She brings her quarter of the pie to her seat and flips open to a dog-eared page. "'Robby runs a hand through his hair, his eyes falling on Hallie like it was the first time he saw her, like they weren't best friends since they were in diapers. He looked at her like he knew she was the only thing of any real worth to ever exist.' I mean, *come on*. How can the author give us that and not expect us to want more? They had more chemistry than the main characters."

"Huh." Elyse flips open her book now. "I didn't even really think about that. You're, like, kinda right? Maybe?"

"I don't know. I don't think I would want to read about him; he's pretty awful." Nikki shrugs.

"It's character development," Faye insists. "It's proof that everything his sister has gone through with her love has rubbed off on him. He learned that maybe love isn't so bad."

We spin in conversation—well, they do—and I listen. The thunder rolls on and the lights continue to flicker. I don't admit that I haven't read the book. I'm happy to listen and to be out of my own brain for a little while.

"Babe!" Elyse calls back to shelves. "Can you bring the next bottle of wine out?"

Cal Ford, her husband and handyman of the shop, pops his head in from the back hallway.

"If you guys are already on your second bottle, then we may need to set up some pillows and blankets on the floor. I'm not letting you guys find your way home in the rain," he says.

His messy hair is pulled back into a bun, and tattoos cover both of his forearms. I catch Elyse gazing up at him with a dreamy look in her eyes.

"Like the book!" Faye shouts.

Cal looks a bit alarmed at the sudden outburst but then eyes his wife for an explanation.

"In the book, the love interest owns a bookshop, and the girl comes over. They drink too much wine and end up having sex on the floor in front of the mystery and thriller section."

"Oh God." Cal shakes his head as he walks back toward the office, then shouts from the hallway, "This is why I don't join the book club."

Elyse rolls her eyes once he's out of earshot. "As if we haven't done that here."

Faye blushes a bright shade of red and slaps her hand over her mouth. Nikki throws her head back, laughing. And I just take it in. Happy to be included, to be able to sit here and blend into the couch, watching it all unfold.

"Lauren, I still think your book is better." Nikki shrugs. "If I am going to be forced to read about two people falling in love, then well . . . it better be written by you."

"Agreed," Elyse adds very matter-of-factly.

"Well, my next one isn't so love-y," I tell them, leaving out how sharp and pointed the book I have spent the past nine months writing is. The romance, though there, has been laced with heartbreak. I also don't tell them how I haven't felt any love worth writing about.

"When will it be out?" Faye leans forward, her wide eyes full of excitement. Hope.

Whenever my publisher decides to sign my new deal and when I can get a new editor to edit it. But to her I say, "I'm hoping for next year."

Thunder roars again, and the lights flicker once more before blinking out completely. The sound of the building powering down fills the air. Then nothing. Pure silence. A silence I don't even realize existed anymore. And I'm just thankful I don't need to continue that conversation.

"This damn old building," Elyse mumbles through the dark. The candle is not doing enough to keep up. She pops up and looks out the window. "The other side of the street is still fully lit."

"Let's go to Ninety-Seven's," Faye suggests. "They're on the other side of the street, right?"

And without any further conversation, we are all in tow, running through the rain. Our jackets do a horrible job of keeping us dry while our feet splash through puddles. They are laughing despite it all.

"Are you okay?" Faye asks me as we run across the crosswalk.

"What?" I ask back, pretending to not know what she means.

"Are you okay? You've been quiet tonight." We make it to the other side, and Ninety-Seven's is up one more block. "You've been quiet for the past couple months, really."

"Yeah, you know," I call over to her, "getting this next book ready has been tricky. It's all I can think about most days."

She offers me a small smile and a nod, not convinced with my story, but she doesn't push it any further. Of course, the lie is rooted in truth. But it's just a fraction of the entire truth.

As we step inside Ninety-Seven's restaurant, the hostesses at the front desk look alarmed at the sight of us.

"Table for four," Elyse announces and wrings out her hair onto the doormat.

The shorter of the girls, in her black uniform with a white tie, gives a quick, disapproving glance and then leads us through the dimly lit restaurant back to the tables near the bar. Ones we have always joked were for the drunks who would disrupt the rest of the diners.

Ninety-Seven's is an upscale Italian place, with no TV in sight and a live string quartet as a permanent fixture in the corner. The choppy floor plan gives insight into the home that was once here. And each room is labeled as such. The Foyer. The Sitting Room. The Ballroom.

"The waiter will be with you soon," the woman says and hurries away, leaving us in the Butler's Pantry.

Elyse uses the cloth napkin to finish drying out her hair, then drops it before grabbing Nikki's. "Cal tried calling the landlord last time the power went out, said he's working on it. But he's also said he was working on it the time we called before that, too. The store and both apartments upstairs lose power any time there's a storm."

The apartment upstairs. I reach for the water pitcher in the center of the table, flip over my glass, fill it, and chug it all down. There are two apartments over Ford's, one of which belongs to Elyse and Cal.

The waitress comes around, and Elyse orders a bottle of wine for the table. Faye pulls the book back out and begins to read another romantic excerpt that makes her melt.

"Overall, I think the book sucked." Nikki shrugs once she's finished. "I think the characters were boring. And the twist? You could see it coming a mile away."

Faye shakes her head. "I disagree. Sure, it wasn't the *best* book I have ever read, but it's way better than that horror book about the stalker we read two months ago."

"Nope." Nikki pops the "p."

"Okay, well, what *did* we like about this book then?" Elyse cuts in. "Everyone say something positive about it and one negative thing."

"I liked the brother. I think he was interesting and that he deserves his own book. I didn't like that the main character didn't ever speak to her mom again. I think that should have been more important to her character development," Faye says.

The waitress returns with the wine and pours us each a half glass. Faye motions for her to pour more.

"I like that she didn't speak to her mom again; I think it made it more real. You know? So many books fix every problem the character has within the book's timeline of, like, six months. I like that the author left that to still be solved later. But I do agree. The brother was far more interesting than the main girl." Elyse adds, "Lauren, what do you think?"

I glance up at their expectant faces and shrug. "It was good."

Their eyes all fall on me.

"Why did the girl leave her job at the cemetery?" Nikki questions.

"Because it's too depressing." I sip from my glass.

They all fall into a fit of laughter. "She never worked at a cemetery. You didn't read it!"

I can't fight the smile. "No, I forgot."

That's a lie too. I just haven't been able to get myself to read many books these days.

We talk for a bit longer, but soon everyone starts taking their leave. Elyse goes back home to Cal to wait for the power. Nikki and Faye decide to meet some friends at a bar and try their luck at getting into Kensington Club. I opt out, promising I'm just tired, and make a pit stop to the bathroom once the tab is paid.

The bathroom is labeled as the Office. It has heavy oak walls and warmly lit sconces on the walls, leaving very little light in the room. I wash my hands, and as I walk back, I spot the bar off to the left in a room labeled as the Conservatory. It houses large windows and a long, heavy wooden bar. My eyes land on the only open spot. No better place to hide. I rub the tender scar on my hand and slide onto the leather stool, and rest my arms on the worn, padded edge. The person next to me does a double take, but I keep my eyes trained forward, avoiding any forced conversation. The bartender spots me and steps over, polishing a glass.

"Your house white," the voice next to me says before I even had a chance to speak.

I know that voice.

The bartender picks up a bottle and begins to pour, then hands the glass to the man. I know those hands that slide the glass of white down to me. The ones that now drop some cash and then push off the counter.

I look and try to get a glimpse of his face to be sure, but his hair, that freckle on his neck, him sliding a glass of wine down to me. It all gives him away.

"Rhett." I find his name coming out of my mouth before I can even think to stop it. "Wait. Stay."

2

NOW

Rhett Atwood is standing there with a storm in his eyes. His jaw hasn't been shaven in days—weeks, maybe—and my eyes take stock of his shoulders, his arms, his dark hair. All still so him. Yet all so different.

He opens his mouth to say something. But nothing comes out. When he reaches for his jacket, I know he's leaving. Again.

His glass of red wine sits still full on the bar, so I make a foolish decision.

"Finish your glass," I say quickly.

Though I should *know* better. I guess I am just unable to *do* better in this moment.

"Lauren." His voice is gruff and low. I hadn't even realized until now just how much I missed hearing my name on his lips. It's like an old favorite song coming on the radio. The nostalgia is sweet and sad at the same time.

"Please," I plead softly. "I hate your wine, but if you leave right now, I will drink yours and mine."

I strike a chord. He stifles a smile, and after a moment of thought, he drags his hand down over his face and slides back into the stool with his coat still on. We both pick up our glasses, chug them, and all but slam them back down.

"What are you doing on a Friday night at Ninety-Seven's by yourself?" I ask.

He chews on the inside of this cheek and turns to look at me carefully. His sad green eyes land on mine, then they travel down my arms and to my elbows resting on the padded edge.

"If you ever want to be alone . . ." he begins.

"Go to the busiest place you know," I finish, a small, ironic laugh breaking from me.

It's the first line in *Golden Hour*. The line he always did say was his favorite.

"How is your next manuscript coming along?" He asks like he is asking about the weather in my hometown. Like it isn't the entire axis around which my life revolves.

"I just finished it. Editing starts soon."

"Do you have an editor?"

I instantly regret asking him to sit. I regret playing it cool. Because we are nothing of the sort. Not anymore.

"You can't quit being my editor, then ask about the new one," I tell him. My words come out cold and pointed.

"Okay." He keeps his voice steady. "Then how are Myranda and Runclave? Have they hooked up yet?"

He looks at me, and he's smiling. An actual humored smile. I shake my head, fighting my own smile.

"She's still Myranda, and he's still Charles. I'm sure they have. There's no getting over that for her, I'm sure," I say and immediately am struck with the irony of the statement. Rhett and I sit there, electricity buzzing between us. So much so that I almost expect the lights to flicker in competition. But I talk myself out of saying anything while he sits, watching my hands fiddle with my glass.

"You can say it." He finally breaks the silence.

"Say what?"

He scoffs and rubs a hand over his face. "Lauren."

I take in a shaky breath and really look at him. He looks good. His jaw seems softer now. His hair is longer than even last year. His green eyes still seem to know more than they let on. Shoulders and body — stronger.

Then it slips out. "You never called."

"You asked me to not—"

"You had chances before that to reach out. You could have, and you didn't."

"It's complicated . . . "

Bullshit. I stand and toss some more money onto the counter, just adding to Rhett's money still sitting there.

"I'm glad to hear you got my package in the mail," I snap. The only way he would have known I asked him to not call was if he got my package in the mail with the copy of my book.

"Lauren—" He follows me through the crowded restaurant while curious eyes watch and nosy ears listen.

I try to secure the fastest route through the crowded tables until he and I spill out onto the sidewalk. The bitter chill in the air nearly knocks the wind from my lungs. The rain has subsided into a light drizzle, and lightning stretches horizontally across the sky and is followed by low rumbles.

I turn back to face him, neither of us having the words. Why, even after all this time, do I still feel the way I do? Why do his arms still look like they're where I am supposed to be right now? Those emotions I had effectively bottled up, and played victim to, begin to bubble and burst the top that I screwed on really fucking tight.

My chest heaves with heavy breaths that I count. I count the times he blinks the rain away. I count the moments he could say something, anything. I count the times he lets each of them pass. So I turn and wave my arm, trying to hail a taxi. I have never even hailed a damn taxi. I was always too scared, and now I'm cursing myself for never being brave enough.

Rhett steps in front of me as I try to wave at every yellow car that passes by, the rain falling harder now, blurring what is a taxi and what happens to be yellow.

"Lauren, please." His voice grabs my attention, and my arm falls to my side. "Let me buy you a drink, anywhere but here. Please. I am going back home tonight, but—"

"Rhett." I shake my head like it will clear the fog from my head. "You know I can't."

He drags a hand over his face again, then looks around like he is looking for some magical way to fix this. And part of me prays he would. Or could.

I wave again at the uneasy onset of traffic when God parts the sea, and a taxi pulls over as the clouds open wider over us. I give him a curt nod before slipping into the back seat and pull the door shut behind me. I have never been more grateful for the driver's borderline refusal for conversation. Because I know if I were to open my mouth, I would tell him to turn around.

I tell myself to not look back. I try to, at least. But I turn anyway and watch Rhett with his hands clasped behind his head. A piece of hair grazes his cheek as he stands in the rain. One quick turn at the stoplight and he's gone. And I'm lost again among millions of people. Alone in the busiest place I know.

3

NOW

The late heat of September seems to linger between the skyscrapers as I trudge under construction scaffoldings and around garbage the trucks have yet to collect. The smell of the black tar between the cracks in the road radiates and burns my nose. Sunlight reflects off the near-standstill traffic as I reprimand myself first, for leaving my sunglasses at the apartment. And then again, for even leaving the apartment at all on a Monday. I should have opted for a phone call. Or even a text, honestly. Maybe I can go back home and blame it being Monday. You can always blame Monday.

As I pass through crosswalks, around a horde of schoolchildren and people on their lunch breaks, I am struck at the insignificance of me. And them. People going about their lives, unimpressed by the decades-old infrastructure around them, not charmed by the brass doorways. Or the art spray-painted on brick walls that gets no more than a passing glance.

When I came here as a child—the few times I did—it seemed as if everything stretched so endlessly into the sky above me, the clouds seemed to dance with the top floors of these buildings. It looked nothing like my small Illinois hometown, where the biggest building was a big, ugly brown apartment building on the other side of town that stood floors above everything else.

But what seemed so new and fresh then now seems mundane and boring. The brass-trimmed building that would have blown the socks off six-year-old me, I now know to be a senior apartment complex. Or the marble-columned building that once housed a bank now has been turned into an ill-performing guidance center.

Stepping around a woman and her yappy dog, I narrowly miss the man on his phone, hurrying by just as quickly as I am. We exchange less than a glance at each other. My mind still can't move past seeing Rhett last night. I can't move past his fingers on his glass, his curled hair, his shoulders squarely next to mine, his hands desperately clutched behind his head as my taxi drove away.

I called my sister Hannah the moment I got home last night. She answered on the first ring and told me to pour myself a glass of wine and then tell her everything. I told her about the book club. Walking up to Ford's bookstore in the rain, seeing Rhett's darkened window up next to Elyse and Cal's. Then how I sat at the bar and he was there next to me. And how he slid a glass of wine to me and how I asked him to stay. By the time I finished telling her everything, I had drunk way too much wine, and now I can't even recall the advice she gave me.

"Watch it," a voice spits as I dodge a lady coming straight at me. My mind isn't here. Instead, it is all over the memory of Rhett's arms and his eyes, and how angry I am that I can't let them go. Or that I don't even really want to.

These streets once seemed like a backward maze and the only way through was with the GPS on my phone. Now I take a left along another nondescript building, making a point to not run into anyone else, and jog at the end of the crosswalk light to make it across. All the while my phone stays in my pocket.

Just ahead stands the building that contains the Runclave Publishing offices. It's awfully tall and awfully imposing. When I first visited, before I even moved here, I was coming to meet Myranda and Charles Runclave Jr., the new man in charge at Runclave Publishing. His father before him, as he claims, built the place from the ground up. Runclave Jr. tells of how their family went from poverty to the Ivy League. How he went from going to inner-city public schools to attending Northwestern on an academic scholarship (despite his father's generous donation to their business department). How his fraternity is what encouraged him to follow his dream and follow in his dad's foot-steps of taking over the family business. He joked, that first meeting, how maybe he and King Charles had a lot in common. Waiting for someone's last breath to claim the throne and then being too busy to shed a tear afterward because, well, he has a kingdom to run.

I had rolled my eyes then, and I roll them now as I prepare to hear whatever he has to say. The man who keeps his nose in every aspect of his company. And my work.

"Just a check-in meeting, going over numbers and whatnot," Myranda had promised when she said Runclave wanted to meet. I had all but hung up on her when she told me that. Sure, I knew the numbers were looking pretty good. My follower counts are trending steadily upward and excitement around my next book is growing. However, confrontation has never been my thing. Positive or negative.

My stomach churns at the thought of this meeting, and it sinks as the elevator flies me up past the law offices and insur-ance agents, until I step out into the marble lobby of Runclave Publishing House. Everything black and sharp. The name *Runclave* is on a massive metal plaque above the reception desk.

The young girl sitting behind the desk adjusts her headset as she answers the ringing phone.

"Runclave Publishing House. This is Olivia." She nods, and nods some more. "Okay, yes. Sure. I will let him know. Mm-hmm. Yup. Okay."

She says hello—this time, I'm not sure to me or the phone—but then she waves me up to the desk.

"Lauren?" she asks.

I nod. "Yes, I have a meeting with—"

"Mr. Runclave and Ms. Grant," she finishes and pops up from her spot. "Follow me."

Through the glass doors, I follow Olivia down the hallway past the endless sea of modern desks and streamlined computers. Every person here is a cog in a modern, clean-edged machine. I recognize a couple of people from the few times I have been here, or from pictures Myranda posts of them all going out after a long week. Her attachment here is undeniable. I wonder if she even tried to get my manuscript to other publishers. Bigger names like Hawthorne Publishing. Sibley and Horan Publishing. Or in my wildest dreams, Bird and Darce Publishing. Or if this was my only real option.

"How was your summer?" Olivia asks as we nearly bolt down the hallway, her heels clicking faster than I can keep up with.

"Uh, good," I lie. Thinking about how I spent it writing a book that hurt almost as bad as the actual heartbreak that inspired it. "You?"

"Oh, it was great. I went to Wisconsin to visit some family. My cousin Abe has a boat, and the cousins and I spent the summer boating around Lake Monona with a view of the state capitol. It was a *dream*."

Olivia talks with her hands and her hair, which I didn't even know was possible until now.

"That sounds fun," I force out and spot the conference room

up ahead. Glass windows, floor-to-ceiling, wall-to-wall. A human fish tank of sorts.

"Oh, it was. I didn't even know I liked beer so much. But when there's music and water and sunshine? Then you love beer, I guess," she says happily as we make another turn and Olivia motions towards the glass doors. "There is coffee ready for you; help yourself. I'll let Mr. Runclave and Ms. Grant know you're here."

I step into the fish tank, set my bag on the chair, and pour myself coffee from the pot nicer than one I have ever owned. The creamers are the fancy kind with intricate flavor combinations. I settle on the caramel-brûlée and lavender dairy-free oat-milk one and choke it down while I wait, burning my tongue as I do.

Soon, a flash of red hair and a pantsuit swing in and hold the door for the balding man behind. Myranda and Runclave. Myranda laughs like whatever he just said was the funniest thing she has ever heard.

"Ah, my sweet debut rosebud," Myranda calls over to me, heading straight for the coffee pot herself. "Hope you like the creamers; I encouraged Charlie to pick these out."

I look at "Charlie," who seems to not even have heard his nickname. He's a thin, stretched man with a trim, graying beard and a shiny, polished head. He wears suits every day except on Saturdays. Like today. Because he golfs.

"Looks like numbers are doing great," Runclave says, resting in the chair at the head of the table, the farthest seat from me and closest to the door. "You have quite an impressive debut on your hands."

Myranda hurries over and delivers one cup to Runclave and another for herself. She sits next to him and adds, "And the interviews she has given are getting great feedback as well. People are loving her *and* her book."

"We are looking at your next contract today, correct?" Runclave asks haphazardly like we are going over my lunch order. Like I hadn't thought about getting my new contract all summer. Like I may ask for no tomatoes on my sandwich.

"Yes, sir. I have another manuscript ready to be edited, and I was thinking of having a different editor—"

"Well, I would like to see this manuscript *after* it's edited, and then we will look at renewing your contract then. I don't want to gamble a four-book deal on a debut that did just okay, you know? We will pay you like a freelancer, so don't worry about funds. You will probably be better off this way."

My heart plummets, and I look at Myranda to give me some clarification on what's going on here. That surely, he isn't holding off my next contract after the success this book has had. But she doesn't give me anything. Her eyes are cast down toward her cup. Like she's bracing herself.

"You just said it was impressive and the numbers look great. We could do a two-book deal and then go again from there—" I start, but he shrugs and clasps his hands over his abdomen.

"I run a tight ship here. A business. A good business. I can't go and take huge risks. Besides I don't foresee us *not* signing your contract, as long as you give us the quality you gave us last time. Now"—he sits forward in his seat, checking his watch—"on the other hand, I have one condition for this next project. I want it edited by Rhett Atwood again. The work you two did together? Taking your messy manuscript and make it sellable? I want that again."

"Oh, I don't think that would be a great idea—" I begin to argue, and then look to Myranda for support, but she gives me a pity shrug and sips her coffee.

"You don't have to marry the guy. Just work with him, okay? He's the best in the game, and the fact he is even willing is a win for us. I know the talk of the land around here, but he's a good editor. In fact, he's phenomenal. Be appreciative I am even allowing this. Someone with his talent and working on a rookie's work? Now *that* was a huge risk. But I'm lucky it paid off."

Allowing this? I can't seem to pick my jaw back up or get any words to come out. Instead, I sit there looking between him and Myranda, who is all too happy to nervously sip from her steaming mug and fidget with her jacket.

"Okay, if that's all. I have an important meeting with the green and a bourbon." Runclave huffs as he shuffles out of his seat. "Also, I want to see some edited pages soon. Get them to Myranda to get to me. Let's say in three weeks? Is that good? Yes. Let's do three weeks." He salutes us with his two fingers and leaves.

A silence follows the door shutting behind him. I wait for Myranda to fill it. But she doesn't.

"What the hell?" I ask. Anger pierces my vision.

"Rhett is a really good editor," Myranda pleads. "I don't know exactly what happened between the two of you, but trust me. The work you two did together was beautiful. You had a good manuscript, but the two of you together made it amazing. And besides, Charlie is right. You don't have to *work* with him, just email."

"Myranda. I can't work with him again."

"What if I come to your meetings, like a mediator? I could sit between you to keep things civil."

"Like a divorce mediation?" I groan and drop my head into my arms on the table.

I could "agree" and then edit it myself. Claim we worked on it together, and nobody would be any the wiser. Or I could pay a freelancer to do it and pay extra for them to pretend to be Rhett.

"Do we even know if he even *wants* to edit my work? Has anybody talked to him about this? Like, are we going through all this just for him to not respond again and leave me high and dry?"

Myranda sighs and looks at me directly in the eyes. "If you're in, he's in."

My stomach flips at the idea of Rhett being on board. But then the flutters are quickly replaced quickly by anger at the fact he hasn't called but is willing to do this. We sat side by side last night, knowing this was on the table, and he didn't mention it?

I drag my hands over my face. "What if I do this? I agree to work with him and Runclave doesn't even sign me on again anyway. All of that, for what?"

She stands and sits right next to me. "Don't plan for your demise before you've even really begun. Listen, I have another meeting I have to go to. But we are still meeting Elyse at that Mexican place right, okay? We can game-plan this together. Don't let him ruin this for you."

I don't say anything, which she must take as not a no.

She blows me a kiss and hurries out of the room. Everything has changed, and my shitty lavender coffee hasn't even cooled yet.

4

———

LAST FALL

I woke up to the early September sun peeking in through the blinds that did an awful job at keeping the apartment quiet last night. Somewhere in my delusional three-in-the-morning mind, I was convinced that if I just shut the blinds, then it would buffer the sound of the city.

I have been in the city for an entire week now, and I still spend the nights counting the time between loud voices or car horns. Like when you're a kid listening to the gap in the streaks of white light and the thunder cracks that follow, knowing the longer you count, the farther away the lightning is. The safer you are.

But I lie awake now in this barren apartment with little more than a photo of my sister, Hannah, her daughter, Winnie, and me, smiling on her fourth birthday. There are few other possessions that I brought along. A few books I clung to as if my life depended on it sat at the bottom of one of my duffel bags with a couple of notebooks and journals. Not much else made it when my mom remarried and we moved from my childhood bedroom and over to her new husband Paul's house. Even fewer things made it to college and back again. I had long ago traded my

Barbies for American Girl dolls, which I handed down to Winnie. I traded posters of boy bands for dramatic quotes about chasing your dreams, which were all eventually tossed in the dumpster behind a Goodwill because even *they* didn't believe in such good fortune. And now with these blank walls, what I wouldn't give to have one of those inspirational posters back. Or maybe even a Harry Styles one at this point.

Forcing my feet out of bed, I try to stretch out the lack of sleep and get my head on straight. I have a meeting with my agent, Myranda, and my editor, Rhett, in a few hours. I sent over some of my pages last week like Myranda had asked, and she must have forwarded them to Rhett, because I got an email from him with a blank subject line. The only thing in the email was an attachment. When I clicked on it, I saw that he had printed the pages, taken a pen to them, and then scanned them back into an email. No greeting or clarifying who he was. Just pages, *covered* in red ink. With more arrows and slashes than I could stomach. Comments scrawled across the margins and entire paragraphs crossed out.

Not strong. Fix this.

I don't like this scene.

Fix this.

Okay, but this could be better.

I scrolled in horror as I watched my work be dissected before me. Then I slammed my laptop shut and ordered carryout. I cracked a window, sat in an oversized T-shirt with a bowl of Chinese in my lap. Nobody was coming to check in on me. Nobody was stopping by or popping in. I was alone here. Alone with my words and Rhett Atwood's red pen marks.

But now, today, I face him. I push myself out of the bed and get in the shower. Scrubbing my face and body until I feel even remotely awake and until the nausea subsides.

When I get out, I see a text from Mom asking how the city

feels. If I feel more inspired. A slight dig, to which I respond to with a thumbs-up and give no other bait for her to reply to. I don't know if it's the lack of sleep or if it's just nerves from this impending meeting, but regardless, I am chugging caffeine like it will help. It doesn't.

When I visited the Runclave offices a few weeks ago to sign the official contract, I was introduced to some of the people in the office. They stood around like we were at the water cooler, telling me who to avoid whenever I came in. They mentioned rumors about Runclave and Myranda, and how the DoorDash guy is hooking up with the chatty receptionist in the bathroom when he brings her salads on Thursdays. They laughed about all kinds of salacious things, but what they mentioned in hushed tones was Rhett Atwood.

In passing, Myranda told me that she had gotten me an amazing editor. She gave me very few details otherwise. But these people had firsthand experience with him. One of the women asked who was signed up to be my editor, so I mentioned it was something Atwood.

"He's arrogant." She groaned, clutching her coffee. "Like a borderline narcissist. He thinks he's hot shit because he's young and hot. But it's all gone straight to his head."

"Well, he *is* hot shit," another girl countered. "I mean, you've seen him *and* the books he has worked on? They're best sellers. He *is* as good as he thinks. Even though I haven't seen any of his work recently."

"You know Meg, over in communications? She tried asking him out at the break station when he came by a few weeks ago, and she said he hardly even looked at her. He made some random apology about being busy or some lame-ass excuse."

"Maybe he's gay," the shorter brunette whispered like a schoolgirl at her locker, offering up her only contribution to the gossip.

"I've tried too," the guy next to me in the circle admitted and gave a shrug. "I saw him out at Kensington Club a few weeks ago with some friends. He is totally straight, unfortunately for me."

"Let's be real, though." The first girl tipped her head. "If we had a chance with him, there's no way any of us would turn him down. His arrogance *is* kinda hot."

"Oh, I would marry him on the spot if he offered," the short girl chimed in.

I laughed along like I wasn't getting more scared as the stories continued. How was a best-selling editor going to edit *my* book? Or maybe the question was, *Why* would he? Maybe there had been some mistake, or he had no idea what he was getting into. And maybe my career was over before it had even begun. Maybe.

I shake the memory from my head and wipe down the counter again and even manage to remake my bed one last time before setting out for this coffee shop.

I checked the directions more than once in the night while I should have been sleeping. But as I walk, I try to take in the city around me. Take in the shiny cars and passing people. The way the sun glints off the windows of the magnificent buildings, tall and ornate, details that people are too busy to slow down and look at. I tell myself to appreciate it. Convince myself of the beauty around me and hope soon I will feel it too. In a city as busy as this one, you're invisible in a crowd. Indistinguishable from every other wide-eyed dreamer. No number of shiny billboards or dramatic art murals filled that loneliness. It all just made it worse. I pulled out my phone and made a note to change the first line in my book.

If you ever want to be alone, go to the busiest place you know.

A few blocks later and after a few wrong turns, I approach the front doors of the little coffee shop that Myranda chose for this meeting. It's next to a bookshop called Ford's.

A bright-green poster in the bookstore's window catches my eyes, and when I step over, I realize it's flyers for a book club. I grab one, shove it in my bag, and duck inside the coffee shop.

Inside there are tables crammed in among mismatched chairs, and almost every single one is full. It doesn't take too long, however, to spot Myranda's red hair. It bobs as she talks to the man she's with. The man who happens to be the tallest man in the room. His legs are stretched under the table, and his brow is heavy with questions as he stares back at me. He's young. I don't know what I expected from the gossip but he's no more than thirty and he looks as if he was waiting on anyone else other than me to walk in the door.

Myranda pauses, realizing she must have lost his attention. She follows his eyes to see what he is looking at. She beams as she waves me over, making it too late to run. As I approach, all I can think about are all those cautionary tales from the office. How arrogant and cold he is. He has dark hair that curls at the ends. His eyes, dark green and set just so perfectly atop his cheekbones. He has full lips and a strong jaw. It almost makes me mad that he is as good-looking as they said he was. Of course, someone who looks like this probably is every bit arrogant as everyone says. How could he not be?

Myranda leaps to her feet and wraps her arms around me. She smells of designer perfume and clothes fresh from the dry cleaner.

"You made it!" She squeezes me tight. "How have your first few days been?"

"Good," I say as I untangle myself from her. "Thanks."

"How does it feel to actually *be* here? I mean, you finally made it. You're an *author* here in the city." She speaks of Chicago as if it were New York City. Or the next great frontier. The place where dreams come true.

"Good," I say again, feeling the burn of Rhett's eyes on me.

"Oh, Lauren! Right, sorry, this is Rhett Atwood. Your editor. Rhett, this is *the* Lauren Dorada. The wondrous brain behind the debut novel you've been assigned."

He clenches his jaw as Myranda pulls me into the seat between them. "Getting Rhett on board was not an easy task." She clicks her tongue. "I had to all but beg on my knees. The work he has done on projects similar to yours was just magic, and I know both of your creative minds will mesh so well. He doesn't do debuts, so I had to send him an early copy of your manuscript, but after he read it, he was in."

I look from her to him, and maybe it's my imagination, but I think I see a slight blush crawl up under that tortured artist's collar.

"I need a latte," Myranda announces and stands. "Do you guys want anything? They have great espresso and macchiatos here. Or if you're in the mood for—"

"I'm good," Rhett and I say in unison. And Myranda, unruffled, is off to the counter.

"She already had a cup before you got here," Rhett says once she is out of earshot.

"Was I late?" I check my phone, anxiety rushing through me at the idea. How, on my first day, first *real* day, could I be late?

"No. I got here early to get some work done, and she said she needed extra caffeine for Pilates later."

"Is she always this—"

"Awake?" He asks. "So far? Yeah."

While Myranda is gone, Rhett doesn't say anything else. He returns to his newspaper and red pen, and I'm not brave enough to ask why on earth is he red-penning a newspaper.

"Okay. Lattes for the table." Myranda sets down three paper cups with a happy smile, knowing full well we said no. Like an insistent mother.

But neither Rhett nor I argue. We quietly accept them and drink.

"So you were a teacher before this?" Myranda turns her full attention to me. Still, Rhett's eyes scan me like he's looking for a secret I could be hiding. I flush under his green-eyed speculation.

"Uh, yeah, just for a year."

"Did you like it?" Myranda asks.

I can't help but laugh. "No. The moment I had an out, I took it."

Myranda spills into her story about her cousin's wife being a teacher and the stories she tells. I'm watching her, but I am picturing Rhett turning that poor girl from the office down. How brutal it would be to be turned down by someone who looks like him. No matter if you stood a chance or not. His expression is impossible to interpret. It's as if he is so buried in thought that it would be impossible to dig him back up.

"I always used to think that maybe I would be a teacher." Myranda sighs. "I loved the way my fifth-grade teacher commanded a room. Eyes followed her. Our attention was on her at all times. I loved it. I wanted that. Maybe I still do. Maybe I'll be a professor when I'm done with all of this."

"Sounds like maybe being a dictator would work well if being an agent doesn't," Rhett quips and I shoot him a glance and see the playful glint in his eye. The little dig gets a deep laugh from Myranda in return.

"Yeah, maybe you're not too far off." She smiles. "So, Lauren, we will run through the developmental edits first. Focusing on story, plot holes, all of that. Then we will get into line edits and copy edits. You can email everything back and forth with Rhett, like you have already started." She stands and reaches for her bag. She smooths out the invisible wrinkles in her pantsuit. "I have Pilates in about twenty minutes; I need a better spot than last time. And Rhett, I know Runclave is expecting you in about an hour at your contract meeting if you want to head out. Lauren, go ahead get started on the edits Rhett already sent over, and get us those next chapters to me as soon as possible."

She blows a kiss and is out the door before Rhett even has a chance to stand. But at the mention of those edits, my feelings grow icy again. My guard comes back up.

He doesn't smile. Just puts his hand across the table, waiting for me to shake it. "It was nice to meet you. I look forward to working together."

I shake his hand, and I would be foolish to say he lingers, or I linger, even a half moment too long. I pull my hand back before that ice melts. He picks up his bag and coffee, then heads out, too, accidentally leaving behind the newspaper on the seat next to him.

I pick it up and see he has red-penned the entire obituary section. Circles here, lines there. There are no grammar mistakes that I can tell, but he must see something of note among the lines.

I throw it into my bag to get back to him at some point and step back into a city that is doing its hardest to swallow me whole.

5

NOW

Elyse is at the cheap Mexican restaurant like she promised she would be, two margaritas at the ready. She raises me a glass as I sit.

"It's a bit early for tequila, isn't it?" I mention, and she shakes her head.

"Not when you text me, indicating we are on the precipice of a nuclear breakdown of your career. And more importantly, at the mention of Rhett Atwood. I think it's necessary."

I accept the glass from her without hesitation and sip it with instant regret. If only that ever stopped me.

"Besides, who is going to tell us no?" Elyse smiles and pulls her hair up into a blond mess of a bun on top of her head.

"She might." I nod toward Myranda as she barrels into the front doors, animated, as she explains to the poor hostess that she is meeting people. The hostess doesn't seem to give a single shit, but Myranda does. Finally, she scans the small restaurant and spots us.

She hurries over, slides in next to Elyse, and lets out a sigh. "So."

"So?" I narrow my eyes at her. "After all of that, *so* is all you can come up with?"

She reaches across and grabs my hand. "I'm sorry, I know what Charlie said wasn't what you wanted to hear. It's complicated—"

"That's an understatement." I scoff and flip over the menu, pretending to read their lunch specials.

"We are having margaritas," Elyse announces. "No objections allowed."

"Well, I'm here as a friend, not your agent. And honestly, after that meeting? I'm surprised you didn't start drinking on your way back here."

"Who said I don't have a flask in my pocket?" I say and make a note to order myself one for any more meetings with Runclave or any further mention of Rhett, the editor back from the dead.

"So. Rhett is going to edit your next manuscript. Right?" Elyse processes out loud.

"That's what Charles said." I wait for Myranda to chime in and tell me I misunderstood. That surely, she would never expect me to work with him again.

"He's like a really good editor, though, right? And I get you two had your thing, but, like . . . he's a really good editor?"

"The best," Myranda nods her head solemnly like we are speaking over his grave.

"It's not about his editing. It's just . . . everything that happened."

"Well, you don't have to fall back in love with him," Myranda says. "Just use him to get your book to be the best it can be."

"I can't believe he even agreed to it," I admit. "I never heard back from him after last fall. Maybe all those office girls were right about him. They warned me."

A look washes over Myranda's face, but she leans in. "Don't for one second listen to anything any of those *girls* have to say.

Rhett doesn't even work for Runclave, and he only goes into the offices on rare occasions, if ever. And you've seen him. He's gorgeous, with all of that hair and those shoulders—of course they all want him. But they can't have him. Hence why they hate him. You were the first one to make it past his walls."

"My point still stands." I snap a chip in half before taking a bite, pretending like I'm not proud of the fact that I was able to infiltrate the fortress. Even if it was for as briefly as it was.

"Don't let your hate for him then, ruin your love for writing now," Myranda counters again.

"You don't have to work with him in person again, right? Can't you just email?" Elyse looks to Myranda. "She can just email everything, right?"

An idea flashes over Myranda's face. "I mean, yeah, technically, she could . . . "

"Email only." I mull it over for a moment, clinging to the tiniest bit of hope that I won't be forced to spend any elongated amount of time with him, because I know damn well I wouldn't be strong enough to stand my ground if he looked at me again like he did last night. Frankly, if the taxi hadn't come when it did, who knows what would have happened? "I could do email."

Myranda doesn't seem so keen on the idea, so I zero in on her.

"Was this your idea?" I ask her. "The whole Rhett thing? Did you scheme it up, thinking we would get back together? Or that we wouldn't be able to avoid each other anymore if we had to work together?"

"No!" She throws her hands up to show she's innocent. "I had no idea until about ten minutes before we walked into that meeting. I swear, this time I didn't know."

"I just need to get out of the city." I groan and push the rest of my second drink to Elyse.

"Hold that thought." Myranda sets down her glass, whips out her laptop, and begins typing furiously.

"What?" I ask her. "What are you doing?"

"Hold on." She clicks a few things and then turns it to me. A wood-planked cabin appears on the screen.

"What is this?" I lean in close to get a better look.

"Take a writing retreat. Take the next three months and work on this manuscript. Get out of the city. Edit it from there." She taps at the screen.

"Where is this?" Clicking through the pictures, it seems too good to be true.

"It's up in Michigan. A little town called Green Branch. A friend of mine's family owns it. Let me look into it and see if it's available. I could even find a way to get Runclave to cover it. You know, guilt him into it because he didn't sign you back on yet."

"I was kinda just being dramatic about leaving the city." I hesitate, but the looks on both their faces tells me I won't be going down without a fight.

"I think it's a great idea," Elyse chimes in. "It's exactly what you need. Get your mind out of, well, here." She waves her hands around generally, like the city has me trapped.

"I can't just up and leave. I have, like—"

"What?" Elyse leans in, her eyebrows narrowed. "Me? Book club? Shitty coffee shops? All those things can wait, like, a few months while you get this book finished up."

"Well, that and . . . it's just a big decision. We aren't talking about just a weekend; we are talking about *months*."

Elyse chugs down the remainder of my drink. "Take advantage of the fact that Rhett is willing to do this, and take a trip on your publisher's tab. Three months with not even a single chance of running into Rhett Atwood? Even though I wish the two of you would hook up in the cab of his truck and get this angsty shit over with, I feel like this is your perfect out."

Elyse has mentioned very little about Rhett in the past few months, leaving me to assume she didn't know the extent of our relationship, or exactly what went down between us.

Myranda hesitates but then nods. "It's Michigan in the fall. Nothing can be better than that, right?" Her phone buzzes on the table. "Oh, sorry, I have to grab this. I'll call you later with details." She chugs her margarita and stumbles out of the restaurant, blowing kisses as she leaves Elyse and me with this idea floating between us.

"You can literally put your apartment up on a rental site, or a subleasing website. People are dying to get into your neighborhood."

"I can't imagine why."

"You are not a city girl," she acknowledges with a laugh and looks down at the menu.

"You have no idea."

A few beats of silence filter between us before she folds her hands and looks up at me, more intense this time.

"How serious *were* things with you and Rhett?" she asks now. "I mean, obviously, there was something going on but . . . "

"I don't know. I felt like we were onto something, you know? Just when we finally figured it out, it dissolved. I saw him Friday night at Ninety-Seven's. When we were out after book club."

Elyse leans in, narrowing her eyes. "No shit. Why didn't you say anything?"

"I didn't even know right away. You guys left, and I sat at the bar because I was feeling sorry for myself. But then this guy is buying me a drink, and I realized it was him."

"Holy shit. What did you talk about?"

"Nothing," I lie. "Just awkward hellos and how-are-yous."

She nods, not believing me for a single second. "Okay, then what happened after that?"

"He acted like he wanted to explain what happened."

"And?"

"And nothing!" I say, my voice high with defense. "There's nothing to explain. I can't afford the luxury of pining over him, and if he explained it, I would have forgiven him and gotten sucked back in. And I can't do that. I can't *be* like that." *Be like my mom*, I leave out.

Not knowing the balance of forgiveness and being taken advantage of. I watched my mom not leave when the door was open, so many times. She busied herself with her real estate career and kept her nose down. And my fear of being like her has kept me mostly single this long. Other than passing infatuations in high school, my short-lived relationship in college, or the single date with a guy from a dating app who turned out to be my student's dad, after which he kindly paid the tab and dropped me off at home. But not before asking if the Christmas party needed more volunteers or not. Letting each of them leave was easier than finding the strength to be the one to leave them.

Elyse bobs her head back and forth. "Before Cal proposed, I broke up with him. I was cruel too. I, like, showed up with all his shit in a box and told him it was over. You should have seen him. Wide-eyed, he had just woken up, pajama pants and coffee in his hand. Confused as hell."

"Why did you break up with him?"

She laughs. "Because I was *scared*. I knew he bought a ring, and I, like, fucking panicked. I didn't even know what to think, and I knew if I talked to him about it, he would talk me out of it, and it would be fine, but I was fight-or-flight. And I was flying because I knew he would fight."

Her words stick like burrs to my clothes. To my heart.

I was flying because I knew he would fight.

Rhett may seem ready to fight now, but he didn't fight for me back then. He was the flight risk I hadn't expected.

"Hey, ladies." We look up and see Cal himself walk in like we had summoned him here just by the mention of his name. "Elyse mentioned margaritas, so I'm the designated driver. But I come at a cost."

"And what is that?" Elyse rolls her eyes but blushes anyway.

"Tacos." He slides in next to me and waves the waitress over. "A lot of tacos."

Elyse looks to Cal suddenly, fighting for her margarita back from him. "What do you know about Rhett Atwood nowadays?"

"No." I put my hands up. "I want to know nothing about him. Please."

Cal shrugs. "I haven't talked to him in months anyway. He kinda ghosted me. I honestly haven't even seen him either. He never leaves his apartment. Or maybe he never comes home. I can't tell. Haven't seen the truck, either, for that matter."

By the time we finish our lunch, Elyse is past the point of tipsy and into the realm of day drunk. So I sit with her in the back seat to make sure she doesn't puke all over herself.

"Driver!" She calls up ahead to Cal. "Could you lay off the swerving? I'm going to be sick."

I look up into the rearview mirror, and I expect Cal to roll his eyes. But he doesn't. He smiles, and he shakes his head gently.

"Go to Michigan," Elyse says, suddenly serious, as we pull up to my apartment. "Do it. Take the jump. Be spontaneous. I can't be, but I can live vicariously through you."

"Fine." And maybe it was that final tequila shot talking, but sober me, I think, agrees. Because the only thing scarier than going to a little cabin up north is being trapped in this city any longer. A rejected transplant. "I will."

When I get upstairs, I pull out my laptop and pull up the link to the rental. It's a small, weatherworn cabin in northwest Michigan. It sits high up, near the trees and a rocky hillside, with a large front deck and lights strung along the eaves. It looks quiet. Quaint. I pull out my phone and shoot Myranda a text.

I tell her I'm in.

6

———

LAST FALL

The early weeks of fall are filled with adjusting to the sounds of the city and getting scans of Rhett's edits, then making the changes and sending them back. Which is followed by Rhett sending over *more* edits, then I make *more* changes. The edits and the coffee are on an endless loop. And the amount of red pen on my pages has me tempted to swap out the coffee for a substance with a higher alcohol content.

If there is one thing Rhett Atwood doesn't do, it's hold back. Paragraphs in their entirety are crossed out, question marks appear on lines I was proud of, and there are little quips in the margins.

What is this?

I don't get this.

This could be better.

Rewrite this and send it back to me.

Each email I get has begun to fill me with dread. His name pops up, and my heart hammers in my chest—and not in the same way it did back at the coffee shop. Yet I open them, read them, and push forward.

It's not until a Friday afternoon that Rhett takes a single break. He says he's going home for the weekend and that he will get back to the edits Monday morning. With that email, I close my laptop with such relief that I could cry.

With my newfound free time, I get my apartment back in order. Cleaning up the fast-food containers I had yet to throw away. The bottle of wine, long ago empty, is put in the recycle bin. I throw out the junk mail still addressed to the previous tenant. I even manage to clean out my bag, which I haven't done in months. As I pull out the receipts and garbage, I notice the little flyer for the book club at Ford's bookstore. It lists the times and meeting dates, and with a glance at the clock, I realize if I leave now, I will just make it to this week's meeting. I've resorted to talking to myself and it's not like I'm making friends anywhere else.

So I convince myself to be brave. I grab my bag and head out with the flyer clutched in my hands, letting my unadmitted loneliness drive me forward and pray this is the missing piece of what I have been looking for here. The piece that is going to make this all feel not so foreign.

Ford's is a tiny, deep-green-painted storefront, set between the coffee shop on one side and a corner mart on the other. This neighborhood is much quieter than mine. There are big trees and sidewalk cafés. Brownstone homes and not a skyscraper on the block. It was quiet the other day, but it's even quieter now at night.

"Welcome to Ford's!" a voice calls out as I step in. A flash of blond hair comes from the back hallway.

"Hi. I'm here for the book club?"

I half expect her to turn me away, telling me I misunderstood the flyer. But instead, her face lights up with a smile, and she waves me over to follow her. "Oh, come in. I'm so glad! I told my husband that flyer would work." She motions to the crinkled paper in my hand, damp with nervous sweat.

"I had a meeting next door last week and saw it," I admit, and she beckons for me to follow her toward the sitting area. A leather couch is accompanied by a few antique-looking armchairs, lamps, and a trunk coffee table covered in a cheese board and wine. The side table holds a bust of a woman's head made into a planter. Green leaves spill out like hair.

"I'm Elyse Ford." She smiles and motions to the two other girls sitting on the chairs and couch. "Girls, this is . . ." Elyse trails off.

"Lauren," I say. "I'm Lauren."

"Lauren," Elyse repeats. "Lauren, this is Faye, our resident romance fanatic. And this is Nikki. She really only reads things that make you uncomfortable. They also happen to be sisters." She motions for me to sit. "My husband and I own the place. Are you new to the city?"

"Yeah, I just moved here."

"Oh? Why'd you move here?" Elyse's eyes are filled with curiosity. Genuinely too. Like she actually cares to know.

"Uh . . . " I stammer. "I write. I'm a writer. I have the weekend off from my arrogant editor," I joke.

"You'll fit in just fine around here then." Elyse winks. "We will start in about ten minutes, if you want to look around. Find a book. First one is on me if you join our club."

I thank her and wander around the maze of shelves that have no real order. Romance seems to be near the front but also near the back, and then a horror book is shoved between the young adult dystopian and current events sections. I step around another shelf and run right into a wall of a man coming toward me. He grabs my elbow to steady me.

But, of course, it isn't just a man. It's Rhett Atwood.

"Lauren." He smiles, looking not nearly as shocked as I feel.

"Rhett," I respond. "Sorry, I didn't see you. Are you here for the book club too?"

He chuckles and drops his hands from my arm. "No, I'm just grabbing a book before heading out of town."

"Oh," is all I'm able to get out. His baseball hat is flipped backward. His chiseled jaw has a touch of stubble, and his dark hair curls peek out from under his hat. He seems a tad less "city slicker" in these clothes. Seeing him standing here, though, I'm also stricken with how tall he really is. My head hardly reaches his shoulder.

"Oh." I reach into my bag and hold up his newspaper. "You left this. Wasn't sure if you still needed it."

An expression flames behind his eyes as he clears his throat. "Yeah, thanks." He accepts it, and when I expect him to explain, he doesn't.

"I'm actually glad I bumped into you." He smiles, eyes crinkling and all. "I really liked that last chapter you revised and sent over last night. I think it's my favorite one yet."

"Thanks," I say, my hands sweating through the cover of this paperback in my hand. Is he *actually* being nice to me?

"Wells Stevens?" he asks.

"W-What?"

He nods toward the book in my hand. I look down at it. It was on a table of new and popular books. It has a pretty painting of a bee on a honeycomb on the cover.

"Yeah." I shrug. "It seems okay."

He nods, smirking at my lack of vocabulary. Especially for someone who writes.

"I love that one," he says like it's an inside joke. "I was thinking we could meet up for coffee when I get back? Like Monday? To go over this next group of chapters. I have some ideas I want to run by you."

I note how much darker his green eyes are in this low light.

In the sunlight, they're a mossy green, but here, in the dim lights, they're almost emerald.

"Sure," I say. "We can meet next door again?"

"We could meet closer to you? Myranda said you live north of Navy Pier. I know a place. I'll send you the address."

"Okay," I squeak out.

He nods to me and begins to walk away but then pauses and says, "Wells Stevens is a bit arrogant, if that's not your type."

My blush of embarrassment turns into full-on, maroon-tinted shame as he winks at me and pays for his book.

I take the book that is now bent from my nervous grip and make my way over to the couch.

"Ooh I have heard good things about that one." Faye nods to the book in my hand.

I look at the cover. "I haven't even heard of it before," I admit, but my attention is drawn out the window. Rhett is on the sidewalk with his book under his arm, newspaper in his back pocket and his hat turned forward now. I watch as he slides behind the wheel of an old red Ford pickup truck.

"Do you know him?" Elyse asks, bringing a winged wine opener over and sits next to me.

"Who?" I turn my attention back to the cheese board, pretending to haven't even the slightest of clues what she means.

"That Rhett guy? He lives upstairs; he's in the other apartment across the hall from Cal and me. He seems like a nice guy. Quiet. He comes down to the store when we host parties or put on the game. But your conversation with him just now was the most I have ever heard him speak."

"He's my editor," I admit, and their faces recognize the great error I made in mentioning my arrogant editor.

"To arrogant men," Elyse says, pouring us all a glass of white wine, and we raise the glasses to each other. I chug it down because before I text him an apology, I will need to be wine drunk.

The three friends argue and tease about the book they just read. Nikki hated it. And Faye loved it. Elyse was indifferent. They banter and finish the bottle of wine while I sit quietly, taking it all in. Nikki and Faye ended up talking more about some party over in Hyde Park.

"If there is a party to get into, these two are going to make it their mission to get in," Elyse whispers.

I listen along, but my mind keeps going back to having to work with Rhett in person. Miserably fixing up my manuscript with his cruel remarks is one thing, but working together means keeping a cool composure in front of him while he rips my work apart.

"Let's read that Stevens book for the next meeting in two weeks." Nikki suggests, bringing me out of my head. "I heard it's good, and Lauren already picked it up."

"Perfect." Elyse claps her hands together. "Next week, have read *Honeycomb*, by Wells Stevens, and we will meet here. Same time."

"Let's go get dinner," Faye says, "All four of us. There's that Italian restaurant, you know right down the block here? I've been dying to try it. It's, like, Twenty-Nine's or Ninety-Nine's or something."

"I'm in," Elyse says. "I can have Cal close up. Lauren? Nikki?"

My first response is to turn down the offer. Tell them I really ought to get back to work. But there will be plenty of that waiting for me when I get home, and Italian food does sound really good.

"I'm in," Nikki and I say together.

⁓

WE ARE SEATED at a table near a massive mural on the wall. Nearly every other table is filled. Low chandeliers hang overhead, gas-lit lamps sit on every table, and the four of us chat like old friends. After the wine, my stomach is less on edge, and my cheeks are now only pink from the alcohol, not from embarrassment. We talk about growing up near Chicago and the eventual migration we all made to the city. Elyse and her husband moved from Indiana two years ago. Faye and Nikki (Nikki the older of the two) moved from the suburbs after college on a mission to live it up in the city. They talk about hitting parties and trying to boost their Instagram following. Their whole schtick is being opposite sisters.

We order pizza and more wine, and they ask about my writing.

"Well, I was a teacher for a year," I tell them. "And I hated it, so I started writing to cope. I just kept writing until I finally had something I was proud of. Then I submitted to agents. I found one was willing to take me on and she was the one who helped me find a place to live out here and everything."

I don't mention the loneliness I felt while writing it. My days were spent poorly managing my students, then coming home to my mom and Paul's house that never fully felt like home. I would hole up in my room and write all night. I was alone, even when I wasn't alone. I also don't mention how the loneliness I have felt since moving to the city could rival that. How the mundane cycle of waking up, drinking coffee, writing until dark, showering, going to bed, then repeating has worn on me. The only real human interaction I have had since being here is Myranda showing up at my doorstep unannounced, trying her best to encourage me or bringing food by.

Yet I kept it up and kept at it. Here I was, getting to wake up and to live in the city, being paid to write. I didn't have to beg twenty little dictators to stop fighting or to put the scissors down.

No more waiting in lines at a copier for assignments the kids were going to throw away anyway.

"That is really cool." Nikki sighs. "Maybe one day, I will write a book."

"You could never." Faye tosses her hair over her shoulder. "You don't have a romantic bone in your body."

"Maybe I'll write a horror story about two sisters learning they aren't actually sisters."

Faye rolls her eyes, and the waitress brings the bills for the three of them.

"Oh, I think you forgot mine," I say, but she looks at me with a growing grin. "The guy over there, the one getting carryout? He paid for it."

The four of us look, and sure as hell, Rhett is standing there with a plastic bag of Styrofoam containers in hand. He gives a nod before turning away.

"I can't let him pay for me," I mumble and stand. "I'll see you guys next meeting. Thanks for everything."

Rhett is out the door by the time I get to him.

"This doesn't look like going out of town," I say, feeling silly as soon as I say it. He laughs and motions to the same truck as earlier.

"I almost got out of town, but my parents always make me bring Ninety-Seven's home. Had to come back for it."

"I can't let you pay for my tab," I say and dig in my purse for any cash I have.

"Please, let me. I'm sorry for being so harsh. Your manuscript has serious potential, and I don't want to shortchange you, you know? You deserve honesty."

My brain can't find a response to that. I just sit there like an idiot, trying to comprehend possibly the most genuine compliment I have ever received.

"See you Monday, Lauren." He nods and gets into his truck.

My name sounds all too pretty from his lips. But I continue to stand, feet melting into the sidewalk, and watch him drive away.

"Holy hell, he really is hot." Nikki is next to me now. "At the store earlier, I thought maybe, but damn."

"A baseball hat is my weakness." Faye comes up on my other side.

"You should see how ruthlessly he edits my work." I shake my head and shove the crumpled bills back into my bag.

"Maybe he would make love the same way." Faye nudges her elbow into my side, and I force a laugh, my entire body probably red hot.

Later, I am sitting in bed, looking over every edit he has sent. I try to match them to the man on the sidewalk, try to find him in these harsh comments, like "Don't love this." Or "Eh, try again." And my least favorite, "Unoriginal."

Then I think back to his backward hat in the bookstore. Or the way he reacted to seeing the book I had chosen in the bookstore. And the smile as he drove off tonight. None of it makes sense. Right now, the only insight into Rhett Atwood's mind might just be that exact book. The one he says he loves.

I go back to my bag, dig *Honeycomb* out, and begin to read. By four in the morning, the book is finished, my bedsheets are stained by tears and mascara, and I am no closer to any understanding of Rhett—nor the author.

7

NOW

With the booking confirmation in my inbox from Myranda, I look around at the bland white apartment that I never got around to fully making my own. The frames that once held stock images now are the only signs of life that I was here. Filled with memories of this city, the ones I cling to. And though I know moving out is temporary, something feels like it's shifted. I don't know if I'll be back here in a few months or not, but I say goodbye to this space anyway.

My car is dusty when I get to it in the parking garage. It hasn't seen the road in a while, and I'm just happy it starts up when I crank the key.

I leave Illinois behind and Indiana too. And once I cross over into Michigan, I begin to question just exactly what I was thinking. That prickly feeling of fear creeps up my neck, but I keep driving anyway. I drive past hills, shopping centers, and off-ramps to towns I've never heard of. My toe is heavy on the pedal as I stay in the left lane so I don't have a chance to veer onto an off-ramp and change my mind.

I keep driving until my phone's cracked screen guides me toward a tiny exit sign that I almost miss. Weaving through tangled back roads and stop-sign intersections, I question whether my GPS is even taking me to the right place. Because the farther east I drive, the farther from Lake Michigan I get and the thicker the evergreen forests grow. Before too long, the "Now Entering Green Branch, Population 2,021" sign shows itself through the trees.

The road leads me through the quiet downtown with little more than a diner, town hall, and a mechanic shop. I blink, and I'm already through it. Turning off onto another winding road, I am directed by the GPS to a neighborhood set back in the trees. It's hilly and rocky, and I can hardly see the houses through the trees.

The GPS, however, points to a single gravel driveway that leads to two houses. On the right sits an old white farmhouse with a wraparound porch with dark-green shutters and a matching porch swing, just begging to have a book read on it. I pull down the driveway until it splits over toward another home farther back. The cabin from the photos.

I pull my car to a stop and rest back in my seat as I look up at my home for the next few months. The cabin is small and settled into the sloping rocky hillside, just like in the picture. It's canopied by rich red-and-golden trees whose leaves are beginning to fall. I even spot a pile of wood on the side. It's like something from a fairy tale.

I open the car door, and the only sound for miles is the wind in the trees and the occasional car in the distance. I inhale the fresh air and can smell smoke from someone's chimney nearby. And in an instant, I know I'm never going back to the city after this.

Over to my right, I can see the side of the farmhouse's porch, where a couple of rocking chairs sit being gently rocked by the wind. The neighbor's windows glow with warm lamplight.

Up the rickety wooden front steps of the cabin, I find the key under the mat, like the confirmation email said it would be, and if the outside is magical, then the inside is enchanted. The dark-wood-paneled walls are covered in pictures of trees of all seasons. Bookshelves overflow, and a large fireplace is topped with a heavy wooden mantel. A box of matches and an old remote sit on the trunk, acting as a coffee table that reminds me of the one at Ford's.

I step through the living room, the floors creaking beneath my feet. The downstairs is just one big room with a view of the front door, back door, and stairs. I run my hand along the kitchen counter and peer out into the backyard. A massive yellow willow tree stands, its leaves spinning to the ground. My heart thumps in the best way. The *home* kind of way. On the back deck, the wind whips the leaves, scattering them across the worn wooden boards as they gather under old outdoor furniture.

I push the window open and breathe in the chilled breeze and force every image or idea of returning to the city out of my mind. Because nothing deserves a spot in my brain right now other than this place. Upstairs, I peek my head into the little bathroom between the rooms. It houses a clawfoot tub and a warped mirror. Big, fluffy towels sit on a stool in the corner. The bedrooms are small, with the kind of furniture you'd expect in an old cabin. A bed, a nightstand, a dresser with a Bible in the top drawer. Plaid lamps on nightstands and faded red rugs underfoot.

Back downstairs, I look through the bookshelf. It's filled with history books, hardcover fiction, and cracked-spine romance paperbacks. There is a book of maps and a book on the mechanics of a 1992 Ford F-150 truck. And at the bottom, next to a cookbook and dictionary, is a book I do recognize. *Honeycomb.* Wells Stevens. It reminds me of the copy Rhett never returned after I loaned it to him. Worn and banged up. As I pick it up, my phone buzzes on the couch behind me. I set the book back on the shelf and see that it's Hannah.

"Hey—"

"Why are you in Michigan?" She cuts me off, her voice nearly shrill.

Shit. "I'm here for work. My publisher is putting me up here for a few months. I meant to tell you." I take a look around the cabin. "How do you even know I'm here?"

"I have your location. And for work? You're not visiting anyone?"

"Uh, no? Hannah, we don't know anyone in Michigan."

She pauses. "Okay, so when can I come visit?"

"Whenever. There's an extra room with little twin beds for you and Winnie and everything. Come this weekend."

"God, she would love it." She sighs. "Ethan's parents have a place on the lake up in Michigan, but they've never invited us up. But Ethan is gone on a golfing weekend with his buddies, and I'm actually enjoying the peace and quiet around here."

"Or do you just enjoy not having him there?"

"Yeah. Same thing." I can hear the smile in her voice.

"Well, when you get a weekend of him *actually* being home, you need to come visit. Okay?"

"Okay. Have fun. Text me with updates." She says it like something's funny, then hangs up.

I lug my bags in, drop them on the floor and pause to sit there in the silence of the house. I don't hear traffic from in here. Not out my window. Not in the distance. Not at all. I can sit with my book and not have a single horn interrupt my thoughts.

And when it's time for bed and I've exhausted the limited TV channels, it takes a bit to find a new rhythm to fall asleep to. This time, though, instead of cars and horns, it's the scraping of tree branches off the roof and the lilting breeze. And soon, I am sound asleep.

8

___

LAST FALL

Half of me was ready to throw in the towel and go crawling home to my mom and my old bedroom. Beg my old principal for forgiveness, a part-time position and refuse to let any more criticism of my beloved manuscript into my brain.

Then I remember what Rhett said when I saw him at the restaurant.

I don't want to shortchange you.

It makes me wonder if maybe there is hope for it. And for me. Those words have been festering in my brain all weekend while I waited on the text from Rhett to schedule our meeting. It's radio silence until the morning of. I am drinking my coffee, reading *Honeycomb* again, when my phone finally buzzes.

Hey, It's Rhett. Myranda finally got back to me with your number. Here is the address to the coffee shop. It should only be a block or two from your neighborhood. Does noon work?

I click on the address and see it is taking me straight to the coffee shop across the street from my apartment building. I agree to noon, then toss my phone aside. I shower and clean up the weekend mess, text my mom back, clean the counter, and then clean it again.

Then I decide on scoping out the place first, get an idea of what exactly I'm looking at. Is this one of those study places? Or Instagram chic places? The latter sounds like an anxiety attack, but I grab my bag and head over an hour early to the small, narrow shop with black-brick walls and old, clunky wood furniture. When I spot him, his focused is buried in a newspaper. He's dressed more formally than at Ford's last week. Back to his *work* clothes. He's clean-shaven, and I have the stupidest desire to feel the fabric of his sweater that's stretched over his chest. I check my watch to confirm that I was actually as early as I thought.

He doesn't see me yet, so I jump in line to order a drink and give myself a pep talk. Or rather, just talk myself into this. The girl behind the counter doesn't look up when taking my order, just scribbles on the cup and passes it off before calling for the next customer. I stand off to the side, where I have a view of the whole shop—and the side of Rhett's face. He's focused on whatever he's doing. Eyes pinched together, mouth a settled straight line.

The barista calls my name when it's ready, and I see Rhett's head pop up, and his eyes find mine. But I also catch the small flicker of a smile on his lips. His jaw is tense, and the fluttering against my rib cage makes me want to swap this drink out for a black coffee. To sober up a little bit. Get this feeling out of my system and calm these mindless butterflies.

"Were you scoping the place out too?" I ask when I approach.

"I always like being early." He digs through his bag, and I see another newspaper poking out.

"How're the obituaries today?" I ask, trying to gauge the level of humor he has in him, if any at all.

And when he chuckles, I continue to question if the person editing my work is the same person sitting across from me right now. Because the comments and this man who has a smile like this don't seem to exist in the same realm.

"Dreary. How's that Stevens book?"

"Ask me after I've had a few too many glasses of wine. Then I will give you an honest review."

"It's a date," he responds quickly, and I'm sure he is mirroring the look of shock on my face after he says it. We both are frozen for a beat. "Your pages," he reminds us both and pulls out a pile of papers from his bag. A stack of papers an inch thick.

"Do I owe you printer ink?" I ask, and he smiles again.

"No. But maybe a new red pen."

He fans through the pages, and I see the red marks, like stretch marks you hated as a child when you grew a little too tall, a little too fast, scrawled across every page and nearly every line. But then my eyes glance up, foolishly, and I catch his eyes— a sleepy shade of green.

"The reason I crossed this chapter out was that I think it diminishes the purpose of their argument later, you know? Like why talk about it now and be okay with it just to argue about it later? But it was really well written. I think you could include this *with* the fight later."

I brace for the impact of the harsh critique. Instead, he shuffles through the papers and points out another page covered in red ink.

"I know it looks scary, but I promise it's not," he says. "This memory was written in a couple different tenses, so I just went through and tried to point out anything that would have needed to be fixed."

Again, the sting doesn't come.

We begin flipping through the rest of the pages, me adding the edits in on my laptop, him explaining each of the edits, even the ones I would have been offended by if he had just simply written them down. Edits I would have rejected originally. But he explains them gently.

After a while, I get us refills of our coffees. His black, mine nearly white with cream. And we continue. The snark and the bite of his words I had envisioned in my brain are nothing more than that: visions. Not even the little backhanded comments on the side hold the same burn when he repeats them out loud. If anything, they're funny. *He's* funny. He's witty, and his comments are almost refreshing compared to the near-constant crossed-out sentences and changed verb tenses. I never was a grammar expert. I just liked getting lost in my own mind.

"I'm really excited about these few pages here," he says, flipping back again. And the pages he shows me are the ones I wrote out in the garden at my mom and Paul's house. I had set up a little blanket next to the pond, and I wrote for hours straight. It also has, of all the pages he has shown me today, the most red ink. "I really like this whole self-reflection moment for the character. It's a little bit of an unexpected pause in the momentum, but I think it's great, and it makes *sense*."

"You know," I say. "You don't have to be nicer to me because I called you arrogant. You can let me have it. It's only fair."

He surprises me with another laugh. His eyes catching the sunlight; the green and flecks of gold reflect just so. His dark eyelashes frame his eyes like they're paintings. Masterpieces, really.

"*Arrogant* isn't an insult. If you said I was a bad editor, then I would be insulted. But I can see where an entire page of red ink can come off as arrogant."

I take the papers from him and add in some more of his edits, feeling a twinge of guilt for thinking him so cruel. To have given in to the water-cooler talk about him. I wonder though, still, if he is bored by me and my work. A debut author with very little to give, except the words from her brain. I wonder if this is all some little side quest to appease a demanding agent like Myranda. The way his phone buzzes on the table before he puts it away proves he probably has a million other far more important projects to be working on.

After our third round of coffees, we inch toward the end of the pile of papers and start to grow a bit weary. When I check the clock, I notice that late afternoon has come quicker than expected. The sun will begin to set soon.

"What got you into writing?" he asks suddenly during a quiet stretch of working.

I shrug at the question I have been asked so many times. It's not one of those things I have an answer for. I didn't have this *come to Jesus* moment, where I was left with tragedy and despair and, in turn, took up writing. I just always wrote.

"This book? Or in general?"

"Before this book," he says and begins to shuffle the papers back into a neat pile.

"I've always written. I still have notebooks from when I was little, filled with crazy stories that I was convinced would be the next best seller. But then, you know, writing doesn't pay the bills the way a salary will."

"I nearly failed English in high school," Rhett admits and slides the papers across to me and gathers our trash.

"You did not."

He nods and stands. "I did. I struggled with reading, and it made writing just that much harder. I didn't know how to get my thoughts out. But I loved editing other people's papers. Making them better, sorting their thoughts out. But then I realized to really edit, I had to write so I could see where both sides came from."

"I almost failed grammar class," I admit and follow him towards the door.

He nods his head with a boyish grin and swings the door open for me "Well, I *do* believe that."

My jaw drops as we both laugh. Rhett places his hand on my lower back as I step past him and out onto the sidewalk.

"I never got into editing. Sorry for not doing you the same favor," I quip and even for just a moment, something flickers in my heart. Maybe it's from the way he's smiling, or the way his eyes linger on mine. But it's quickly stifled by the blaring horns from the street.

"Need a ride?" he asks, nodding toward the vintage, beat-up red Ford pickup truck.

"I live right there." I point over at my building, a bit embarrassed at the blandness of it. And I find myself disappointed that I don't live farther, just so I could have taken him up on the ride.

"Okay, then let's meet up again and work together in person." Rhett rubs the back of his neck. "I think we got more done this way."

"Sure. Sounds good."

"Take the rest of the day off. Let me know what day works for you," he says. As If I have anything else to do.

I walk back up to my apartment, and I pore over the crinkled pages Rhett gave me. His handwriting is small and on nearly every line. It's different now, seeing his pen strokes in person and not over a computer screen. It's possible he may actually even like my story.

I'm halfway through some old edits when Hannah calls, talking a million miles an hour about drama at dance class and how Ethan, her god-awful husband, is refusing to do the daddy-daughter recital performance.

"Whoa, whoa, slow down. He's refusing to do the dance with Winnie at her recital?"

"Yes."

"What's his excuse this time?"

"Business up in Chicago." I can sense the eye roll from here. "You know how he is."

Unfortunately, I do know how Ethan is. A former fraternity president who never grew out of the *brotherhood*. It also doesn't help that Ethan is the son of the infamous defense attorney Anderson Forrest. Ethan followed in his father's footsteps by going into the family business. Forrest Defense Attorney billboards line the freeways going in and out of the city for miles. And Anderson Forrest only liked to represent the hardest of criminals. His two sons, Sebastian and Ethan are following in his footsteps.

"But how are things going in the city? I want to live vicariously through you," Hannah insists.

"I met with my editor, Rhett, today," I tell her, happy to not think about Ethan anymore.

"Oh!" She perks up. "The really harsh one?"

"Yeah. But I don't know. Maybe he isn't as harsh as everyone—"

"Oh no way." Hannah laughs on the other line. "You worked with him for a single *day*, and you already think *he isn't as bad as people say*? They're almost *always* as bad as people say they are. Maybe even worse."

"No, not like that. Hold on." I dig the papers out of my bag and send her a photo. "They're covered in red ink. Like he literally joked I owed him a red pen, but I don't think he was really joking."

"Okay, I just got the pictures. Hold on." She pauses, and I hear her tapping on her screen. "Oh my God. This would make me cry."

"I almost did." I sigh and fall back on the couch. "But then today, he's explaining all of it, all the edits. He seemed, I don't know, hopeful? Is that the right word? I don't know, but he was *excited* about my work. It was strange."

"I can't take criticism to save my life. I could *never* handle that."

"I'm still not sure I can," I admit. "We are meeting up again in a couple days."

"Ooh, for work or a date?"

"If there is anything in my life that I don't have time for, it's dating. Or infatuations. You've seen those edits; I hardly have time to breathe," I say adamantly.

"Okay. Then I am coming to visit you on Friday, and we are going to go out." Her voice was resolute.

"Oh, there is no way. I just said I don't have time—"

"We will find you some tourist to make out with, we can get this little *crush* out of your system, and then you can move forward platonically with your editor."

"A crush? What are you talking about? We already are moving forward platonically. All I said was that he wasn't as mean as everyone said."

"Is he hot?"

"Hannah."

"Oh, he is! Isn't he?" she exclaims. "Oh my God, okay. Then we *have* to go out on Friday. I need to help you shake this."

"Fine. But I have book club first."

"Perfect. They can come too."

"I will. Tell Winnie I say hi."

"Winnie!" she calls out. "Aunty Laurey says hi!"

Then, after a quick shuffle with the phone, I hear my niece's little voice.

"Aunty Laurey!"

"Hi, baby. How are you?"

"Good. I'm four."

"I know. I was at your birthday party, remember?"

She sighs. "Mommy says I need to eat dinner now."

"Ooh, what did she make?"

"We got pizza."

"Of course." I smile to myself. "Well, enjoy your dinner. Love you."

"Love you." She hangs up before handing the phone back to Hannah.

I sit back on the couch and distract myself with my edits for the rest of the night because right now, I would much rather be eating pizza with them than eating leftover Chinese alone on my couch. Again.

9

___

NOW

I blink away the dream where I'm teaching again and It's gone quickly as I stretch and check the clock on the night-stand. My phone is dead, and the clock reads midday. I lie still and wait to see if it's all a dream too. But no traffic sounds come. So, I breathe in the bitterly cold air of the cabin, pull the covers back up over my shoulders, and listen to the quiet of the birds flying south. Before long, though, I drag myself out of bed, pulling the blanket with me as my body calls for caffeine.

Teaching had been the default option for me. I didn't mind school growing up, it came easy to me. And the schedule worked well with my writing so when I didn't get into a writing program I decided on teaching.

Now, the early morning sun peeks in through the trees and through the dust particles dancing in the air. I pull out the generic-brand coffee I brought and set the pot up to go. I watch it like paint drying on an artist's canvas, as each drip falls, more beautiful than the last. I brought a single mug with me from the city. One I made with the intention to smash it against the wall, but now it's my comfort mug. I had painted little tulip blossoms on it with Hannah in the winter.

When a knock on the front door comes, I almost drop my full cup. My heart is zipping off, and I'm sure, for a moment that this is it. *This* is the catch. The murderer is here to collect me. The stalker I never knew about is finally ready to confront me. I peer through the front window and see an older man with graying hair and rose-flushed cheeks, standing there with a golden retriever at his side. Hardly a murderer or stalker. Hopefully. I open the door, and he smiles.

"Hi there. I'm Jack. I own this place, and I live next door. I saw you pull up yesterday and just wanted to stop by and introduce myself. This is Storm." He pats the head of the dog. "She's real friendly. She wanders around, but she finds her way home. If ya mind her, give me a call, and I'll call her back."

"I can't see her being a problem." I crouch down and let Storm lick my face. "I'm Lauren. Nice to meet you." I smile and scratch behind her ears, bringing a tail wag and a smile from her. As if this place were trying to sell me my dream-lottery house, the dog would have been the equivalent of a secret office or built-in bookshelves. I'm sold.

"Here on vacation? Business?" the man asks me, and I take a moment to notice the familiarity in his face. The kind if you were in danger, you would feel safe walking right up to for help. The kind that reminds you of a family member or someone you used to know.

"Uh, work. Yeah," I admit. "And vacation too, I guess."

"Well, that's great. I know you're booked for the three months, but if you need more time, you just give me a holler, and I'll put ya in. We don't get a whole lot of interest around here anymore."

"You don't get a lot of vacationers out here?"

"Oh, golly, no." He chuckles with his hands on his hips. "I bought the place when we were kinda in a pinch, but I thought surely it would rent out. The leaves in the fall bring a little bit of interest but hardly in a small town like Green Branch."

"Well, it's beautiful," I say, suddenly feeling my heart squeezed with pity for this sweet old man.

"Well, thank ya. I'll have my boy swing by in a bit to bring some wood inside for the fireplace. It gets pretty drafty in here. He's just out with his buddy, but he should be back soon. If you need anything, just holler. My number and other local numbers are on the side of the fridge if you need. Don't be shy."

Ducking back inside, I wonder what my mom would think of this place. Would she be impressed? She was over the moon when Hannah showed her pictures of the house she and Ethan were having built. The double doors, his-and-hers closets, the second-story laundry. Even the marble they were having flown in for their counters. Ethan's parents must have felt the need to compensate for their terrible son and pushed money at them to cover a lot of the costs as a wedding gift.

I top off my coffee and head up to the shower, and immediately the water pressure convinces me that I should never leave. It pelts my back and rinses every stress from the city straight down the drain. I stand under the stream and let the steam fill the room and my lungs. Then I reach to the counter and bring my coffee in the shower with me and sip it within the steam. And by the time the water runs cold and my coffee runs out, I have half a mind to call Myranda and tell her I'm never leaving and to beg Jack to let me stay. Permanently.

The towels are fluffy and giant, and I wrap myself in one and throw my hair up in the other. Then in my towel, I go to my bedroom window and crank it open. There is nothing but trees for miles. I let the air chill my shoulders until they hurt. I listen for the traffic I know I won't hear. I listen and listen, yet there's nothing but the wind and Storm running through leaves in her backyard somewhere I can't see.

After a while, I get dressed and pour myself one last cup of coffee before I get back to work. One more thing to help me put off the inevitable.

For so long, I have been focused on getting from point A, teaching, to point b, writing. Sometimes I forget about the me two years ago, elbows deep in lesson plans and testing and behaviors and parents and missing pencils and broken crayon boxes and wondering how I could love these kids but not really like them at all. How I would step in front of a bullet for them (as teachers are expected to do now), yet I won't repeat the directions for a fourth time. I would brush their hair when their moms wouldn't. I would share my snacks when they didn't have one. But if I saw one of them at Target, I would have dived behind a shelf to hide from them. At that time in my life, my favorite artists were releasing music, but I was driving home in silence. The bumps in the roads and the sound of my blinker were the only things getting me home. I couldn't bear to hear a single sound.

And a year ago, I was settling into the city, still impressed by the shiny buildings. The high of being in this big world alone felt scary yet invigorating. I was scared yet wide-eyed. Looking back with rose-colored glasses, sometimes I forget just how scared I was. I had thrown one hard life out the window to replace it with something unknown.

At that time, I was cleaning my apartment every chance I got, buying wine like a real adult, watching the Weather Channel because I wanted to. I went from an impostor in front of a classroom to an impostor in the city. I was just waiting for someone to catch me slipping up. Maybe I still am.

Regardless of the childhood field trips or guilt-driven fifth-birthday trip to the American Girl doll store, Chicago remained this magical little corner nestled along a lake that wasn't even named after the biggest city on it. In my mind, Lake Michigan belonged to us. It should have been Chicago Lake, or Lake Chicago. Michigan has plenty of other lakes to spare. I claimed Chicago from the suburbs as a child, and then as an adult, it didn't claim me back.

At the first meeting with Rhett and Myranda, I had no idea what the next few months were going to look like. I brought them a mangled-up manuscript in hopes they would be able to help me sort it out. It was a promising piece of work, one that Rhett whipped into shape. Through countless long days and late nights, we pulled it together.

Now I have another messy and tangled manuscript that needs a good editor. A good one like Rhett, whether I would ever admit it out loud or not. I know it's time to open my laptop and face it because I'm sure the edits will be coming in soon, and I shouldn't be wasting any time. If I'm not ahead, then I am tragically behind.

Instead of doing just that, I stare at my closed laptop before deciding it can wait until my hair is at least dry. I toss my laptop back onto the couch. Find the TV remote and crash back.

There's a knock at the door and I turn off the soap opera I got sucked into on one of the only stations available. When I open the door, my stomach spirals down to my knees. It takes me a moment to even register what I'm seeing. It's as if my imagination grew legs and is now standing on my front deck. Because those green eyes staring back at me are not that of a teenage boy, like I expected.

"Lauren?"

10

LAST FALL

I have spent the entire last week living on a diet of stale coffee shop pastries and expensive lattes. Rhett and I taking turns buying the next round, at whatever coffee shop we agree to meet at. By the end of the week my fridge is empty. So here I stand, with a small basket in hand and the cheapest and biggest bag of coffee I can find in it. And I'm heading towards the cheese aisle when my phone buzzes in my pocket. My heart lurches when I see Rhett's name pop up as if it hasn't become a common occurrence this week.

Hey, my printer is down. I am going to try and find a printer to get your next pages, then I will be at the coffee shop. I will probably be a couple minutes late.

I don't even think before I send my response. I just do it before I talk myself out of it.

My printer works, come on over. We can work from my place today.

I stare at the screen, my heart beating wildly in my chest, waiting for those three little bubbles to pop up in response. Then they do, and I watch them dance before finally a message pops up.

You're the best. Thanks. Will be over in a bit.

I grab an extra bag of coffee and the pack of red pens that has probably been on the shelf since this place opened and pay. Back at the apartment, I start tidying like my life depends on it, finding any possibly embarrassing item and hiding it under my bed or deep in the garbage can. As if the single sweatshirt on the back of my chair is going to give away some private secret I hadn't even known I was keeping. Or that the empty carryout container will discredit my writing as a whole.

When he knocks on the door, I wipe my sweaty palms on my pants and open it. He stands there, two coffees in hand, his bag on his shoulder and a smile on his face. He's clean-shaven, with hair still damp from the shower. Then I realize I am just standing there, staring at him, and I have to remind my feet to move away so he can walk in.

"Hey!" I step aside. "Come on in."

I watch his eyes work around the little space. They linger on the photo gallery on the wall. I almost miss his chuckle as he hands me a coffee. It's like I'm being forced suddenly to see it all through his eyes. The blanket on the back of the couch that was a mess, then folded, then folded again, then just left messy because I didn't want to come off as trying too hard. Or the kitchen that looks like a department-store showroom—and not in a glamorous way. It's cold and bland, just as it was when I moved in. But my pulse quickens at the image of it all. The cold, uninspiring place. What if he sees my apartment and reports back to Runclave that I actually shouldn't have a book deal? That we should pull the plug before it has really even begun and tell him that I must not have a creative bone in my body? His eyes seem to narrow as he looks around.

"What?" I ask.

"Nothing." He shakes his head. "It just doesn't look like you."

I scoff. "*Look* like me? It's an apartment." But I know exactly what he means.

"I'm not saying it has your eyes or your ears or anything." He chuckles. "I mean, it doesn't *feel* like you."

"What would *feel* like me?" I sip my coffee and lean against the counter while I try and read his eyes.

"Well, this is all too white. Too Ikea. Most of those pictures on the wall are stock photos. I would expect maybe a fireplace or a pile of books on your coffee table, at least."

I push off the counter with a laugh. "I'll get right on the fireplace installation."

"Great." He smirks, and those damn butterflies take flight with the twinkle of his eye. "I really like these few chapters; I can see the first act really coming together now,"

His compliment makes me pause as I pull the printer out of the closet and walk it over to the table. I regain my composure and force my feet forward. "Thank you."

"Of course." He pulls out a couple pages from his bag and slides them across the table to me. "Here are the first few chapters, and I will buy you printer ink for the rest."

These pages are covered in more red ink than all the others so far. "I think we are even for the red pens and the printer ink."

He smiles and step over, leaning over my shoulder to see what page I'm looking at. His hand brushes on my lower back as he uses the other to turn the page in front of me to reveal another onslaught of red markings.

"You're not good at capitalizing your *I*'s."

"I have more important things to focus on than fixing them."

In my peripheral vision, I see a smile appear on his face as he steps away. "Well, that's fair. We will get to more of that in copy edits and line edits."

"Oh, speaking of." I go to my bag and dig out the pens. "These are for you."

He cocks an eyebrow and looks up at me. The smile he's fighting reaches the corners of his mouth as he taps them against his hand. "Thanks. I needed some."

He sits down across from me. I get out my laptop. Then we begin. We slip into an ease of working quietly. His pen scribbling across the new pages, my laptop keys clicking away on these old ones. Soon the nerves melt away, and the caffeine floods my bloodstream. And like some blush-induced trance, we fly through the chapters.

We write like this for hours. Until dinnertime comes around, and instead of calling it a night just yet, Rhett pulls out his phone.

"What carryout do you want?"

"Whatever you want," I tell him. "Wine?"

"Please."

Within an hour, we are sitting on my couch, Styrofoam containers in our laps.

"So. Tell me about the Wells Stevens book," he says, digging in.

I set my food aside and go over to the shelf and pull my copy out. The pages are filled with annotations, sticky notes, my own mindless notes scrawled in the margins. The spine cracked and the pages curled.

"Wow," He gently thumbs through the pages.

"I loved it. It made me cry. A lot. Look at the last few pages."

He flips over to the back, and he can see where the pages are wrinkled from tears and the notes I had made smeared as well.

"Can I read your copy?" he asks. "I would love to read it again and see your notes."

"As long as you promise to return it. It's my prized possession at this point."

"I promise,"

After we finish eating, Rhett begins to pack up his bag, and I'm sad to see him go.

"We should meet up again soon. We get a lot done this way," he offers while his eyes flicker up to meet mine only briefly. It's almost as if he's nervous. I didn't think he had a nervous bone in his body.

"We can meet back here again tomorrow?" I suggest, bracing myself for the rejection.

He pauses and looks back up. "Sounds good. I'll bring more paper and some printer ink."

"I'll have the red pens ready for you," I quip back.

"Good." He smirks. "I'll need them."

I walk him to the door, smiling the whole way behind him and kicking myself while doing so. We say goodbye, and he heads down the hall to the stairs. When I turn back to the apartment, I drop my back against the door and catch my breath.

I check the clock, knowing if I leave right now, I might be only a couple of minutes late for the book club. I change quickly and realize Rhett has my copy of *Honeycomb*, and I will have to lie to the girls and say I forgot it. As I grab my keys, I realize he forgot his baseball hat. I hang it on the hook and head out.

Down on the sidewalk, I am pulling out my phone to order an Uber when I see that red truck parked at the curb.

"Need a ride somewhere?" Rhett asks through the window.

"Book club at Ford's," I say.

He unlocks the door. "Get in. I'm heading there anyway."

"I can Uber—"

"Get in," He says again with a single tactful nod of his head. I don't even try to argue this time. I slide into the passenger seat and take in the inside of the truck. It smells like him. Sunglasses in the visor, a box of gum in the cupholder, the floor mats ingrained with gravel.

"What?" he asks playfully and puts the truck in drive.

"Nothing." I say like he did earlier. "It just doesn't look like you."

He smiles. "I've had this thing since I was sixteen. My dad and I spent an entire summer fixing it up in our garage. It's a ninety-two F-150."

"So maybe it's Chicago that doesn't look like you." I buckle in.

He pauses for a moment. "What do you mean?"

"Did you grow up here in the city?"

"No. I grew up in a tiny town in the woods." He laughs.

"Exactly. Maybe you're a small town, gravel, pickup-truck kinda guy. But here in the city, you're a suave, handsome literary editor. Maybe it's the city that doesn't look like you."

I peek over just quickly enough to catch the clench in his jaw as the corner of his lips quirk into the tiniest smile.

"Did you just say *handsome* literary editor?"

Shit. I glance away, blushing. "You know what I mean."

He chuckles and taps his fingers on the steering wheel.

"My mom was a writer." He smiles. "She would come into the city once in a while for meetings, and she would bring me and my brother and sister. We would do all the tourist stuff. You know, the museum, the aquarium, the zoo."

"Did you, like, fall in love with the city and move here as soon as you turned eighteen?"

"Not really. None of us did. My dad worked too much to really ever take time to join us, and we all pretended to like it. I just thought this is where you came if you wanted to work in the industry." He looks from the road to me then quickly back to the road. A flash of sadness crosses his face.

"You have siblings?"

He nods. "Gwen and Jack . . . we call him Jackie. They're twins."

"Twins? Your poor parents."

He chuckles. "They were wild kids too. My mom had cancer when we were young, and my dad was always taking her to doctors' appointments, so I was left watching them."

"I'm so sorry about your mom."

His lips soften into something almost resembling a smile. "Me too. But I love my brother and sister. They were worth the work."

He pulls off onto the quiet street I recognize now. The trees have fully turned and are losing their leaves. And at this point, I feel as if maybe this is the only street in the city that fall has found.

"You?" he asks as he parks. "Do you have any siblings?"

"I have an older sister. She basically raised me," I admit. "I know it was terrible for her, but my life was better for it. You know . . . to be raised by her."

Rhett looks at me with those eyes and nods. Like maybe he hadn't considered that before.

"Thanks again for the ride," I mumble and get out of the car, overthinking. Wondering if I said too much, or maybe not enough.

Instead of digging a deeper hole, I just walk straight into the bookstore. Elyse greets me with a stack of books in her arms. She sets them on the counter.

"Oh my God, I'm so glad you came back. I was afraid we scared you off." She sighs and wraps me in a hug.

"Lauren!" A voice calls from the couch, and I see Faye cradling the *Honeycomb* book to her chest. "This book."

"Did you like it?" I ask and join her on the couch.

"I *loved* it." She sighs. "I can't even fully process what I read, but I loved it."

Nikki comes in and nods along. "Honestly? I loved it. What did you think?"

"I thought it was brilliant," I admit. "I haven't read anything like this in a long time."

"It is so moody." Elyse sits on the couch. "I don't know. It was good—don't get me wrong—but it was so, I don't know, sad? Is *sad* even the right word?"

"It felt very nostalgic to me. Like he really missed his child-hood or just this sense that nothing will ever be the same. Wistful almost."

"Exactly." Faye is on the edge of her seat, eyes wide with excitement. "I think it was my favorite read of the year so far."

Elyse gives a smile and shakes her head. "You have said this at least seven times this year."

"I mean it this time."

We spend the next two hours talking about the book, going over it again and again. I pick up one of the few copies left on the front table and try to remember all the notes I made inside my own copy. The one that Rhett carried under his arm up to his apartment. The others talk while I look over the cover and run my finger along the author's name.

We are wrapping up our conversation on the book when Hannah calls.

I step into the lobby to take it. "Hello?"

"Hey, I'm almost to your apartment," she says. And I look back at my phone to see the date and realize I totally forgot she was coming up.

"I'll send you the address of where I am now. Just meet me here," I tell her and glance back in the sitting room. It's been a long day as it is. Now going out?

"Okay, great. Mom and Paul have Winnie for the night, so I can pretend I'm not just someone's wife for at least tonight."

I roll my eyes with a chuckle and tell myself that for Hannah, I can make it a late night.

"My sister is in town; she's going to swing by for a minute," I tell the others when I rejoin them. "She is dying to go out."

"Oh my God, Cal is going out with some friends tonight, and they are getting into the Kensington Club. I'm sure he could get us all in too!" Elyse says and whips her phone out. "Let me ask."

Nikki's and Faye's jaws drop while I question what the Kensington Club even is.

"It's this club with a rooftop space that's open all year. They have enough heaters to keep it warm, and it's hard to get into. You have to be a member of the club or have a member invite you. It's like *the* ticket around here."

"Is Cal a member?" I ask Elyse.

She shakes her head. "No, I think he has a friend who is."

Twenty minutes later, Hannah is walking into the bookstore and greeting the other girls like they're old friends. Her dark-brown hair is swept back into a low bun. She wears her jeans better than anyone I have ever met. She has big gold hoops and perfect skin. She's always been so pretty, and I don't know if she even fully realizes just *how* pretty she is.

"Lauren was telling us you were wanting to go out tonight?" Elyse asks her.

"Actually, Lauren needs to go out. I'm only here for the night, but she needs to get out and get over this little crush she has."

Elyse looks over at me with raised eyebrows. "Then the Kensington Club it is."

11

NOW

It's bearded, flannel-wearing, stupidly tall, goddamn Rhett Atwood.

Those bright-green eyes are looking at me, filled with as much shock as mine are. The wood is shoved under his arm and his face is nearly impossible to read. I sit in a stunned silence. Actually, *we* sit in a stunned silence. We sit in this momentary gap in time where he and I are on this porch, with a million questions worth asking that neither of us will ask.

I half expect him to set down the wood there in the doorway and leave, like he has before. To mumble some desperate apology as he all but runs away again. Instead, his eyes dip from my face down to my body, and I am suddenly completely aware of what I'm wearing. Leggings and a T-shirt with no bra. The cold air blowing in only proves that fact. With a small curse under his breath, I wonder if I'm imagining the flare of heat behind his eyes.

"Can I bring this in?" he asks, his voice gruff.

I nod and step aside. He comes in and sets the pile of logs into a designated alcove next to the fireplace. My eyes are unable to leave his body as I see him in the daylight. New muscles pull across his shoulders. The curls in his hair are more obvious now, with their new length. I had noticed a glimpse of this at the restaurant just a couple of weeks ago, but seeing him here in the morning sun just highlights it. Observing him had been so second nature. Watching him. Seeing him. Maybe it still is.

A low, dimly lit anger begins to burn in my belly. Angry at him because it's his fault that it's come to this. Us being uncomfortably silent in the same room. The one thing we never were. Our communal silence was where we prospered. Now it's awkward.

"Myranda set this up for me—" I try to defend myself, proving I hadn't gone so crazy that I booked a cabin up in the woods just to speak to him again. He turns, and my body flushes with warmth when we lock eyes. He takes up the entire room like he always has. This is the backward-hat version of Rhett. The one who drove a red pickup truck with gravel in the floor mats and never took a rideshare anywhere.

The flash of annoyance on his face is gone with an almost gentle laugh. "Of course she did. I should have known when my dad said a lady named Myranda was booking out the cabin for a few months. We hardly get renters anymore. I guess we half expected the person to bail anyway."

"You live here?" I ask, and he nods slowly.

"Grew up here. Moved back here in the winter."

Winter.

After he left. I chew on my lip and look around, biting my tongue. My little magical cabin, my hidden getaway, is now suddenly saturated with him. His hometown, his family's house. Just his stepping into this place took my little veil of secrecy and tore it straight down the middle like some biblical prophecy. Like the priest opened the door into my confessional and squeezed in next to me. Or maybe I invaded *his* little shoe-box-sized place of solace and comfort.

He makes a few more trips with the wood piles, and I'm too stunned to protest, to tell him I am fully capable of bringing in my own wood. But watching him from this close isn't something I thought I would ever do again. So, the weak part of me savors it. I let it last. I let my eyes wander over his back. Watching his muscles pull under his shirt. Studying him as he carries the wood, exposing that little sliver of skin below the hem of his shirt. Where the trail of hair stretches south.

Too soon, the alcove is full, and Rhett stands there with his hands on his hips, breathing heavy.

"This fire." His eyebrows raise. "It's awful."

My jaw drops, and a laugh escapes my throat. "I'm sorry?"

With an almost smile, he kneels, messing with the fire, rearranging the logs. Instantly the smoke is gone and the fire roars. He stands and brushes his hands off on his jeans.

"The other night at the restaurant—" I begin to say, not even sure where I'm going with the thought.

"It's my fault," he says quickly. "I should have just left when I saw you walk in. I owed that to you."

I want to argue. I want to tell him I wish he had called; I want to tell him that I have been waiting for that moment for a year, yet I can't get any words out. Because he's right. He did owe that to me. I asked him to leave me be. Now I am standing before him, wishing I hadn't asked that of him.

"I got your first few chapters from Myranda just a little bit ago," he says, changing the topic. "I can drop them off through the mail slot in the door."

I wrap my arms around my body. If he wants to keep things distant and safe, then distant and safe it shall be.

"Once we finish the manuscript, if you want to talk about things. . ." his voice trails off.

The mention of my manuscript sobers my love-sick heart. I am here for one very specific reason. And honestly, the idea of listening to Rhett explain to me that he didn't want me, and he didn't love me like I loved him, makes me want to die. I would rather live in a safe oblivion.

"We don't have to talk about it. It's over. We're coworkers. Once we finish this, I can push for a new editor, and you can work on other projects. We can forget about . . . this." I motion between us, and he doesn't argue.

The sting of my words is evident in the clench of his jaw. He bobs his head up and down a few times as he turns back onto the deck. Just as he gets to the steps, he turns back. Those clouded eyes lock on mine but he turns away again without a word and leaves.

I watch out the front blinds as Storm runs over and circles at Rhett's feet as he approaches the porch, his face lighting up at the sight of her. He scratches her just behind her ears.

His home, his dog.

That's the driveway where he learned to ride a bike, and that's the garage he and his dad spent that summer fixing up that damn old truck. This neighborhood, the one he spent his summers probably running around with friends, coming in when the lone streetlight came on.

My phone buzzing on the table pulls me away from the window.

"Hey!" Myranda's voice squeaks.

"Are you kidding me?" I say before she can get another word in. The low hum of anger, now bubbling up and over. "When were you planning on telling me where you were sending me?"

"Lauren, I'm—"

"His *family's* cabin? Are you insane? Do you realize how actually crazy this is? I sat there and told you how I couldn't even imagine seeing him again, that I was going to send all of my chapters through email, yet you think it was a good idea to pull this? He was literally just standing at my front door. At my fucking door. Or, well, *his* front door. Which makes this even worse."

"I'm so sorry. I know I should have given you a heads-up, but you never would have agreed—"

"Myranda! Of course I wouldn't have agreed! I'm not going to stay. I am going to pack up and head back to the city. I will stay with my parents or my sister until the sublease is up. I don't know, I—"

"Lauren, please don't leave. I can call him and tell him not to bother you or go near you, please. But you two are brilliant, and your debut is greater than you even realize, and you guys are the perfect team. Your next book is going to be huge as long as you work together. And you needed a break from the city."

A year ago, I probably would have agreed to this whole scheme. How naturally Rhett and I came together, how quickly our friendship grew until it was more than friends. I would have agreed because I was so blinded by his smile and his quiet disposition. God, I was a fool for him. And he for me, or so I thought. Yet it still wasn't enough. No matter how great the book turned out to be. No matter how effortless things between us were. Personally, or professionally. It wasn't and still won't be enough.

"I am leaving tonight," I say defiantly, letting my confidence convince both of us. "And I want a new editor."

I end the call and dial Hannah.

She answers on the first ring. "Hey, how's the forest treating you?"

"I'm leaving tonight."

The pause on the other side is nearly deafening.

"What?" she responds flatly.

"I'm leaving. Tonight. I'm going to call Mom here in a bit and I am going to stay with her until the sublease at my apartment is up. Or unless you have an empty bed—"

"Lauren, what are you talking about? What happened?"

"Rhett is here."

A pause, then a chuckle. "What do you mean?"

"I *mean* this cabin is owned by his family, and I met his dad this morning. At the time, I had no idea, but he offered to send his son by to bring some firewood in, you know, before it gets *too cold*. I pictured a *kid* to come help. Then just now, at my door, with wood in his arms, is Rhett. Just standing there. Turns out *he's* the neighbor's son, and this isn't just like his property investment but his hometown. They own the house next door, and they rent out the cabin. Myranda set this all up and blindsided both of us."

Another pause, a moment longer than the last, then her giggle turns into a deep belly laugh.

"Hannah, this isn't funny. This is actually *very* bad."

"Lauren, I mean, like, it's shitty of Myranda, don't get me wrong. But also brilliant."

"Brilliant? I just about begged to not even work with him, and now she's setting me up at his cabin? This is psychotic level insane."

"I don't know. I think it's smart, if you ask me. Maybe it's the universe, or God or the stars or whatever, giving you another chance. To work together and figure your shit out. Listen. At least give it a week. Okay? If he can stay at his house, and you can stay at the cabin, what difference would it make? And money shouldn't be a problem, use the money from Dad's insurance to skate by for a while."

"First off, Myranda isn't *fate* or *God*, and it makes all the difference. I'll see him outside, at the store. In the driveway. It's just going to bring up all those memories."

"Lauren. The whole book is about those memories. You wrote a book that anyone who knew you during that time will know what you went through. You'll be working through those memories anyway."

"That is exactly why I didn't want him reading this book or editing it."

"Well, it's too late for that. And you are not going to trade in a magical cabin in Green Branch for the fall to live in a spare room at Mom and Paul's house. I won't let you. Listen. A week. Give it a week. Use Rhett to get what you want. And what you want is a best seller. And you can hate him all you want, but he's a damn good editor. Use that to your advantage. Don't let him win this."

"You're not the first person to suggest that," I say and give up on pacing, dropping down onto the couch. Maybe she and Elyse are right. Even Myranda. Maybe I can put aside whatever we had for a few months. For my dream job, right?

"One week." I cave. "I will stay for one week."

"Okay. Tell Tanner I say hi when you—"

"Goodbye!" I drag out the word so she doesn't have a chance to respond before I hang up.

Swapping out my coffee for a glass of wine, I sit by the fire Rhett started, which is much better than the smoky mess I had going earlier. I spend the rest of the day avoiding my laptop. Avoiding apology texts from Myranda and flipping through whatever books that are on the shelves. Busying myself and pretending I'm not sneaking looks out the windows, seeing if I catch a glimpse of this flannelled version of him. The only thing I see is his red truck in the driveway through the trees.

On Myranda's seventh attempt, I finally pick up her call.

"Please. I am about to fly to Michigan to beg at your feet for forgiveness. Let me explain," she says the moment I answer her call.

"I'll do it," I say, before I change my mind.

"Wait. You will?" She falters.

"I will. But on one condition."

"Anything."

"I want a bigger royalty for this next contract."

She pauses for only a moment. "I'll put it in there. Thank you. I love you."

"You better," I say and hang up.

What the fuck have I gotten myself into?

12

LAST FALL

The rooftop is scattered with well-dressed people lounging around glass-stone fire pits in designer chairs. Even the chatter amongst everyone sounds expensive and out of my tax bracket.

My eyes land on him like my brain had subconsciously been looking for him. Rhett Atwood is standing with a crowd near a fire pit, a beer in hand, and he sees me as I'm seeing him. He tips his beer to me with a smile. I smile back and force my attention back to following Hannah, who is walking us over to Elyse.

"This is amazing," Hannah coos to her. "I cannot believe we got in here."

There are a few couples lingering about, drinking overpriced dirty—borderline filthy—martinis in frosted glasses. These people all have gorgeous haircuts, expensive wedding rings, and perfectly shined shoes. We are the youngest ones here by a long shot, with everyone else probably halfway toward cashing out on their retirement plans and Roths and jetting off to an island I've never heard of.

I even spot Faye and Nikki taking some pictures that I will see and like later when they post them, informing all their followers they made it to the *Kensington Club*. But I'm all too aware of the pair of eyes looking at me over the neck of a beer bottle from across the way.

"Are you okay?" Elyse bumps her hip into mine, and I shake my head back into order.

"Yeah, sorry. Tired."

"Then let's get you drinks." She waves over the bartender and adds our drinks to her tab, no matter how much we implore that we don't need her to.

"How is that book coming?" she asks, swiftly moving the conversation from the overpriced and undersized drink in my hand.

"It's coming. I feel good about it. We should be moving along pretty quickly now."

"Oh my God, that's right." Elyse's eyes light up with some divine realization. "Rhett is the one who got us in tonight. Your editor, right?" She turns and looks through the crowd. "He wasn't supposed to make it. He was just going to call ahead, but look, there he is."

We all turn, doing a terrible job at looking inconspicuous. Rhett's tall frame is easy to spot among the crowd, and though I saw him hours ago, it's like I'm seeing him for the first time. His gaze hits me in the heart and maybe even lower too. Even though we were just together, somehow here, across the crowd of indistinguishable faces, the sight of him has my heart pounding in my chest and in my head. He has a hand in his pocket and nurses his beer with his other while a sandy-haired guy next to him talks. Rhett doesn't seem to be listening.

"Wait, *that's* your editor?" Hannah asks. And I nod. And even in the dark, I see Rhett smile.

"Well, I'll be damned. No wonder you wanted to move out here so bad. He's gorgeous. Introduce me. Let me live vicariously through you for tonight."

I go to argue, but she loops her arm in mine and drags me away from a giggling Elyse and right up to Rhett.

"Hi," I say as we approach.

"Hi, Laure." His smile is soft. Small.

Laure.

He shifts his gaze to the guy standing next to him. Rhett is tall but this guy is even taller. He has long, windblown golden hair that's being held back by a backwards baseball hat. With jeans and a white t-shirt, he is the most underdressed person here. The smile on his face tells me that he couldn't give a shit even if he tried. And honestly, when you're as handsome as he is, you can get away with it. And he's looking at Hannah like she has arrived just for him.

"Tanner, this is Lauren and—"

"Hannah." Hannah pushes her hand forward to them both. "Lauren's sister."

Rhett shakes her hand. "This is my buddy Tanner. He's visiting from our hometown."

Tanner manages to unglue his eyes from Hannah ever so briefly and looks at me. "Wait, *this* is Lauren? Like *the* Lauren?"

"Yes, *the* Lauren," Rhett confirms, and Tanner's face lights up with a mischievous spark in his eyes.

"Holy shit. Nice to meet you." He puts his hand out to me. "I've been visiting for a week, and you're just about all I have heard about."

I eye Rhett, and he doesn't even bother to argue. He is just fighting a smile.

"And this is *the* Rhett." Hannah shakes her head. "Tanner, how about you and I go compare notes?"

"I would love to." He smiles. "Let me buy you a drink."

"I'm married." She spits the words out like they were bitter and past their expiration date.

And when I expect this conversation to come to a halt and

for Tanner to bail on his nice gesture, he only shrugs. "Then we can buy our own drinks."

She nods quickly and gets swept away, chugging the nearly full glass already in her hands as she goes.

"You're friends with Cal?" I ask, and Rhett nods his head with a laugh.

"Yeah, you could say that. We trade favors back and forth, being neighbors and all."

"What did you owe him this time to land him an evening at the Kensington Club?"

"Long story." He shrugs and sips back the beer. "But you need a better drink." He motions toward the red wine in my hands that Elyse ordered for me.

"A better drink?" I ask.

"You hate red wine." He states as if that were common knowledge. "Your counter has, like, three bottles of untouched reds, and your recycle bin has about three empty bottles of white."

"Maybe I want to learn to like red." I counter, and he tilts his head, beckoning me on.

His hand graces my back as he guides me through the crowd and up to the bar. We sit next to Tanner and Hannah, who are laughing like two kids. I don't know when or if Ethan has ever looked at her that way. Or smiled at her that way.

"Your house white," Rhett says to the bartender.

It's odd, sitting this close to Rhett in a dimly lit space with no papers or laptops to play buffer. In a room full of people, we are, unequivocally, alone. And yet, with a glass of white wine in my hands, I feel utterly seen.

"This doesn't seem like your scene," I say.

"What? A rooftop bar with this many people?" He teasingly cinches his eyebrows together. "It doesn't seem like yours either."

"It's not," I admit. "I told Elyse that my sister wanted to go out, and well . . . " I glance over at Hannah, who is beaming. "She needed a night off."

Suddenly Rhett straightens just a touch, and he nods behind me. "Look who just walked in."

I turn and see a suit-clad Runclave and a stiletto-propped Myranda stroll in, handing their jackets off to the door attendants.

A drawn-out, thin man like Runclave looks gaunt next to a woman like Myranda. Her hair is styled into the most perfect bob, cut just below her sharp chin. Every curve looks perfectly carved by lots of Pilates and highlighted with perfectly tailored clothes. They walk side by side over to a little section on the other side of the rooftop, where a crowd greets them. And I recognize one of the women as the one who told me the horrible stories about Rhett.

I duck so I'm hidden in front of him. "We cannot be seen," I tell him. "I will never hear the end of it."

"What?" he teases in a low voice. "Having drinks with your coworker? Is that not what they are all doing?"

I shoot him a glance. "You know what I mean."

A playful smirk tugs at the corners of his mouth. "What *do* you mean?"

"Rhett." I shake my head, fighting my own laugh.

"Lauren," he responds, a deeper gravel to his voice, and it makes my stomach flip.

"I don't need to give Myranda any more ideas than she already has. She has more schemes up her sleeves than I can count."

"There are worse things than to be seen together."

"Yeah, except when all those coworkers have all admitted to trying to get with you, and here you are."

"Here *we* are," he corrects.

"Can I ask you a question?" I finish off my drink, and I wave down for another.

"Anything," he says quickly, telling the bartender to add it to his tab.

"How do you have a membership here? Everyone here is at least forty-five. And I'm pretty sure that guy over there is that actor from that new show on Netflix, and he's like, very famous right now."

"You have to apply," he says, and finishes his beer. "Then you have to give a reason, or some qualification as to why you should be given membership. There's an interview and everything."

"And?"

"I told them how many best sellers I have edited at my age. They accepted me."

"How many is it?"

"A few." Another smirk.

"Yet you took on my debut?"

"It's good."

"But why would you want a membership *here*?"

"I usually just come to the restaurant. They have good steak."

It occurs to me then that this would be the perfect place to take a girl to impress her. Rhett's a big-city editor, and looking the way he does, a steak dinner at Kensington Club will seal the deal.

"Lauren!" a voice calls, and I know immediately that we've been caught.

I turn and put on my best face for Myranda, who is hurrying over. Rhett doesn't flinch. He stays leaning an elbow against the bar, with his body still angled toward me. Not a single thing about our positions looks casual.

"What are you doing here?" she asks, her curious smile growing.

"How's Charles?" Rhett asks instead.

"Intolerant." Myranda shakes her head. "He asked for a bourbon. They brought him top shelf, not the stuff in the locked case."

"Oh, tragic." Rhett shakes his head, feigning disappointment.

"Exactly. How is the book coming along? Everything I have seen looks really good so far!"

"Great," Rhett answers for me. "You were right. It's a really good manuscript."

"You wouldn't know based off the amount of red ink on the pages." I laugh, and Myranda smiles at me.

"Are you guys just getting some after work drinks together?" she pushes, and Rhett is saying yes while I am telling her we simply bumped into each other. "Well, it was good seeing you both." Myranda kisses both of my cheeks, then waves to Rhett. "I won't keep intruding on your date." She winks before getting the whiskey from the bartender and struts back over to Charles's side. She says something, and the group of them all turn and look at us. Charles gives a friendly wave; the rest of the marketing department shoots daggers through the dark.

"They're going to hate you even more now," I say, turning back to him, and he's inches from me.

"Good," he says, low and steady. "As long as you don't."

"You make it hard to hate you, Rhett."

"My arrogance did scare you off yet?"

"Let's get out of here," Hannah interrupts. "There's a place nearby I want to check out."

13
____

NOW

The morning comes as gentle as one would dream a northern Michigan October morning would. The leaves twirl toward the ground and tap off the windows as they pass. When I go down the stairs, I see a pile of papers tied with twine like an old-timey Christmas present. They have come in through the mail slot in the door and landed on the floor. The red ink finds me anywhere. My stomach twists at the sight of his handwriting, and I will the pricking of tears to subside. I leave them sitting there menacingly as I pour a massive cup of coffee.

When I finish the cup, I decide to continue my strategic avoidance of work and strap on my tennis shoes, stepping over the pile of papers out the front door. I decide to find my way around the gravel roads of the little neighborhood in some grand attempt to walk the emotions out of my system. I purposely go right out of the driveway to avoid Rhett's house, and I pull my baseball hat on low. The one that was once his. Another thing I can't bring myself to give away. Or give back.

The hilly road is lined in massive red-and-orange trees.

Deep-green spruce and pine trees are sprinkled among them, and its tunnel vision up ahead, with broken wooden fences lining the sides of the gravel road. Birds flutter between trees, and the breeze tumbles a few dried, crinkled leaves alongside me.

I follow the winding road down the hill until I find a small, rickety wooden bridge over a rushing creek. Colorful leaves of all kinds travel down as the water trips over itself. I grab the biggest rock I can find and smash it down into the water. I throw another, but harder this time, and mud flies up this time too. Then another and another until lungs surge for air. And somehow the silliness of it feels good.

"You all right there?" a voice calls from back up the hill. I turn to see Jack, working his way down to me with Storm at his side.

"Yeah, all good," I say, resting my hands on my hips while steadying my breath. Part of me hopes he keeps walking past. Leave me to my little pity party, considering his son is the reason for the occasion.

"You know, when my kids were young, they used to come down here and try to dam up the water. They would take big rocks and line them up against the flow."

"Did it ever work?" I play along, chewing on my nails as I watch the water rush.

"No. The pressure always built up, and then it knocked it over. Every time."

I know there's a story in there, some greater life lesson, but I'm too distracted by the little brown leaf stuck behind a rock. Fighting its way out.

"You're here for work, right?" he asks, coming down closer to me—Storm, too, who sits at my feet. "From Chicago?"

"I am."

"What do you do?"

"I write," I say, knowing exactly how this conversation is going to go. People are always impressed or rolling their eyes.

"My wife used to write. She wasn't too bad either. But my son is an editor. The one who I sent over yesterday? Not like he ever stood a chance to do anything else. My wife had him editing her books before he could walk into town by himself. I always thought he would be a writer too. He was an editor on a best seller by his seventeenth birthday."

"What is your wife's name?" I ask, wondering just how this never managed to come up when Rhett and I worked together. Sure, he mentioned he edited best sellers and that his mom was a writer, but never did those two facts cross over.

"Joanna Atwood. She went by Jo Atwood to sound more neutral."

I jerk my head to look back at him. "Jo Atwood? Like *the* Jo Atwood?"

He smiles, a deep, pride-filled smile. "That's my girl. Met her right after she graduated college. She had a dream and a book, and we made it work."

My heart clenches. He isn't just a young editor who stumbled into success. He's Jo Atwood's son. Best-selling author Jo Atwood's son. Are *those* his best-selling projects?

"Well, I am a huge fan of her work. There isn't a Jo Atwood book I didn't love."

Jack leans over and tosses a stick into the creek, and Storm goes traipsing into the water and splashes about, unfazed by the chill.

"Her books are works of art." Jack smiles more to himself, then points past me. "Walk up along the creek here. There's a small trail up to a little lookout spot. Beautiful in the fall. All these colors."

Jack calls for Storm to come back to his side, "Also, make sure to check out the diner in town. It doesn't look like much, but it's pretty good."

"Well, I don't think I trust my own cooking so I will have to stop by," I say. His smile is like Rhett's, rooted and genuine, with deep smile lines framing his eyes.

My dad was a thin, sharp man with angular shoulders, a straight jaw, and slick blond hair. Nothing about him was warm or kind or soft. Instead of smile lines around his eyes, he had deep frown ridges between his brows. My dad spent more time wining and dining his mistresses and frequenting bars than spending time with us. He chose them and alcohol until the very end.

Dad had left a few months before with a bag packed and a promise to never return. Which was a promise he unfortunately never kept. He always came crawling back, even when we wished he wouldn't.

I recognized the male officer who knocked on our door as one of the men my mom had dated to get back at my dad for his countless affairs. I think his name was Daryl. Daryl's partner said my dad lost control of his car and veered off into oncoming traffic on the highway. He crossed a grass median, and a semi-truck hit him. While Mom talked to the police, I sat at the dining room table, eating the dinner she made us. Which was overcooked and bland.

They handed my mom their cards and offered their condolences. I took another bite of the pasta on my plate. Mom thanked them. They left their number for her. I took a bite of carrots.

I didn't know then exactly what it all meant. Mom came back in and shoved their cards into the junk drawer with dry eyes.

"Did you guys hear that?" she asked plainly.

Mom had warned us, from the time we were very young, that our dad was going to kill himself. And that we needed to be prepared for it to happen. Either it could be on purpose or an accident. But regardless, we needed to know it would be coming.

He would often leave, and we would think maybe this was it, but then he always came back. He would swear he was doing better or getting help. Mom would let him back in, then soon he would be gone again for days, weeks, sometimes months on a bender. This had been the longest amount of time that had passed with him being gone. Months this time, almost a full year.

The cop said he was living at a motel about ten minutes up the road. He hadn't even gone far. He still probably shopped at the same grocery store. Got gas at the same gas station on the corner that sold the good pizza. The one he always brought with him when he inevitably came crawling back. Hannah and I would walk past the motel when we would walk to get ice cream in the summer. We were never the wiser.

We sat on the couch that night watching *Shrek*. And we didn't talk about it. None of us knew how. We should have been sadder than we were, but we lost him so many little times that the final absence didn't cut as deeply.

Though the winds pick up and I see the dark clouds begin to roll in, I decide to head up the little trail anyway. Quickly, I learn that *trail* is a generous word for what this is. It's nothing more than some flattened grass that winds up the hill. Roots jut up through the ground and low-slung branches brush my head as I approach the top. I come to a clearing that looks out at the forests of trees around us. The late summer green is fading into early fall yellows and a creeping-in of an amber-rich orange that is soon to take over.

I can't believe this place even exists. I've been living with a view of a brick wall when something like this could have been an option. It makes me think of just how much Rhett didn't tell me. We spent nearly every waking moment together for months, and I didn't know he was from Michigan. I didn't know his mom was *the* Jo Atwood. I didn't know a damn thing. He didn't tell me a damn thing.

Peeking through the trees, I can see the tips of roofs and smoke coming from their chimneys. Beyond that, dark clouds form and roll in as the birds seem to scatter to safety among the trees. Nowhere in my hometown looks like this. Not even on its best fall day.

I stay until I feel drips of cold rain on my head. When I'm back on the gravel road, the clouds seem to open up from the bottom and let down every drop they've been carrying. The trees aren't able to hold it back, but I don't bother running. This is the kind of rain that feels baptismal. Cleansing. Holy, even.

Soon I'm soaking wet and standing on the front deck, catching my breath. I try to fight the urge, I really do, but I cave and look over at the white house next door. Rhett is sitting there in a rocking chair under his covered porch with a steaming mug resting on his knee and a folded paper back in his hand.

He looks at me like the first time we met. He isn't just looking at me. He's *watching* me. Studying me. Even from a distance, he looks at me like too many thoughts have rendered him motionless. I was hardly ever able to read him up close, let alone from this far. We watch each other for a moment. He nods. I chew on the inside of my cheek and head inside, a touch breathless.

I change into dry clothes, then build the fire as close to what Rhett did yesterday as I can. Taking his advice, as usual. Then, finally, I get the pages and settle into the couch. I trace my finger over the words he's written in the margins. The little comments and the *I*'s he continues to capitalize. His edits are gentle, kind, thoughtful. There's no snark or bite. I flip through them, looking for the constructive comments, the honest critiques. I don't find them.

If he were to be honest about anything, I wish, at least, it would be about my writing. He was never soft with my work; he was honest but never soft. Now, his gentle scribbles are nothing more than that. Gentle. Soft. Passive. And it breaks my heart all over again.

14

LAST FALL

The four of us are soon walking down the cracked city sidewalk through the dark, leaving Kensington Club behind. Hannah and Tanner are a few steps ahead, giggling, bumping arms, and catching each other's eyes every chance they get.

"Your sister said she's married, right?" Rhett asks me quietly as we trail behind, our own hands gracing each other's every so often.

"Yeah. He's a real piece of shit. We're trying to get her to leave him. But they have a daughter, and it makes things tricky. What about Tanner?"

"He dated this girl all through high school. Got engaged. Then she cheated on him with his boss at the mechanic shop. It messed him up."

"Oh God." I sneak a glance up ahead at Tanner, who is smiling from ear to ear as Hannah tells him about Winnie. He's handsome and rugged. His baseball hat is now curled and shoved in his back pocket and his entire face is glowing down at my sister.

"He had to stop by the auto shop to pick up a jack to help me with my truck. He saw the light on upstairs and went up to turn it off, and he found them together. Turns out they were hooking up before Tanner and her were even engaged."

My heart breaks for him, just watching him smile at Hannah like she's the prettiest thing he has ever seen. A still-married single mother. He walks on the street side like Rhett does and guides Hannah gently away from drunk pedestrians and cracks in the sidewalk.

Hannah leads us toward a little red door off to the left, one you would miss if you weren't looking carefully enough. Tanner opens it and lets us all go in first. I wouldn't have been surprised if inside there were an actual hole in the wall. The ceiling barely reaches over Rhett's and Tanner's heads and the tables look like old used office furniture. By the looks of it, the bar is just a few pieces of plywood slapped together and painted black.

"I saw this place online; people say it's a hidden gem," Hannah says over her shoulder as we take the up stools at said bar.

The woman working serves the bikers next to us their beers and then shifts toward us.

"Tequila shots. Please." Hannah hands over her card.

The air is smoky and stale, the sound of late-nineties grunge music blasts overhead, and I'm questioning Hannah and every ounce of her judgment.

The shots are passed out, and Hannah raises hers to us. "To new friends and shitty bars."

We raise ours, tap them to the bar top, and throw them back together. Tanner whips his head back and forth, as if he's doing everything in his power to keep it down. Hannah giggles and is already ordering herself and Tanner beers.

"I'm not sure this is any better than that stuffy party on the rooftop," I say to her, and she shrugs.

"Wait for it."

"Wait for what?"

She smiles, and sure enough, within minutes, the little place is packed. Bodies all crammed in and watching a worker begin plugging in a karaoke machine.

"Oh, there is no way," I shake my head.

Her laugh is maniacal almost as she leans over the bar to wave down the bartender.

"Another round of shots," She calls out.

"No thanks," Rhett and I say in unison, but the woman doesn't hear. She slides over four. Rhett and I meet eyes and without a word, we both slide ours to our Romeo and Juliet.

The DJ takes volunteers for the first song of the night, and Hannah has Tanner by the hand, dragging him toward the stage. He seems nothing other than thrilled to follow her and to have her holding his hand.

Hannah says something into the DJ's ear, he nods, and the opening notes of "Smooth," by Santana and Rob Thomas begin to play over the speakers.

"Oh my God." I shake my head, and Rhett leans in.

"She must have him under a spell," he says into my ear over the pounding instrumental music. "I have never seen him like this."

I'm momentarily frozen at the feeling of his lips against my ear. He must sense my goose bumps because his fingers trace them down my arm. My body leans into his touch on its own volition.

I force my eyes upward to watch Hannah twirl around the makeshift stage, getting tangled in the microphone's wire while Tanner sings the words to her like they belong to her. She is beaming and God, I missed this.

"I haven't seen her smile like this in a long time," I say to Rhett. But when I look over my shoulder, I see he isn't watching them at all. He's watching me. "What?" I ask, feeling self-conscious but the heat behind his eyes only draws me in.

"I . . . nothing. Nothing." He shakes his head and nods back up to Hannah and Tanner, who are receiving a standing ovation and chants for an encore.

"No, not nothing," I push, the tequila speaking for me.

His eyes drift between mine, to my lips, and back up again. I could close the distance. In fact, suddenly, I want nothing more than to close the distance. To taste his lips, the ones, I realize, I have been watching all night. I want kiss that smirk off them.

He leans down and into my ear once again and says, "You're beautiful."

Heat flushes my skin as I shake my head. "You can't say that."

"It's the truth."

"We're coworkers."

He pulls back and looks at me, his smile melting into a more serious gaze. "It's still the truth."

I roll my eyes. "That's the alcohol talking."

Though I am trying to play it cool, the stool beneath me is the only thing keeping me up. Through the dark, I search his eyes for some ounce of a joke. A point of safety to retreat to because I'm afraid I will say exactly what I'm thinking if I sit here any longer with him and that look in his eyes.

A Paul Simon hit about a girl named Betty booms over the speakers now, and Tanner's voice takes over.

"Let's dance." Rhett stands.

"You don't seem like the dancing type," I tell him.

He puts his hand out to me and shrugs. "I'm not."

"And you're going to go dance anyway?"

"No. *We* are," he insists. "Come on, Laure."

My hand melts into his as he tugs me through the crowd until we are directly in the middle of the dancing bodies. With his free hand, he pulls me by my waist back into his body. We sway together in a crowd of people who don't see or care about the red flush in my cheeks. Rhett's hands keep me placed firmly against him, and it's like there are little pricks of electricity from each of his fingers into my hips.

He leans down, bringing his lips back to my ear. A place I'm quickly learning how much I enjoy his lips being. I have to will every muscle to not lean into it. To not stretch my neck out for him.

"Do you know why we came out tonight?" he asks gruffly while his chin grazes my neck.

I turn back and catch his eye, but he leans back to my ear before I can ask why.

"I was just going call ahead so Cal could get into Kensington without me. But then I heard you were coming out too. So, I changed my plans."

"Rhett. We were just together this morning." My heart pounds.

"But this isn't work. This is different." His eyes dip back to my lips, and I think I have him. His face is only inches from mine, and every ounce of gravity tries to close the gap.

But the song ends and now Hannah and Tanner approach, both out of breath and laughing.

"I'm going to the bathroom," Hannah announces, and pulls me by arm away from Rhett and through the crowd. "Come on."

My eyes are anchored to Rhett's as she drags me away and I hear Tanner drunkenly say, "We're going to marry sisters, aren't we?"

The bathroom door closes behind us, and Hannah is smiling wider than I thought she still could. She splashes her face with cold water and dabs dry with a paper towel.

"So?" she asks me through the mirror before spinning to face me.

"Tanner seems nice." I shrug and narrow my gaze on her.

"No, I mean his friend. Your editor. He's totally into you."

I roll my eyes. "Hannah, we work together, and we really don't even know each other that well. It's not like that."

"Surely you aren't that blind. I saw you two on the dance floor. His lips on your ear like that?"

"I'm not blind," I counter. "I'm realistic. And besides, I can't afford any distractions right now. What I want to talk about is Tanner."

She leans against the bathroom counter, and she shakes her head. "I can't."

"You can't what?"

"I can't let myself think this is real because real life isn't this nice." She pushes back off the counter and rolls her shoulders. "I need to go before I start to sober up and remember that a man could be this nice to me. It's better to get plastered and forget before going back to my life."

I open my mouth to say something, anything, but before I can she is pulling me back out through the crowd. She waves to Rhett and Tanner back at the bar to follow, and they are quickly on their feet, following us out.

Out on the sidewalk, Rhett gently grabs my arm and holds me back while Hannah and Tanner walk ahead; neither of them noticing our absence. His hand on my arm shouldn't be sending pulses of electricity through every inch of my body, yet here we are.

The Uber pulls up to the curb. Tanner holds the door for Hannah to slide in and across the seat. He says goodbye then steps away. Rhett walks over and takes the door for me. And just before I get in, I turn around to face him. He is only inches in front of me, with one hand on the door, the other on the side of the car, caging me in.

"You know why *we* came out tonight?" I counter now, clinging to the final drops of courage in my veins. Rhett leans down, almost challenging me, a smirk pulling at the corners of his mouth. His lips are only inches from mine.

"Why did you come out tonight?" His question a whisper.

"So I could get you out of my head. My goal was to make out with a stranger and not think about you."

"And how did that go?" he asks, fighting a full-of-it grin.

"Terribly," I admit. "I'll see you at my place tomorrow afternoon."

"Good." He pulls his hand from the doorframe and tucks a hair behind my ear. "I'll be there."

I sit down into the seat and swing my legs in. As I go to pull the door shut, Rhett grabs it and leans in once more. "Too bad I wasn't the stranger you chose. Tonight could have gone very differently."

And before I can respond, he gently presses the door shut. My jaw hangs open as the smile on Hannah's face only confirms how much trouble I am in.

15

NOW

It's not even eight o'clock in the morning, and Myranda has already called twice. Once for another apology and another to see if the edits are going okay despite everything. That despite my broken heart, she wants to make sure things are coming along according to plan. *Her* plan.

What I didn't tell Myranda is that Rhett and I have this unspoken agreement to a faceless and impersonal way of shoving edits through the mail slot in my door. I don't tell her that we have drifted from working quietly together in my apartment to being unable to say a single word to each other in person without it being painful.

I don't tell her how it reminded me of those years before Dad died, when my parents were nothing but passing ships. They usually just missed each other as they were coming and going. Mom would be picking up some papers from her office before heading out to a house showing, while Dad had just disappeared into the garage with his beer and sour expression complaining about how dirty the house was. Hannah wouldn't ever acknowledge it. She never said much. If anyone was good at putting their head down and withstanding it, it was her.

But when my parents did cross paths at dinnertime, or Sunday mornings, or those few in-between moments, it was war. Small passing comments and passive-aggressive notes became a battle. A cold war on our own home turf.

Dad would leave out his shoes or leave his dirty plate on the table. Mom would ask him to put them away or pick it up. The other person, in their eyes, was always wrong. A misplaced dish resulted in a screaming match, a personal attack on the other's character. A single moment would uproot years of distrust and anger between them.

"What is so fucking hard about putting the damn plate in the sink? Honestly!" Mom would yell from the kitchen. Which would arouse Dad from whichever locked room he was hiding in. He would come stomping out, his words flying before he even made it to her. His red face said as much as his voice.

"Can I not even leave a single plate out without being reprimanded like a fucking *child*? Can I not exist in my own house? Huh, Rochelle? It's not like you ever lift a finger to clean. I should just move into the garage, damn it. Maybe then I could live in fucking peace." He picked up the plate and tossed it into the sink. It must have hit just right because it exploded on contact. Tiny pieces of blue ceramic shattered into a cataclysmic expanse across the kitchen. The shock of it silenced all of us.

Hannah and I were in the living room; she was helping me with my homework while probably overdue on her own assignments. We were on our stomachs, knocking our feet as she would correct yet another math problem I had gotten wrong. We would giggle when she drew little frowny faces next to the wrong answers and smiley faces next to the right ones.

But then, a small little piece of the blue plate had found its way right in front of us. A little chip no bigger than a penny, just sitting there like a warning, a "Do Not Enter" sign. The little delicate flower printed on it was broken in half. Neither Hannah nor I dared to move. I was scared if I breathed, it would pop the momentary bubble of silence. That more little ceramic flowers would go flying.

"You're a fucking idiot," mom had grumbled under her breath before storming into their bedroom, slamming the door shut behind her. Followed by the deafening whisper of the lock click. Their favorite weapon of choice.

Dad sat there, still. Grasping the edge of the sink, gazing through the darkened window in front of him. Looking back now, I think he was probably reconciling with his reflection. He took in ragged breaths, then swung open the fridge, the condiments in the door clattering about. He grabbed out as many beers as he could hold and wordlessly stepped around my sister and me to the front door. Moments later, we listened in silence as his car rumbled out of the driveway.

Of course, he had left before. Hannah and I had grown numb to the slamming doors and the broken-hinged fridge. We were immune to the bitter fighting between our parents. We were all too familiar with sitting still so that maybe, just maybe, if we didn't flinch, neither of them would see us and wouldn't sling any of their verbal garbage at us. Lucky for us, I guess, their entire world was consumed in hurting each other. Like some ultimate retribution for this shitty double life, we lived. Pretending to be a happy family when we left the house.

But in those few moments I didn't have Hannah's shoulder to hide behind, I would scurry to my room. Like my mom did. Like my dad did. Hiding. Closing doors. Silently clicking the lock. I would get out my math notebook from school and sit with my back against the door. It started with drawing pictures, then the pictures turned into stories, then the stories soon filled notebook after notebook. Each filled with imagined worlds with families that didn't lock the doors within their own home. Families with unchipped plates and unbroken fridge doors. A dad who kissed his daughters' foreheads good night each night, no matter how the day turned out. And just looked at them. Saw them.

A bark from outside pulls me from the memory. I stand and peek out the window and see Storm rolling around in the front yard. Her ears perk up when I open the door and she is bolting past me through the door before I can even call her.

"Storm, come on. Your family will be looking for you." I try to motion her back to the door, but she plops herself right on the couch, placing her head on the arm of it. Her big brown eyes begging me to not kick her out. "Okay, fine. Just for a little while." I leave the door open a crack, to give her the option to leave if she wants, but I secretly pray she doesn't.

I pick my laptop back up, and with Storm breathing softly next to me, I work away at the edits, telling myself that once I'm back in the world of my book again, it will be good. That I will slide right back into my happy place and it will distract me from the fact that Rhett is just next door while his dog is resting against my leg. It will help numb the pain caused by the fact that Rhett and I—even though we are now only separated by a gravel driveway and a mail slot in the front door—can't even be in the same room.

And it does work, for a short period of time while I sort through sugarcoated corrections and sweetened-up suggestions. Until a whistle wakes Storm up. She lifts her head up.

"Storm!" Jack calls out, making her stand and stretch.

"She's here!" I shout back.

"Oh, did she come in?" Jack asks, coming up the steps. "Sorry, she forgets we don't live here anymore. Usually, she'll just lie on the front deck."

"You used to live here?" I ask him.

"Yeah, my wife's Alzheimer's worsened about a year ago; she got a bit volatile. So, I moved in here, so we didn't have to disrupt her from our home. That was before we had to move her into a nursing home."

Jo Atwood is in a nursing home?

"Well, Storm is always welcome," I say. Afterall, it's her home too.

"Careful . . . she might not leave then." He laughs before leading her back to his house.

That sacrifice sits heavy on my mind. That Jack was so willing to keep his wife comfortable that he would buy a house and move out of his, rather than displace her. Not that money was a problem for a best-selling author like Jo Atwood. But the movement of it all. My dad couldn't even tolerate my mom existing within our own house. And she couldn't even tolerate him existing at all, for that matter.

Against all my better judgment, I leave the door open after Jack and Storm leave. Because I can in a place like this, or maybe because I am hoping that next time, it's Rhett who wanders in the door.

A week after Dad walked out with those beers in his hands, there was a party at the district attorney's home that my mom had gotten us invited to. Apparently, she had sold him his vacation home up in Wisconsin and this would be the perfect networking opportunity. Hannah was excited to dress up so mom let her borrow one of her dresses, and Hannah let me borrow one of hers. I found myself spinning in the mirror, watching the fabric twirl around my knobby legs.

But then Dad had come home only minutes before we were supposed to leave. Hannah had me up on Mom's bathroom counter. She held up Mom's lipstick, telling me to pucker. The front door slammed open, and dread swept through the house. Mom stood in the bedroom, trying to slip into a red dress that didn't fit like it used to, or so she said. She wiggled and craned her neck back at the zipper until Hannah stepped over to help.

When the bedroom door swung open, and we could smell him before we saw him. He reeked of liquor and bad temper.

"Can you get out of my bathroom?" he snapped, coming into the room. "I have to get ready for this damn party. And if you actually wanted me there, you would at least not be in my way."

Hannah hurried over and helped me down. Before we could leave their room, we heard Dad bark, "They look like hookers. Is that your attempt to get back at me? Dressing your kids up like hookers?"

"Our kids," I heard Mom say. Hannah and I both froze there in the hallway. "They're *our* kids. Our daughters."

"I'm not so sure about that," he slurred and slammed the bathroom door shut.

That night at the party, we managed the show of the century. Mom and Dad walked in holding hands; Dad had shaved his stubble and slicked back his hair. He looked handsome. Hannah and I got to keep our dresses on, but Dad did make us wipe off our makeup on the way there.

Now I settle on the couch for the rest of the evening. I miss storm and pretend that I don't miss Rhett.

16

LAST FALL

I send Hannah home the morning after with ibuprofen and a corner-shop Gatorade. She was teary-eyed as she pulled her minivan away from the curb, and I can only wonder if it's because she's returning home to Ethan. Or because she's leaving Tanner behind.

Later, after getting some work done, I get a text from Rhett telling me to meet him at Ford's. I call an Uber and meet him on the sidewalk outside the store.

"Hey, you," he says, as I slip out of the car. I'm suddenly aware that I should be nervous. But I'm not. If anything, I am missing the pounding music that gave me the excuse to lean into him.

"How was Tanner this morning?"

"Hungover and heartbroken. How was your sister?"

"Heartbroken and hungover."

His mouth quirks into a small grin. "They're going to give us a run for our money, aren't they?"

"I think so."

"Come on." He tilts his head toward the store and holds the door for me. Part of me hopes that Cal and Elyse won't be in today, but when the chimes on the door ring, I see them both unloading a box of books onto a shelf.

"Welcome to—" Elyse turns and sees us, and a curious smile replaces any words she was about to say.

"Hey, guys." Rhett places his hand on my lower back as he ushers us inside. My spine goes stick straight.

Elyse's expression asks a million questions as her eyes dart between Rhett and me. None of which I have an answer to.

"How's your book coming along?" she asks, squeezing in another book onto the shelf.

"It's going," I say as soon as Rhett says, "Really good."

"She's modest," Rhett insists.

"I believe that." Elyse smiles. "Are you guys looking for any books specifically today?"

"I'm heading home and want a book for the weekend," he says.

"Speaking of home, where do you—" I start to ask, but Cal's cursing under his breath.

"What's wrong, babe?" Elyse asked, the conversation moving swiftly on.

Cal glances down at the book in front of him, thumbing through the pages. "These are all misprinted. Look." He fans the edges. "The cover was put on upside down."

"Throw them in the misprint shelf," Elyse grumbles. "I'll call the distributor."

"The misprint shelf?" I ask, and Cal points next to the register counter, where a small shelf filled with an array of books sits. The shelf is painted yellow and looks a bit crooked itself.

"All misprinted, but readable." He picks up another and shows me. "Upside-down cover, the cover page is missing, or the forty-fifth page missing. For that one we just typed it out and shoved it where it was supposed to be. We don't get as much for them, but we just give the distributor a hell of a time when it happens. They actually sell really well. You know. Saving the earth and all that."

I scan the titles until I find one, a kid's book, that strikes me.

"That's another upside-down one."

"I'll take it," I say and put it on the counter.

"Great. Feel free to keep looking around. We have some new titles that just came in." Cal begins moving the books to the yellow shelf.

"What's your genre?" I ask Rhett while we wander around the shelves.

He pops his head around a shelf. "Huh?"

"Genre? What genre do you like to read?"

"Oh." He shrugs. "Anything."

"Anything?" I narrow my eyes at him.

"Sure." He picks up a book. "I liked this one. It's a horror mystery about northern Michigan. I also liked this one." He slides the bloody-handprint one back on the shelf and pulls down another. "This was a mystery about a serial killer."

"Do you read romance?"

He eyes me. "For fun or for work?"

"That's a no." Now I nod for him to follow me. "I'll pick your book for your trip home."

He runs a hand across the spines, but his eyes are on me.

"What about this one?" I hold up a classic best-seller, happy-ending romance with cartoon people on the front. "Have you read this?"

He shakes his head no.

"Okay, what about this one?" I pick up another that Faye swore was one of the best she's ever read. Another head shake no.

I reach for one I would recognize anywhere. "This is the one."

"The one?" he asks, taking it incredulously from my hands. He flips it around like a piece of meat.

"Never mind." I take it back at some attempt to keep it safe. "I cried at this one."

"Perfect." He takes it back again, leaning in close. "I'll take it."

With a wink, Rhett turns from me and walks away. Suddenly, I want nothing more than to pull him back behind the shelf. But instead, I follow him with unsteady feet.

"What's the last book you cried at?" he asks me after he buys both books, and we say goodbye to an amused Elyse. The sky seems to have grown a lot darker in the past ten minutes.

"That *Honeycomb* book. Wells Stevens," I admit.

He turns to look at me, eyebrows raised.

"It was really sad." I shrug. "I think the author had a sad childhood."

Rhett nods, not saying a word.

"Did you not think it was sad?"

"No, not it's not that, at all. I just think that was insightful. I had never thought of that before. And I have read it a lot of times."

"You just had to have had a hard childhood to spot when someone else has too."

I wonder, for a moment, if he is going to respond. He seems lost somewhere deep in his mind. He motions toward his truck, and I don't argue. I just slide back into the passenger seat, no argument, and place my book safely in my bag and turn on the radio.

I don't know if it was some divine inspiration or the refusal to call it quits, but we end up working through more chapters once we get back. It was nearly midnight before we sat back in our chairs, each letting out a sigh and throwing in the towel.

This was the time our conversations usually ended in unsaid

things, neither of us brave enough to say anything more. He makes a polite exit, I watch him leave, and then I recount all the things I could have said.

But tonight, I sense a slight hesitation in him when it's time to leave. I motion toward the kitchen.

"Wine?" I offer, willing to prolong our night.

He looks up, an unreadable glance. Almost smiling. "Yeah. That would be great."

I pour him a glass of red wine and myself a glass of white. I hand him his, and we both sit on the couch.

"You said your mom is a writer?" I ask.

"Yeah. Lifelong too. Even when she was going through cancer. It was like a life jacket for her. She could be drowning in treatments or surgeries, but if she could write, then she was good."

"She got better?"

He smiles. "The cancer stopped coming back."

"I can't believe she wrote through all of that," I say as I cling to every little piece of himself he gives me.

We finish our glasses of wine and soon we are hesitating by my door. Trying and failing to say goodbye when he steps closer.

Suddenly the flash of fear that I thought I had gotten out of my system floods back with a dizzying punch. I am here in the city pursuing my dream career and in no way can I jeopardize that. Especially not for a fling. And Rhett Atwood, I'm learning quickly, is anything but.

"No distractions," I hear my voice say just above a whisper while my heart pounds in morse code in my chest. It's begging him to ignore me. To kiss me anyway.

But he hesitates, then kisses my forehead. "No distractions."

~

HE COMES BACK the next day. And the day after that. We continue to blame his broken printer, but after an entire week passes, we stop blaming things and just work. Even on days when he is working on other projects. We sit in this comfortable silence at my dining room table, pretending to not look at each other.

There are these moments, even though I say no distractions, where he gets these looks on his face that are impenetrable. And then I am sure that he will bring it up. Talk about what we are avoiding. But when he doesn't, I convince myself that whatever was said between us back at the karaoke bar was purely the influence of overpriced drinks and dimly lit rooms.

17

———

NOW

Rhett and I spend an entire week exchanging edits through the mail slot in the door like a secret affair neither of us are willing to face. I hear him walk up the steps some mornings. I smell him on the pages once they crash to the floor with a thud. Sometimes, I see his shadow hesitate on the front deck before he turns back again to walk across the driveway. And my heart aches each time he doesn't knock.

This Morning, I decide to throw the edits in my bag and finally venture out to the diner in town. It's the only place to eat other than the pizza shop and the deli counter at the grocery store, it seems.

The inside is filled with wood-paneled walls, worn green-vinyl booths, and table tops sticky with cleaner. The woman clearing a table calls for me to sit anywhere, and I head up to the counter for carryout and sit on a creaky, spinning stool.

A girl with wild blond hair comes around the corner, and I almost mistake her for Elyse. "Hey there!" She smiles, a twang to her voice. "Carryout?"

"Yeah, if that's okay."

"Of course. Here's a menu. The name's Mayben if you need anything."

"Thanks," I say.

"Maybe, your car is done." A voice booms, and I know the voice. And it's not Rhett's.

I turn, and in the flesh stands Tanner. Rhett's best friend Tanner, with sun-streaked hair and dark eyes.

"Holy shit." He laughs. "Lauren Dorada?"

His entire face lights with a smile, lines carved into his cheeks from smiling like that often.

"Tanner." I smile and give him the hug he was already coming in for.

"I see you've met my sister, Mayben. Maybe, this is Lauren."

"Rhett's Lauren?" she asks, standing straighter, and I am frozen between them, unsure of exactly what that could mean.

"The very one." He pats my back and motions for me to sit back at the counter. "I heard you were in town."

I scoff. "Yeah. I'm sure he's ready to run again."

Tanner gives me a side glance. "He called me and said he was delivering wood for the renter and that I never would have guessed who the renter was."

"My agent set it up. I had no idea he lived here or that this place even existed before a couple weeks ago," I admit.

Mayben smiles. "He told me about you. Last year. When everything . . . well, you know."

Ended, I think.

"Hey, Tanner." The voice comes from behind us. Tanner turns, and I know that voice. This time, I don't turn.

"Hey, Jack, look who I just ran into." Tanner nudges me, and I begrudgingly turn to see Jack and Rhett standing there at the door. Rhett's eyes are on mine in an instant.

"Hey, kiddo." Jack waves. "Have you eaten yet? Come join us!"

"Oh, I can't—" I begin to argue.

"I insist. Tanner, care to join too?" Jack looks between Tanner and me.

"I have to get back to the shop." Tanner tips his head. "Just came to let Maybe know her car was done." He walks over and shakes Jack's hand and pats Rhett's shoulder with a mischievous smile. Halfway out the door, he stops and turns on his heel to face me. "Tell Hannah I said hi?"

"Sure." I nod, and his lips smirk as he chews on the inside of his cheek.

"Come on, kid. Breakfast is on me." Jack waves me over again. As if I could really fight him on it. He sits in the middle of one side of the booth, so I am forced to slide in next to Rhett.

"How are you liking the cabin so far?" Jack asks. "Anything I can do or get ya?"

"It's great," I assure him trying to pretend that Rhett's leg doesn't bump mine under the table. "It's so beautiful out here."

"We could have moved anywhere, but nowhere else compared."

Mayben comes up now, dropping off waters and pulling the pen from her hair. "You guys ready? The usual, Rhett?"

"Yeah, thanks Maybe."

For some reason, when Mayben's brother calls her by her nickname, I find it cute. But when Rhett says it— well, a twinge of what I would never admit to being jealousy boils up inside of me. I stifle it down with a sip of water.

"I'll have the number four," Jack orders, not even glancing at the menu. I order the cheapest thing on the menu.

"Great. I'll put that in for you." She smiles and all but sashays away.

"He dated her in high school," Jack says, leaning forward like he has the inside scoop on Green Branch drama. "And now she is—"

"Dad." Rhett snaps.

I nearly choke on my water only to take another sip to hide my red cheeks. Hide my irrational jealousy. Of course he dated Tanner's sister. A girl like that? Sunshine with a smile. It would make sense for someone like him. The opposite of me. He needs someone not as serious as he is. Maybe he needs someone as plucky as a girl called Maybe.

"I heard Storm found her way over the other day." Rhett, thank God, changes the subject.

"Yeah, she helped me get some work done. It gets lonely." I force a smile before I see Rhett's frown and realize what I just said. And he dares to look at me with sympathy in his eyes.

"I loved working alone," Jack says. "All those handyman projects around town. It was a peaceful career. Sometimes the homeowner would try to be nosy, so I would send them away with some project to keep them busy. Especially when the kids tagged along. I sent them on whatever mindless task that would keep them out of my hair."

When Mayben swoops in with her arms full of plates, I'm struck by how pretty she is. She has the small-town beauty you can't pay a plastic surgeon to recreate. Big curly blonde hair, round nose and full cheeks. And Rhett only stops looking at me to look up at her. I feel that flare of jealousy again. Then to top it all off, Mayben winks at him before walking back to the counter. I glance over and see Rhett's cheeks blush. This may be a whole lot bigger than a high school sweetheart.

Jack is an expert already at filling Rhett's and my silence with story after story. He has a joyful smile on his face as he tells the silly stories that Rhett has to cut in and correct details. Like when it took place or who was actually there. I even catch Rhett watching his dad with a boyish grin as they recount a time at Lac Dunes, when Rhett buried the twins, Jackie and Gwen, in the sand up to their necks, and ran away.

"I just needed a few moments of peace." Rhett smiles softly.

When Mayben brings the single bill, I reach for it, but Rhett is quicker.

"I have it," I say, digging my wallet out.

Rhett laughs, and it touches a soft spot. "No chance. My dad didn't all but force you to eat with us for you to pay for our food."

"Rhett—" I begin, but he's already motioning for me to let him out.

Jack looks between us, and I can feel his concentration. Like he's trying to figure something out, figure us out. Rhett must have never mentioned me to him.

"Well, thank you." I cave, attempting to get out of his questioning eye. "I appreciate it."

I slide out of the booth so Rhett can take the bill up to the counter. I watch as Mayben smiles her charming smile and flips her beautiful hair over her shoulder and laughs a big laugh as he speaks.

"Missing Chicago?" Jack asks, drawing my attention back to him.

"No." I laugh. "Not even a little bit."

He smiles. "Rhett lived there for a few years too. Once the twins could stand on their own feet, I think he finally felt like he could move on with his life. He did a better job raising them than my wife and I did some days. Her cancer took up so much of their childhood. All just for her to get Alzheimer's anyway. Have you ever been to Kensington in the city? My Jo and I loved their steak. We went there when she finished her cancer treatment."

"Yeah, I've been once." The heat of the memory floods back into my system.

It's then I notice he's playing with his wedding ring.

"How long have you been married?"

"We married in 1982. I had a custom ring made for her and everything. It was an emerald on a gold band. She always said she wanted something that reminded her of here. At the time, I didn't know what that meant, but I drew up a million pictures and presented it to a jeweler in the town over. The green is for the trees in the summer, her favorite season, and gold because the name of her first book was called *Gold Lock*. Her books were just starting to get published, and we had no money, but I used every last penny I could scrounge up. And I wanted to make sure it was different and that nobody else would have the same one. To this day, I think the ring is why she said yes."

"That sounds beautiful. I would love to see it—"

"Ready, Dad?" Rhett walks back, dropping a stack of bills on the table.

"Sure, sure." Jack nods to me. "It was sure nice chatting with ya, young lady. Feel free to come over anytime, breakfast or dinner. We would love the company. I know Storm sure would."

"That sounds nice," I lie and follow them toward the door.

Outside, Jack walks over to Rhett's truck, but Rhett nods down toward my car. "Here, I'll walk you."

I dig out my keys, fumbling with them before they clatter to the ground. Rhett doesn't hesitate to pick them up. But he does hesitate to hand them back.

"We could work together. Just meet and work here." He nods back towards the diner.

I can feel the rise in my eyebrows at the suggestion. Does he *want* to work together? Is Myranda putting him up to it?

"I promise we can keep it strictly work," he insists. "We work better in person."

"Fine." I relent, knowing damn well this is going to hurt.

"Fine." He hands me back my keys, our hands brushing, and I spot the satisfied grin as he walks away.

18

LAST FALL

Halloween tumbles into the city with thunder and slow, steady rain. After nearly three weeks of working together, I've run out of coffee and printer ink, so I call Rhett while digging through the messy closet looking for the rain jacket I could have sworn I packed. My phone is pinched between my ear and shoulder as I dig around. There's a casualness to it now, hopping on the phone to ask a question or make plans.

"Hey!" he answers, his voice light, easy.

"Hey. My printer is down, and I don't have coffee."

"Come over," he answers quickly. His words, the exact ones I wanted to hear, send shivers down my spine.

"Okay. Do you have coffee?"

"Yup. I'll start it now. I'll see you soon." He hangs up, and I find the deep-green rain jacket I got from a thrift shop in college. I grab my green-handled bag, the L.L. Bean one my mom bought me for my high school graduation, with my initial, *L*, in script on the front. I fill it with my laptop, notebooks, and red pens. God knows we will need them.

On the way out of the lobby, I catch my doorman Herman's inquisitive eye. "Are you going to see him this time?"

"Him?"

"Him. That man that's been coming over. He tips well." Herman's eyes are mischievous. Glinting with questions.

"Uh, maybe," I admit and adjust my bag on my shoulder.

"Good." Herman nods and turns back to the security cameras. "I like him."

On Rhett's street, carved pumpkins sit on brownstone front stoops, and plastic-pumpkin buckets hang in the rain from the branches overhead. Ford's displays Halloween books in the window. Ones about witches, sorcery, and haunted houses. The whole street is encapsulated into a cozy Halloween bubble.

Between the coffee shop and bookstore is a single brown door you would glance right over if you weren't looking close enough. I pull up my hood and dive from the car to the awning. On the call box, there are two names: Ford and Atwood. My heart races suddenly. Even though working together has become our regular routine, something about going to *his* place has me freaking out a little bit. I press the button next to *Atwood* and wait, listening to the sound and inhaling the scent of the rain, chewing on my cheek. But instead of me being buzzed in, the door opens, and Rhett is standing there, ushering me in out of the rain.

"You could have just buzzed me in," I tell him as we stand in the cramped and narrow entryway at the base of the stairs neither of us taking a step back.

"I could have." He smirks, "Come on."

I don't know what I expected from his apartment, but the moment I step in through the front door, that comment he made about my apartment not feeling like me makes sense. This space feels like him. The walls are a deep gray, covered in pictures and bookshelves. He has a padded leather couch, with throw pillows and blankets over the back. The little kitchen off to the right has deep-brown cabinets and some dying plants draping from the top of the fridge.

"You should water those," I say, and he looks over his shoulder, a curious smirk on his face. I continue to look at the quotes held to the fridge with magnets and the stack of well-read books on the floor near the window. Everywhere my eyes look, it just looks like him.

"It's your fault they're dead," he quips.

I whip my head to him, shocked at the snarky poke. His arms are crossed over his chest as he stands in the doorway watching me. His eyes are lit with a smile.

"*My* fault?" I question.

He pushes off the doorway and helps me out of my jacket and nods. "You're the reason I'm never home to water them anymore."

I open my mouth to argue, but I can't. He's right. There isn't a day anymore that he isn't over. Unless he goes home to his parents for a day or two, we are stationed at my dining room table or on my couch with glasses of wine in our hands.

Rhett hangs my jacket on a hook near the door. "Coffee?"

"Please." I tell him as he pulls a coffee pot from the corner of the counter and fills it up. "No way."

"What?" He freezes like he had done something wrong.

"You're a coffee snob." I motion toward the pot and the grinder he is plugging in.

He laughs. "A bit."

"Rhett. I buy the grocery store generic pre-ground coffee and use whatever pot the apartment came with. You have been suffering in silence."

"I bring coffee over sometimes."

"Yeah, from coffee shops."

I watch as he takes down paper travel cups, identical to the ones he brings me, from his cabinet.

"I just don't want to bring two ceramic mugs of coffee through the city. But I could if you wanted me to."

"Rhett," I say, not knowing what else to say, but a laugh bubbles up in my chest.

"Besides . . . the company outweighs the coffee," he states, and I spy a slight pinkness to his cheeks before he turns back to the contraption in front of him. "Pick yourself a mug." He motions toward the cabinet next to him.

"Which is your favorite?" I ask.

"That one." He points to the top shelf, a green one that reads, *Don't Be a Prick. Tyler, Arizona.*

"My sister got it for me when she went with her friends for spring break. She said I was the biggest prick in the family and needed humbling."

I laugh at the idea of him receiving criticism and pull out that mug and one from a place called *Darcie's* on *Main* for myself. Rhett fills up both mugs, then opens the fridge. I peek and see it's filled with real ingredients, leftovers, a few condiments. And I can't help but notice the hinges on it aren't broken. But what catches my eye are the bottle of white wine and the coffee creamer. He doesn't even need to ask. He just pops the creamer open and pours it in, then hands me the mug. My heart flutters at the sight. God, *flutters* isn't even a strong enough word.

Atop Rhett's coffee-ring-stained table there is a neat pile of paper and some pens in a cup. Baseball plays silently in the background, and I catch him humming an Elvis song. When I pick up my bag and pull my laptop out, Rhett points to something in my bag.

"That book." He's pointing at the children's book he had bought me the other day. *Where the Wild Things Are.* The one I put in my bag and haven't taken out since that day. "I meant to ask why you wanted it."

"I just like it," I say quickly and get out my laptop charger.

He eyes me. "Remember when you said after reading *Honeycomb*? You said you can tell when someone has had a hard childhood? That book is the same way. Kids with easy childhoods don't love that book."

"Do you like it?" I countered.

"My sister did. She loved it."

I let out a shaky breath. "Hannah would read it to me. Whenever my parents were fighting, she would read it to me in my room to help drown out the sound of them screaming. Or things being broken."

Rhett looks at me with sadness, but I'm thankful to not see any pity in his eyes. Which strikes me because it's always pity. My teachers. My mom. The men she brought home. They saw me as this little broken thing. Not something strong from withstanding what I had been through. There isn't a trace of that pity in Rhett's eyes.

After Dad died, Mom started dating publicly. This time she could bring guys over without sneaking them in, like she had before.

One time she was dating this guy, and they could argue like they were being paid to. And about anything too. About the answers on *Who Wants to Be a Millionaire* or what to get on the pizza. Or how many times they spent at her house versus his.

After dinner one night, I went to bed, or so they thought, and I heard them arguing about going to some Realty event. Of course it wasn't just about the event, because soon they were screaming at each other. I thought, so hopefully, that the version of my mom who screamed when angry died with my dad. But I heard shattering glass and knew she had never left. The anger had just grown dormant.

One night, while Hannah was out with friends, and I didn't know what else to do. Pretending to sleep wasn't working and I didn't have a car, so I couldn't just drive around town until they stopped screaming. And the pillow could only drown out so much. So, I crept across the hallway and went into Hannah's room to find the book. The one she read to me when Mom and Dad would fight. The one with the little boy leading the monsters across the cover. I dug under her bed and through her knickknacks and clothes. I checked her closet and her dresser, but it wasn't there. It wasn't in her nightstand or the bookshelf that was mostly filled with perfumes and makeup now. I turned over every book twice, in hopes that I had just missed it.

Suddenly, I was beside myself. I was angrier about the book than I was about another man coming into our house screaming about God knew what. The book was nowhere, and I grabbed a book that wasn't it, and I threw it hard against the wall. Then another and another. And for a moment I understood why my parents threw things so much. It felt good to not just feel this anger inside but also to let it out.

"Lauren!" My mom came in suddenly, shaking her head, the red-faced man over her shoulder watching with wide eyes. "What are you—"

"The book!" I yelled. "It's gone."

"Lauren." She looked between me and the man and then came to my side and tried to usher me out of the now-destroyed room. "Stop crying and go back to bed."

"The book. The one with the monsters, it's gone. The one Hannah read me. *Our* book."

"Oh sweetheart, I donated all her old books last week. I don't know which book you mean."

"*Wild Things!*" I yelled.

"*Where the Wild Things Are?*"

I nodded through the tears, and I saw a crack in her stance.

A softness appearing in her eyes. She didn't react when the man left. Instead, she sat with me on the floor, our backs against Hannah's bed. "I'm sorry I got rid of it. I didn't know it was special to you."

I cried that night, for the first time since my father died. I don't know what I cried for. I remember laying there, my body racked with sobs. Maybe I cried for my dad or because of my dad. Maybe for Hannah, for my mom, for the continuous loop of men who treated my mom the way my dad did, or how she continued to take out her anger with my dad on those same men. That night, Mom helped me clean up Hannah's room. Putting things back where they belonged. Her dance shoes back on the shelf, her book on gardening to their spot on her nightstand. After, I crawled into Hannah's bed.

She came home late; I heard her and Mom whispering in the living room. Then the door creaked open, and she crawled into the bed next to me. She smoothed the hair on my head and recited the book from memory until I fell asleep.

The next morning, my mom said she was going to a working lunch with the owner of a land-development company. That she was hoping to get a job with him and his company. It would be a big salary and commission. She said Paul Ayers could be the answer to her prayers. She came home from that meeting, and I never heard her yell again. At the time, she thanked him for giving her career new life, but I thanked him for this new version of my mom.

Now, all these years later, Rhett has this misprinted version of *Where the Wild Things Are* open and is reading it aloud. I sit and listen with my chin in my hands and tears in my eyes.

"And Max the king of the wild things was lonely and wanted to be where someone loves him best of all," he reads softly.

"That's my favorite part." My voice cracks as I say it, tears threatening to spill over, no matter how hard I willed them to stay put. "I thought maybe that Hannah had written the book about me when I was little. I didn't know other people knew about it until my first-grade teacher read it to the class."

Rhett glances up and I see tears of his own forming in his eyes. He doesn't say anything; he doesn't try to tell me he's sorry or that it's okay or tell me not to cry. He pulls my chair closer to him, then returns to reading the book.

I usually can blame a glass or two of wine for making me teary, but this time I have no excuse but the softness in his voice and the gentleness in his eyes. The way his fingers separate the pages and turn them. The softness I didn't know at nine, or eight, or seven. A softness I only knew in the form of my sister.

"Come here, Laure," Rhett says and puts the book down. He pulls me into his lap and wraps his arms around me.

"I'm sorry." I choke out while embarrassment tries to crawl in as the tears escape down my cheeks.

"No. There's nothing to be sorry for," he says into my hair. "You're golden."

And we stay like that. This time, the story and hug aren't soundtracked by arguments and yelling. And maybe that relief is what makes the tears finally fully break loose.

19

___

NOW

Downtown Green Branch is ready for Halloween with pumpkins at most storefronts, and fake (I hope) cobwebs are strung up in store windows. There is a new chill in the air today, like October is saying goodbye and winter warning us of its arrival.

Rhett and I agreed to meet at the diner at nine o'clock, so I get there just after seven to get settled. When I walk in, he is already sitting in a booth along the windows. Two cups of coffee sit on the table in front of him. My heart doesn't just skip a beat; it doubles in pace at the sight. He looks good. As good as the other day—if not better. His baseball hat is on backward; his flannel hugs his arms just right and his dark eyelashes grace his cheeks as he blinks with laser focus on his laptop. I sit down across from him, and I almost see a smile on his face. Almost.

"Good morning." His voice is low and gravelly, and I have half a mind to dump this cup of coffee on him. How dare he come here with that voice and those arms, ordering me coffee, and expect me to continue to be angry.

"Hi," I force out.

"I had a feeling you'd be here early." He nods to the cups of coffee. "Scoping the place out?"

"I couldn't sleep," I admit.

He nods. "Me either."

I relax a bit when an older, rounder waitress brings over silverware and menus. She has a Halloween pin on her apron and glasses on a crocheted loop around her neck. She warms our coffee and drops off a glass jar of sugar and bowl of little creamers.

"Here's the creamer and sugar you asked for. I'll be back for your orders soon." She winks at me and turns to leave.

"Since when do you drink cream and sugar in your coffee?" I ask and reach for them.

"I don't. You do, though."

I chew on my lip.

"So your manuscript. It's—"

"Rough. I know."

He rubs his chin and glances back down at his laptop. "It's not rough. It's actually quite incredible. This is beyond your debut."

A flare of annoyance rises within me. Of course he would like this. The book that is saturated in the pain he caused. I wonder how much of it he realizes is inspired by us. Or if he didn't notice at all. And frankly, I'm not sure which would hurt worse.

"Thanks," I mumble and dump an extra cream into my cup.

"Don't be modest now. I think this is really something great."

A slight blush creeps up my chest at his words. A compliment from anyone would be nice, but coming from him? It feels as good as it hurts. And that's a lot.

"How are your sales on your debut looking?" Rhett asks like he is searching for conversation.

"I don't know. I thought they were good, but I'm not sure."

His head tilts in confusion. "What do you mean?"

"Runclave hasn't agreed to take this book on yet. He wants a finished product on his desk before he'll decide. He may not re-sign me."

A thought passes over his face, but he shakes it away—"Then let's get this book to be a best seller, and we won't even have to worry about that."

"Let's."

We order breakfast, and I continue to drink my coffee as we sit at that booth for hours. Him working on a stack of papers and then back to his computer, then back again.

I add in some of his edits. My lack of capitalization and weak sentence structure. There is no ignoring the few compliments he scribbled in the margins. I ask him about some marks or edits he's made. He gives me gentle explanations.

Lunch comes and goes, Rhett tips out the first waitress and we start fresh with the new one. Another older woman, and I'm glad again that it's not Mayben.

Despite the mountain of papers in front of me and tension in my heart, I keep finding my eyes on him. I'm having a hard time believing he is even real and in front of me. I want to reach over and touch his hand. After all this time, he had become a memory more than a real person. I have thought about him endlessly over the past ten months, so much so that I had this entirely new version of him in mind.

In my head, he was no longer this quiet, caring man who watched me when I spoke, who held doors for me or kissed my head. I had begun to envision him as this coward who got too close and then ran away, vowing to never cross that line again. Leaving me in the dust while he continued with his big-city life, editing *real* best-selling books and writing me off. I made him the ghost I was afraid to spot in the city.

"Everything okay?" he asks, catching me staring.

He looks older. Lines by his eyes, and focus lines in his forehead. He looks wiser. Even more handsome than he was last fall. I talk myself out of reaching across the table and feeling the scruff that suits him better than I thought it would.

Instead, I say yes, that everything's fine. I mumble a quick apology with a lie about the lack of sleep catching up to me and turn back to my laptop and type. I force myself to keep my eyes down. To not look at the way he still runs his hand through his hair like he used to. To not look at him and miss him, even when he is sitting just across from me, separated by only two feet and cheap diner food between us.

Dinner comes and goes; we eat whatever our newest waitress said is on special. We hardly stop to eat, just taking bites as we go. Finally, the crowd around us fades away again, this time for the night. Waitresses begin closing up, and we both look up, almost shocked that we have been here all day. Shocked that old habits die hard, I guess.

"We should call it quits for the night," I say and begin packing up my things. "Want me to email you whatever I have next?"

"Sure," he says and follows suit in packing up. "Want to meet here in a week?"

I shove the disappointment deep into my pockets, embarrassed that I even hoped he would say we could meet again tomorrow. Or that I wished he would tell me to not even bother emailing to just bring it over. That we could work at his place, or he could come to mine. Disappointed that this distance between him and I even exist at all. I force a smile and nod.

"Sure," I say. "See you in a week." Throwing my bag over my shoulder, I head out to my car.

But as I step off the sidewalk, I notice that my car has sunken forward. A flat tire on my driver's side.

"Shit." I set my bag down and kick the wheel like it will solve the problem.

"Do you have a spare?" Rhett comes up next to me. "I can change it."

I shake my head and point to the back tire. "It's already on."

"Come on." He picks up my bag.

"It's okay. I'll call the auto shop. Tanner works there, right?"

"They're closed now. I'll text Tanner so he can take care of it first thing in the morning. I'll drive you home in the meantime." He carries my bag over to his red truck parked a few empty spaces away. The street is streaked in dim moonlight and the fading streetlight. The same layer of dust and dirt cover the old thing. I miss this damn truck.

"It's okay," I say. "If you give me my bag, I can call a cab or an Uber."

He chuckles. "Not out here, you aren't."

"Sure, I can. Everyone has Uber."

He shakes his head. "The one Uber driver in town is a college kid named Nate who is currently up at Northern Michigan University until the end of the semester. Come on."

I reluctantly follow Rhett as he walks ahead and opens the passenger door for me. He hands me my bag once I'm sitting and even goes as far as grabbing the seat belt and handing it to me.

"I got it," I snap but he only smiles, sending my stomach into a tailspin. But the place where our hands touch is on fire.

"I never doubted that." He pulls his hand back and carefully shuts the door.

We drive for a while, the silence sitting between us on the bench. Taking up every inch of room we've allowed to grow between us. We pass trick-or-treaters on each side. Kids and teenagers dressed up, parents lugging the wagons behind with their pillowcases filled with candy.

"Did Myranda tell you I lived here?" he asks, coming to a bend in the road, where a few kids dart across dressed like the Sanderson sisters.

"No," I admit. "I wouldn't have said yes if I had known."

He's quiet at that for a moment. "Where would have you gone instead?"

I shrug and let out a laugh. "Anywhere. Not here, though."

"Don't hold it against Michigan that I live here," he says as I catch his eye for a moment.

"I held it against Chicago that you left," I admit and regret it the moment I say it. I zip my heart up and flip on the radio; it crackles to life, playing a country song.

"You listen to country?" I ask, moving the conversation on, not wanting there to be any space where he can question what I meant.

He looks over at me, a playful challenge on his face. "Do I listen to country?"

"That's what I asked."

He laughs at the annoyance in my voice and turns his eyes back to the road. "Go ahead. Find another station."

I bite, even though I should have known better. But channel after channel. Static. Or oldies. Or a Christian station. Then we loop back to the country station.

"Oh." I lean back in the seat.

"We don't have many options out here. For anything," he says. "Not in restaurants, grocery stores, or radio stations."

And girls, I think to myself. Yet it's been a long time since high school. He has left and come back, and she still winks at him.

"Has Tanner moved on from Hannah?" I ask.

Rhett shakes his head. "No. He's been inviting her out since he met her, but he said he'll wait for her."

"If I hear anything, I'll let you know," I offer, like some peace treaty or an olive branch. Pretending like my sister, maybe one day, dating his best friend won't break my heart. But I know it sure as hell will. Because if our lives aren't tangled up enough now as it is, watching him move on through my sister's life will just about kill me. That is, if she ever actually leaves Ethan.

We drive the rest of the way in the quiet of the winding roads until Rhett turns the car up the driveway. I get out, mumble an awkward thank-you, and close the door.

I'm halfway up the steps when I hear his door open.

"I had to leave," he calls out. I freeze and turn around. He is standing next to his truck, like he has half a mind to follow me up. And if I didn't know better, I would call his tone desperate. "I didn't have a choice, and I couldn't come back. It's all just—"

"Complicated?" I finish for him. I wait for him to explain any further, letting the silence sit heavy between us. But he doesn't. "It always is. I'll see you in a week."

I go inside with a pounding heart and peek back out the window. With his back to me, Rhett hits the hood of the truck and runs his hands through his hair. And, God, I am so mad at him. I'm even more mad that he's the reason I can't walk out there and wrap my arms around him and talk this shit out.

But something about what he said earlier strikes me as odd, so I pull out my phone and call Hannah.

"Hey, what's up?" She answers on the first ring.

"Are you busy?"

"Just taking Winnie trick-or-treating. Mom and Paul have an eye on her. Why? What's up?"

"Tanner has been inviting you to visit since you met?"

She laughs nervously. "Yeah. He told me the first night we met that Green Branch would be waiting for me."

"So you knew," I say. "You knew where I was when I first got here."

"Well—"

"If he had been inviting you, telling you that Green Branch

was waiting for you, then when you called and asked why I was in Michigan, you knew Rhett was here."

"I assumed you knew," she insists. "I mean how did you *not* know where he lived? It wasn't until you called me all mad that he was there that I fully realized that you didn't know."

"Myranda set us up."

"She has a habit of that. Oh, Winnie, watch where you're going!"

"I'll let you go, but we're coming back to this."

"Okay. I love you. Tell Tanner I say hi."

I roll my eyes hang up. Something stings about the fact that even Hannah knew more about these people than I do. So I flip my lights out so kids don't come for candy because all I can offer is my untouched groceries and a cautionary tale about falling in love.

20

LAST FALL

After hiding from the storm at his apartment and getting through some copy and line edits, the storm knocking the power out, Rhett and I decide on Ninety-Seven's. The very restaurant we had made fun of all day saying that some nepo baby probably took his bottom-tier inheritance and opened a restaurant, naming it after the year he was born. We laughed about it until suddenly, we ran out of work and found ourselves starving.

"You live right here and you're telling me you have never eaten here?"

"I get carryout. And my dad loves their breadsticks. He makes me bring some almost every time I come home. And who would I sit in there with? Sit alone at a white-tablecloth restaurant?"

"I don't know. Girls? Don't you bring girls here? On dates?" I force a glance up to see his reaction. To see if maybe I caught him in something, but then he tilts his head to the side. He doesn't think I'm serious. He promptly lets out a laugh. "Is that what this is about? Are you trying to gauge if I'm dating other people?"

The way he says *other people* makes me shake my head. "You know what I mean."

"I'm bringing you right now," he says. "What do you call that?"

"I call it coworkers getting food after a long day of work," I lie.

Rhett hooks his pinky through mine, and we dash out of his apartment and across the road. We stand in the entry way dripping wet and out of breath.

"No," he says low into my ear. "I'm not bringing other girls here. I'm not dating anyone else."

"You keep saying 'anyone else,'" I whisper back.

He looks at me with a seriousness that challenges me to look away.

"Two?" the host asks, forcing us to break eye contact and look at her.

We are seated in a room labeled the Living Room, and it's immediately clear that we are severely underdressed for this place. It makes me miss the dingy no-name Karaoke bar.

"I only had one serious girlfriend," Rhett says once we order wine. The confession makes me choke on my water.

"What are you talking about?" I use my cloth napkin to dab at my mouth.

"I'm just laying it out there. You asked if I was bringing other girls here. And I want you to know I'm not. And that I only ever had one serious girlfriend. She was a couple years younger than me; we dated all through high school. But then I ended things when I went away to school. I have been on a few dates since her, of course, but . . ." His voice trails off.

"But?"

"But I don't want you to think I am pulling these cards I know work on women."

"Are you not going to ask about my super serious boyfriend

whom I am madly in love with?" I tease, but instantly a hint of fear flashes in his eyes before he registers that I'm joking. Then he shakes his head stoically.

"Nope. That's none of my business."

"I had a single boyfriend in college. He was a finance student and we had the same pre-rec humanities class. He was as unremarkable as a guy named Matt could be. We dated for the semester, and then he broke up with me for his lab partner."

"Yikes." He grimaces. "Were you friends with her?

"Nope. I didn't know *him*." I shake my head, giving him a look. "His name was Matt too," I add, and it's his turn to choke on his water.

"Damn."

"Damn, indeed. However, he did send me a card after they eloped last summer. So, I mean, at least it was the one."

My phone buzzes periodically, so I silence the calls from Myranda and messages from Mom about a time to come visit or how much better it would be if I were just to come back and visit home again. Rhett cancels a handful of calls from his sister and brother until we both turn our phones off entirely.

"My brother and sister will call me before ever calling our dad. My brother even listed me as his emergency contact once I had a car because we never knew if my dad would get service in the hospital. But he was pretty easy. He usually just called wanting food or a ride somewhere. But my sister—" Rhett shakes his head. "She was a product of her surroundings."

"What do you mean?" I ask carefully.

"She's a wild child. Always has been. A menace, honestly. If you tell her to jump off a bridge, she won't. But you tell her not to jump off a bridge, she would be halfway down already. One time, I was taking Jackie to some study group while my mom and dad were at the hospital, and within the half hour it took me to get him there and to get back, Gwen had gotten herself stuck on the roof with the dog."

"How old was she?"

"Fifteen? Maybe Sixteen?" He shakes his head. "It was like chasing a cat with a death wish that summer. Every time I turned around, she was into something she shouldn't have been. Breaking into the high school pool. She had this boyfriend, *Patrick*." I chuckle at the way he says his name. "He was a good kid, and I swear his parents thanked God when he got into the University of Wisconsin and she didn't. She was always dragging him into trouble right along with her."

"Well, my sister spent most of her time hiding me from our dad's screaming fits. Then he died, and she married a man just like him. But Hannah being Hannah, she sees the best in him and is waiting for him to go back to the way he used to be."

"Does he hurt her?"

"Not physically. Just emotionally. He can be really charming. But they have a daughter. She isn't one to cause waves."

Once we finish eating, the string quartet shifts songs, and the sound grows. It takes me only a moment before I spot one of the violinists making their way through the room. It then takes me another moment to see him join up with our waiter and head straight towards us.

"What is going on?" Rhett asks me, as if I have a clue.

I shrug as the waiter approaches us and places a plate with a dessert and one spoon in front of both Rhett and me.

"Your friends over there told us the good news." He points over his shoulder at the couple who are craned around with smiles plastered on their faces.

Cal and Elyse.

The plate has "Congrats on the engagement," written in chocolate sauce.

"On behalf of Ninety-Seven's and myself, we wish you the

happiest of lives together." The waiter leaves the violinist to finish their song as my jaw hangs open.

"Oh my God." I shake my head, feeling the eyes of everyone around us stare with contented smiles.

"Congrats to us then, babe." Rhett smirks, playing along and raising his wineglass to me.

Maybe it's the wine, or the candlelight, or the violin, or the pretend promise of a lifetime with Rhett, but I raise my glass to him. "You're too much."

Just when I think we could sink back into obscurity, the sound of metal tapping glass travels around the room.

"You're supposed to kiss when people hit their glasses," the older woman next to us says and motions for Rhett to get to it.

Rhett laughs, a real deep laugh. "Is that okay?"

"Anything for a free dessert." I say back through a gritted smile and pretend that my heart isn't pounding viciously in my chest. Rhett stands and steps over to me, offering me his hand.

Is he really going to kiss me? Is this really what our first kiss is going to be?

I slip my hand into his, and he pulls me up into his arms. With my chest pressed to his, I realize I can feel his heart pounding as hard as mine is. He loops a hand around the back of my neck, tilting my head up, then pauses, just there before my lips. A single breath of hesitation, or maybe it's anticipation. With a final smirk, he leans in and meets my lips with his. And when I expect him to pull away, I can feel his tongue run along my bottom lip ever so briefly, and I pretend along with the rest of the restaurant that this isn't just a free dessert, and that this isn't the first time he's kissed me. And that this doesn't feel as real as it does. I let my hands wrap around his waist as he pulls me even closer, his lips greedy.

The cheering is what breaks us apart. We stand there staring at each other, arms and hands still clinging to each other, breathing heavily. Both of our eyes are filled with question.

What did we just do?

I am thankful for the low lighting that hides my red cheeks. All I can think to myself is that surely that wasn't fake. No way there was zero emotion behind that kiss. Right? But Rhett doesn't say anything else. He pulls back my chair for me to sit, then tops off my wine as Cal and Elyse approach.

"We just closed up the shop and wanted some dinner. We saw you over here looking at each other like you do, and, well . . . we just had to," Elyse teases.

"Join us." Rhett motions toward the empty seats at our table. "How are you guys?"

I'm still in a daze when Cal pulls out a chair for Elyse, and she sits without question.

"Great, we just had a book signing for an author from New York that went really well, and we have a company wanting to put their book-themed goods in our store." Elyse leans in. "Plus, I think the news station wants to do a special on us. One of their marketing people reached out last week. Said they had a source telling them how amazing our shop is and how we don't waste misprint books and all of that."

"Elyse!" I exclaim. "That's amazing!"

She nods and looks at Cal with such pride in her eyes, and he looks at her like she is, well, everything. He reaches over and rubs her back.

"How much longer until your book will be done?" Elyse asks me. "I would love to put out a whole table of them once it's out."

I smile at her offer and thank her. "I don't know exactly. We should be wrapping up edits here soon."

"Great. You will have to come in and sign some copies once it's out, okay? Promise?"

"Promise."

"Well, we should go." Cal stands and gives Elyse a look.

Elyse blushes and hurries a goodbye before linking her hand in Cal's, then kissing him.

"I'm so excited for them. That news piece will be huge for them," I say, watching them go.

Rhett nods and doesn't say anything.

"What?" I ask.

He pulls his head back in mock confusion and hands his card to the waiter. "What do you mean, what?"

"You're guilty. What did you do?"

"Don't say anything, but I have some connections at the news station. I don't want her to think it was like some inside job —" he says, looking a bit embarrassed. "They run a good business, and they've always been good to me, and I wanted to return the favor."

"I won't say a thing." My heart swells.

The waiter returns his card and offers us another congratulations.

"Thank you. Come on, *Fiancée*." He puts his hand out to me. "Let's get you home."

I let him take my hand and weave me through the sea of congratulations and well wishes. When the crowd disappears behind the closed doors, Rhett doesn't drop my hand. Even though there is nobody around to keep this charade up for, he keeps his fingers locked with mine as we walk back toward his apartment.

"Want to come upstairs?" he asks, nodding at his door. The answer I want to give and the answer I need to give are two completely different answers. I shake my head. Not letting the wine win again. Or my heart.

He studies me, but he doesn't push it. If he were to, I would cave in an instant. I think maybe he knows it too.

"I would drive you home if it weren't for that second bottle of wine." He motions for my phone and types around. "My card is on your uber app now. Your car will be here in a minute. I think we will be done in a few weeks."

I know he means the edits. But what if it also means our time together? Or whatever this is?

Deep in my belly, the fear of him growing tired of me inflates. Every day that we inch closer to the deadline, the more my brain is convinced that he will lose interest once the scandal of this is gone. Once he can, in fact, have me, he won't want me. He taps the back of my arm, bringing me out of my wine-soaked brain.

"Stop," he whispers.

I look up at him, and he nods toward my fingers, on which I have been chewing on what is left of my nails.

"You chew on them every time I bring the deadline up," he says, reaching over and taking my hands in his so I couldn't bite them if I wanted to.

He pulls me into his chest. With his head resting on mine, I breathe in the scent of him and let this moment stain my brain the deepest shade of gold I can imagine. The sound of his heart beating in equal measure to mine soothes me before too soon a little black four-door pulls up to the curb. Rhett places a kiss on my head then pulls away to open the door for me.

"Listen, I have to go home for the weekend again," he says once I slide into the back seat. "I will call you when I'm back, okay? Take a day off."

Of course I won't, but instead, my stomach just sinks at the idea of not seeing him when this wine wears off in the morning. And it sinks because he didn't kiss me goodbye when no one was watching.

21

———

NOW

The colors, seemingly overnight, have delved into their richest shades of orange and reds backdropped by the faded browns and burgundies of the changing leaves. And I know Michigan has already planted roots in my heart. Visions of its trees and horizons will follow me anywhere I go from here.

Frost has begun to creep in on the windows each morning and is gone as soon as the sun rises. I watch it melt away while drinking my coffee and waiting on Storm to find her way over to the cabin. Each morning, she pops her little head up into the front window until I let her in. We sit in front of the fire, working in a peaceful silence.

The book-club girls keep me in the loop over text about the book they're reading this week. Even Herman sent me a brief email about the lady subleasing my apartment while I'm gone. He said she's a retired teacher who got tired of mowing her grass and left Wisconsin behind, and she loves the apartment and the city. I feel that with every update, the ball is going to drop. That somehow all of this will be taken from me. But in reality, nothing has changed back in the city. Which, in all honesty, only proves how insignificant my role there was.

Every couple of days, Rhett drops the edits back through the mail slot and is gone before I find the courage to open the door. Tanner dropped my car off to me the day after Rhett brought me home. He told me it was taken care of, and he wouldn't accept any of the money I tried to shove at him.

"Listen, I know things with Hannah are tricky, but I'll wait for her. I know you and Rhett have your thing." He said "thing" like the word itself was fragile. "But when she's ready, I'm ready."

"She says hi," I called out as he walked away.

There was a hesitation in his stride. I also couldn't miss the smile on his face as he got into the passenger seat of the waiting car. I don't know why I've carried so much hope for the two of them when I know it's only going to make it difficult for me in the end.

Now I'm walking into the diner to meet Rhett at our booth, and I see Mayben, in her apron and a pen in her clipped-up hair, sitting across from him with two cups of coffee between them. The sight of it stings. She is leaning in and smiling at him the way I used to. Hanging onto every word he says. It's like seeing a mirror of us a year ago. Rhett's back is to me, so I can't make out the smile I'm sure he has on, enjoying a simple conversation with a nice girl like her. She tilts her head back when she laughs, and I can't even hate her. She's nice. And pretty. And local. Maybe he was right to leave. Especially if she was here to come home to.

"Oh, hey!" Mayben says, spotting me. She pops up from the booth and smooths her apron. "Rhett ordered you guys coffees; do you need anything else?"

The coffee isn't hers? "I don't think so."

She smiles and gives Rhett a sure tip of the head before going back to the counter.

When I sit across from him, I notice he has a book in his hands. My book. *Golden Hour.*

"First time?" I quip, nodding to the book and pick up the coffee I guess he ordered for me.

He shakes his head, straight-faced. "Nineteenth time."

I look at him, looking for the lie. But it's not there. "You've read my book *nineteen* times?"

Looking closely at the book, I see the cracked spine and curled pages. It's beaten up and in bad shape. It's what I've always considered a well-loved book.

"Well, I have finished it eighteen times. At least once a month since I first read it, and all the other times. This will be my nineteenth once I finish it."

I shake my head, knowing I will never be able to crawl into his mind and understand it. Understand why he does what he does, and more importantly, why he doesn't do what he doesn't.

"You don't believe me," Rhett says and sets the book aside.

"No—it's not that. I do believe you. I just don't know why you would," I say simply.

He nods. "After working on your new one, I was wondering if this sadness was in your first one. So I picked it up last night. I was wondering if I was too distracted to see the melancholy in it the first eighteen times."

Too distracted. The only title we ever gave this was "distraction." I guess even though we talked about it, it still stings to hear him say it out loud. I see his bookmark is close to the end.

"Did you sleep last night?" I ask, gentler this time.

He shakes his head. "No."

I nod and pull out my laptop. "Me either."

"Why? Because you were also up reading your debut book until the sunrise?"

"Because you were next door," I admit and watch his face for the reaction. All I want is a reaction. Not this nicety we have been playing at.

"Lauren—"

"Mayben is nice," I push, suddenly unable to keep the lid on my mouth. Tired of keeping it quiet. "Seems like things are going well."

I can see his expression change; I can see the buttons being pressed. There's a flash of amusement in his eyes. "What?"

"If you had told Myranda that you were preoccupied here, she wouldn't have bothered sending me out here." *And that you would be too distracted to truly edit my work.*

"Lauren, what are you doing?" I feel a twinge of guilt at the hurt on his face. But I just need him to push back. Fight back, for once.

But he won't take the bait, so I just shake my head and turn back to my laptop and look over these gentle marks in the margins. And after a while, he finally sets his pen down.

He leans in. "Say it. What is going on in your head, Lauren? No more beating around the bush."

There it is, I think to myself. The fire in his eyes. The clench of his jaw. The honesty I have been craving.

"Stop being so nice. You aren't doing me any favors by all of —" I wave my hands around the half-assed edits "This. Your edits are a fraction of what they were before. Your comments are compliments, not critiques. *You're* the one who told me that my work was worth making better. You were never nice before. You don't get to break my heart and then come back with the gentle gloves and not give this book what it deserves."

His eyes are narrowed on me like he's waiting for more. But instead of saying another word, I stare back. Letting him be the one to crack for once. Let him fill the silence.

"Fine," he says, sitting straight. His face is expressionless as he reaches over for the stack of papers. He skims through a couple of pages until he finds what he's looking for. "This chapter sucks. It's lazy. You give me these eloquent and beautiful lines, then suddenly you stop here." He stabs his finger into a spot with a single question mark.

I look at the scene he's talking about. It was one I wrote earlier this summer while sitting with Hannah at a café in Wicker Park out on the sidewalk. I had a lot of writing to do, and she needed to get out of the house. I may have been up to my eyeballs in deadlines, but she needed me. One ear was on her, and the other on this chapter.

He's right. It was lazy.

"What else?"

Then it's like the floodgates open. He tears apart my pages with his red pen and comments. Pointing out passive voice and lazy writing and whatever else he could find. He gives it his best, so, in turn, I can too.

After we hit a lull and take a break to eat when Mayben walks by, shoving her apron in her purse. "Bye, guys!"

"Let me walk you out," Rhett offers her.

And this, I'm sure, is to push back. To just prove my comments further. A knife twist in the wound of watching him move on. He stands up and follows her out the door.

I ignore the stinging of tears in my eyes while they stand on the sidewalk by her car. The few sneaking glances I do take, I notice her smile is gone. Rhett is rubbing the back of his neck. He is probably telling her they need to cool it off while I'm around so he can keep his job. I angrily slam my keyboard.

"Baby doll, you all right?" I turn and see the waitress standing there, a soft smile of concern on her face. A turkey pendant pinned to her apron.

"Yeah. I just—"

"Looks like maybe you should talk to him about it." She nods at Rhett and Mayben out the window.

I shake my head. "Oh, it's not like that." My voice is not as resolute as I wanted. She gives me a quick smile and tops off our coffees.

When Rhett comes back in, he doesn't say a thing. So I don't say anything either. I slam out a few more edits until I can't take it anymore.

"I need to get groceries," I say suddenly. So much so it catches Rhett off guard.

"You what?"

"Groceries," I say, swiping my things into my bag. "Meet here in a week?" I ask, but I am walking away with tears in my eyes, before I can hear a response.

22

NOW

At the grocery store, I fill my cart. My grumbling stomach thinks everything in here looks good. So I throw it all in. Sweets, breads, Doritos, Cheetos Puffs, you name it. The words I said and the look on Rhett's face play over and over again, and all I want is to tear into this frozen pizza. On my way to the check out, I pass down the miscellaneous aisle where all the paper products and office supplies live. I have half a mind to buy the rest of their red pens out of spite and toss them in with the fire tonight. But I don't. Instead, I take them and bury them beneath the notebooks. I can at least make him work for it. The cashier gives me a look when I unload all things onto the belt.

"Are you staying in town for a while?" she asks me, like a damn interrogator.

"Not much longer," I say. "I just have to finish some work up in the next few weeks, then I'll stop clearing out your frozen pizza section."

She chuckles and loads the bags. "The owner was wondering why there has been a run on them. I'll be sure to let him know."

I nod. And wish Rhett would be the one to leave. Because I

like this place. I like these people. I could even like Mayben, worst of all.

"You're the writer, right?" she asks.

I look up at her waiting for some clarity on how she knows that. "Sorry?"

"The writer, Lauren Dorada? Right?"

"I am. How do you—"

"When the town heard that Jo Atwood's son came out of retirement to edit someone's novel last year, we didn't believe it. And then I heard he came out of retirement again for your newest project? Well, we were all curious as to what would make him willing to work again. But I think I think I get it now."

Retirement? I shake my head at the thought. There's no way he had been retired. People were still talking about his work in the office. All those best sellers. Jo Atwood hadn't put out books in years, but surely, he had done other projects.

"The bookstore up the road here even has a table of your books right in front. They've had it up since it came out. I'm honestly surprised there is a face to the name."

"Which bookstore?" I ask.

She chuckles. "There is only one in town. Green Branch Books, just up the street here on the left."

"Right, thank you."

I put my groceries in the back of my car and head down the road, past the auto shop, until I see the "Green Branch Books" sign hanging from a white brick building that is sandwiched in-between the others. I park my car along the curb and go inside, and sure enough, a small table is stacked with copies of *Golden Hour*. A small sign accompanying them reads, "Hometown Editor, Rhett Atwood."

I pick up the hardcover book and run my hand along my name on the bottom. Turning it over, a small photo of me smiling on the back. Flipping to the acknowledgments I see where I thanked Myranda, my publisher, my mom and Paul. I thanked Hannah for helping me cling to stories in times of need, and then toward the bottom of the page, I wrote:

"My biggest thanks go to you. The one who taught me the magic of not being alone. And who reminded me how much I still hate red wine."

"Can I help you?"

My eyes flash up and see an older woman with wire-framed glasses.

"Oh, I just—"

"That's a good seller. But I think everyone in town probably has one at this rate." The woman comes over. "Rhett Atwood is Jo Atwood's son. They're from right here in Green Branch. Do you know the family?"

"I don't know Jo. I heard Rhett was in retirement before this book?"

"Yes, he really only edited his mom's books. Give or take a few. He edited hers since he was in high school. That boy was a best-selling editor before he could vote in an election. Joey wouldn't let anyone else touch her work once he got ahold of it. He retired once his mom's Alzheimer's took away her writing. I remember when he first started editing her books; she was just thrilled."

"You knew Jo back then?"

"Oh yes." The lines in the woman's face deepen as she smiles. "She would bring the kids in to get books pretty often. Rhett and those crazy twins in tow. I don't know how he did it."

"Who? Jack?"

"No." She shakes her head. "Rhett. He basically raised those two. Once Joey got her cancer diagnosis, Rhett would be the one in here buying books for their classes, or at the grocery store shopping. Joey wrote most of her books in the hospital those days and Jack hardly left her side. Which left those twins for

Rhett to care for. People joked he was a single dad at thirteen. And from what I've seen, they turned out pretty all right. Then to hear he's working again? Well, I was just shocked. After everything that happened."

"Hi, Dollie." A voice calls from the back of the store and it's Tanner carrying in a big cardboard box. "This was at the post office for you."

"Oh, Tanny, come in. Come meet . . . " She looks to me for the answer.

"Lauren," I say quietly.

"Tanner, meet Lauren . . . " Dollie's voice trails off, and she adjusts her glasses, looking down at the book in my hands.

"Lauren Dorada," I confirm, and she waves me off.

"Gosh, girl, you let me talk your ear off about what you already knew!" She chuckles.

"Lauren is in town for a few weeks," Tanner says. "She and Rhett are working together again."

"So, it is true?" Dollie shakes her head with a mischievous grin. "You must have some hold over him."

"You have no idea," Tanner says flatly and sets the box on the counter. I can't read his expression. Is he mad at me? Or is he mad at Rhett? Is he even mad at all?

"Well, Miss Lauren." Dollie goes behind the counter and pulls out a Sharpie. "Do you mind signing the stock of your books? People might buy a second copy if it's signed."

"Sure." I take the marker as Dollie urges Tanner to bring me a chair. I open the cover of the first one and scribble my name right above my printed one. The autograph I perfected my senior year of high school when I thought I would get accepted to the creative writing program at Michigan State University and my career as an author would follow graduation.

I got rejected from State and ended getting into the teaching program at the University of Illinois. I promised myself it was temporary. That teaching was just for now, as I worked toward my dream. But with each professional development meeting, the fear of not being able to get out creeped in. And as I sit in a bookstore in a town I hadn't even heard of a month ago, signing my book, I almost forget about all of that fear.

"You should talk to Rhett," Tanner says as he shuffles by with another box.

"I do talk to Rhett. We started working together at the diner—"

"No. I mean really *talk* to him. I'm not saying forgive him, but he has some explaining to do."

He holds my eyes for a moment before moving past. "All right, Dollie, you need anything else?"

"I'm all set. Thanks, my boy."

I gave Rhett that chance to talk when things ended. And then again, the other night as he stood in my driveway. But he didn't. And I don't think I could handle reopening the already bleeding wound because it may sting now, but if I find out something I don't want to know, I don't think I could sew my heart back up next time.

23

LAST FALL

I'm six episodes deep on whatever Netflix show I got sucked into when I almost miss my phone buzzing from somewhere deep within the couch cushions.

"Hello?" the voice says when I answer, and it's not Myranda like I had dreaded. It's Rhett.

"Oh, hey." Pulling the phone to my ear, I prop myself up on my elbow.

"Can I come see you?" he asks.

I look at the clock. It's six in the evening.

"I was starting to think you got lost,"

It's Wednesday. He went home for the weekend on Friday, and I have hardly heard from him since he left. He sent a few edits over, but I'm caught up and haven't heard when he was coming back. There's a knock on the door, so I look back down at my phone and see a text come in from Myranda, asking to stop by again.

"Let me call you back," I say and hang up, wanting him to feel an ounce of the wondering I felt this week.

In my oversized T-shirt and no pants, I answer the door for Myranda. Only instead, it's not Myranda standing there. It's

Rhett shoving his phone into his pocket, tulips and a full plastic bag from the grocery store in hand.

"Hi Laure." He smiles.

"What—"

"I'm making us dinner," he raises the bag to me.

I hesitate for a moment, trying to process that he's standing there. His broad shoulders take up the doorway, and his green eyes seem a touch brighter, or maybe it's just been too long since I have seen them last.

"Do you have some more edits in that magic bag of yours too?" I gesture to the bag on his shoulder.

He smirks. "Covered in red ink too."

I step aside as if that is the secret password to get in.

"Things got tricky at home," he says, pulling out a mason jar from the cabinet. He unties the twine and brown paper from the flowers and puts them in the jar. Tulips. All different shades of pink. It's like butterflies have taken up residency in my stomach.

"I love tulips." I tell him.

"I know. You write about them a lot."

I watch him arrange them and place them on the center of the table.

"When did you get back into town?" I ask.

He checks his watch. "Just a bit ago."

"Have you been home yet?"

"Not yet."

"Well, once we finish eating, you need to go home and sleep."

He shakes his head like it's a silly notion. "I'm good. I'll sleep in tomorrow."

I think about arguing, but I don't dare, because I am happy he's here. "Then we can meet at your place tomorrow," I suggest. "Just text me when you're awake, and I will head over."

"That sounds perfect," he smiles and begins prepping dinner.

"Spaghetti?" I ask.

"It's not Ninety-Seven's, but the recipe is good," he promises with a glint in his eye. "Want to pour us some wine?"

"Hm." I pour us each a glass, then lean against the counter, watching him work. "He can edit *and* he can cook?"

"I've been trying to convince you, kid, I'm a real catch." He winks.

"As if you've needed to prove it." I sip my wine, hoping the glass hides my blushing cheeks.

He glances over at me, but he shakes his head with a deep grin instead of responding.

We eat on the couch, and it's divine. I want nothing more than to only eat food cooked by Rhett for the rest of my life. And not only in the romantic sense, but in the garlic and cheese sense. I catch him smiling at me, and maybe I do mean the romantic sense.

After dinner, we silently pick up our dishes and stand at the kitchen sink side by side. It's a revered respect for the quiet, and we don't see a need to fill it. Just when I expect him to go to the table to get to work, he doesn't. Instead, I flip on some lamps, and something across the room catches his eye.

It's the old record player Elyse gave me a few days ago when I stopped in. Truthfully, I was hoping to catch a glimpse of whether Rhett was back home yet, but then she had handed off her old record player to me to make room for their "new" vintage one for the store.

"What records do you have?" he asks.

"I'm not sure," I admit. "Elyse just gave me a box full."

He kneels and flips through the collection. I am in a trance, watching his fingers carefully flick through the records until he finds one. It's *From Elvis in Memphis*.

He pulls a record out of a torn cover and places it on the player. "Wearin' That Loved-On Look" comes on.

"Isn't it about his girl cheating on him while he was gone?" I tease while Elvis's voice croons through the room.

"You didn't cheat on me while I was gone, did you?" he teases and puts his hand out for me.

I take it hesitantly, the wine flooding my cheeks with a deep red blush. "Wouldn't I have to be your girl to cheat?"

"Are you?" His eyes are locked on mine, and it sets my spine straight.

"Am I?"

He pulls me against him, and we sway around the living room. "Will you be?"

I laugh as he dips me, and all I can think is that there never really was any other option for us. The moment I saw him sitting there at the coffee shop, I think I knew I was a goner. All these tiny moments were just building up until neither of us could deny just what has happened here. The quiet moments in crowded rooms. The conversations lit by lamplight. The longing stares over coffee shop tables and cups of coffee.

He kisses me gently at first, like the kiss back at Ninety-Seven's. Then he pulls back to check my eyes, to see if we are on the same page. I hate even the few inches of space between us, so I pull him back and feel his smile against my lips. He kisses me harder, like he needs it this time. Like he has been waiting for this as long as I have. His tongue grazes my bottom lip before he bites down gently.

"Rhett." I moan into his mouth as our hands snake around each other pulling the other closer and tighter. Each place his fingers touch simmers with heat.

Rhett walks backward, pulling me with him so our bodies stay connected. He sits back into the couch and tugs me down on top of him, so I'm straddling his lap. Our mouths search each other like every pent-up ounce of tension between us has erupted. Our hands cover enough ground on each other's body in attempt to make up for lost time. My mind is completely centered, steady right here, feeling the electricity in each fingertip as he buries them into my upper thighs. Every imagined moment of this dulls in comparison to the fire that is igniting through my body. So, I push out every ounce of warning and fear and let the flames consume me.

My hands find their way under his shirt, and something about the feel of the hair on his chest and his skin on mine is intoxicating. Any nerves melt away as he leans forward and lets me pull his shirt off over his head and toss it aside. I whisper his name between kisses, making my name fall from his lips in a moan. His hands reach higher up my thighs and around, squeezing as he goes. He moves his lips from mine to my jaw, down my neck, and along my collarbone like he's finding his way home. My head falls back as he pulls the collar of my T-shirt down, revealing just a few extra inches of my shoulder, then laces it with kisses and bites, ones I know I will count when he's gone. Inch by inch, his lips trail from one shoulder to the other. With a mind of their own, my hips rock against him and I feel how much he wants this too, and I almost come undone just at the thought.

"God, Lauren." He groans into my neck. The drop in octave has my head dropping back. "Leaving marks on your neck might be my new favorite hobby."

My shirt is almost off when my name is being called out and not from him—but from the front door. "I hear your music; I know you're home. Can I just come in?"

Myranda.

Rhett keeps me pinned there for a moment, fingers digging into my hips while we stare at each other with our chests heaving, trying to catch our breath. Then I silently scramble off him despite his silent protest, and I find my phone. I have a missed call and several follow-up texts from Myranda reminding me that not only did she want to come by, but that she was also already in the area.

"Uh, yeah, one second," I call back, pulling my shirt back in order. I motion for Rhett to go into my bedroom, and I close the door behind him. I smooth my hair and my clothes, and let Myranda in. "Sorry, I was—"

"No, don't be sorry." She smiles and strides on in. "You look cute! All flushed and airy. Maybe the city is growing on you."

"Maybe," I mumble, and spot Rhett's bag on the back of his chair still.

"Looks like things are going well between you and Rhett?" she says, and I can't gauge what she means exactly. Does she see his bag too? Or is it the stretched collar of my shirt? I scratch my head and wince a bit at the understatement. "Yeah. He's a good editor."

"I mean seeing you guys out together at Kensington Club. Date night?"

"No," I say quickly, and pray she doesn't pay any attention to the two empty glasses on the coffee table. "We have some mutual friends. We just ran into each other."

Myranda scans around the room, and as I nervously fold the blanket, Rhett's shirt tumbles from it, and I nearly dive to shove it in between the cushions.

"Mm-hmm." She sits at the counter, missing the action. "Anyway, I just wanted to stop by and let you know Charlie is wanting to push up the deadlines a little bit. You guys are flying through these edits, and he thinks we could get the edits even faster. I'll email you over the new schedule. Rhett said you two have taken to just working here together?"

"Uh, yeah," I say and nervously wipe down the counter. "I have a better printer than he does, and it just works."

"Great." She smiles a devilish smile, "I had a feeling you two would hit it off. I'll let you be. I'm sure you had a long night last night." She winks and wiggles her fingers goodbye and is out the door. I watch as the elevator opens and she steps in, giving one last wave.

"Where's my shirt?" I turn, and Rhett is standing there with a playful grin on his face.

His chest is on full display, and I want to go back to pressing mine against his. His arms are strong with rounded shoulders, and God, I want to crawl right back into him.

I need to snap out of it, put my head back on straight. But standing here, watching him look at me the way he is, isn't sobering me. Not even a little bit.

"Uh, your shirt is—"

"Not on," says a voice that doesn't come from either of us.

I spin, and it's not Myranda in the hallway but Elyse, jaw dropped in amusement.

"Oh God." My hand flies to my forehead. "This isn't—"

"I texted you earlier that I had more records to drop off, but you were obviously busy." She wags her eyebrows at me.

"Hey, Elyse." Rhett smiles that unbothered smile.

"Hey, Rhett." She smirks back and walks past me and into the apartment, investigating. Then she turns back to me. "I ran into Myranda in the elevator. She warned me that you may have already had company."

Rhett, seemingly unfazed, finds his shirt between the cushions, slips it back on over his head, and begins collecting his things. Meanwhile, my feet are cemented to the floor, and half of me is ready to dart out this door. Spare myself any more embarrassment.

"Nothing gets by you guys," he says to Elyse. Then kisses my head and whispers, "I'll call you tomorrow." Then slips out past me and to the stairs.

I take my time closing the door, and once it clicks shut, I turn to Elyse's jaw on the floor.

"Holy shit!" she yells out. "I knew you two were, like, *into each other*, but I didn't know you were hooking up instead of writing!"

I roll my eyes and grab our abandoned glasses and rinse them out. "That's not what is going on here."

"Did you guys have sex? Like just now?"

"No!" I splash water at her, and she erupts into laughter. "We just kissed."

"*Just* kissed?" She laughs, "Lauren, you have a hickey forming on your neck, and his shirt was shoved into your couch cushion!" My fingers fly to the sore spot just behind my ear, and I blush at its tenderness.

"Listen. It is more complicated than just making out," I say and finish cleaning up the kitchen. "Myranda can't know. She could have him reassigned."

"She is the one who warned me about the hickey, the two wineglasses, and his bag still being here. Herman the door guy warned me he's been here a lot. I didn't even believe it. I had to come see for myself. So much for getting him out of your system." She raises her eyebrows. "Looks like you just got your first real taste."

24

NOW

The coffee sloshes in my mug as I step off the gravel path and onto the tree-lined trail. The creek is rushing even faster than it was last time. I find my way past the rushing water and up the hill to the top of the lookout spot. The cool air bites at my lungs as I push up through the trees. At the top, I sit among the damp leaves and impending dark clouds.

It's been days since I saw Tanner at the bookstore. Both his words and Dollie's continue to loop through my mind. If Rhett really had wanted to tell me why he left, he would have. But the question nags at me. Why would he come out of retirement for me?

"Mind some company?" I turn and watch Rhett himself step into the clearing with a large thermos in his hand as if I had summoned him. "I brought coffee."

A peace offering.

I pat the ground next to me in the form of a cease-fire and he sits, leaving a safe gap between us. I hold my mug out for him to top off.

"My dad said you might be here." Rhett says as he pours the lid of the thermos full for himself. There's creamer in the coffee.

"I ran into him and Storm down by the creek the other day."

He laughs. "He knows this place is where I disappeared to in high school when things at home were crazy."

"I couldn't imagine having this all in your backyard." I motion toward the view before us. The hill and horizon are something from a postcard. It's breathtaking.

We don't say anything for a long while. I keep my elbows on my knees, and so does he. I wonder if we could just forget everything between us. Could we continue like coworkers and like nothing ever happened? Rather than beating around the bush or even acknowledging it, we completely forget it.

"Where are you going after you're done here?" Rhett asks gently.

The right answer is the city. I know that, of course. But now, just these few weeks out of there, I can't even imagine returning to the busy sidewalks and incessant traffic. But I also know I can't stay here.

"I have no idea," I admit.

"At least you have the freedom to go anywhere."

"Or it's really just paralyzing that I have nowhere to call home."

I feel Rhett's stare after I say it. The envy is buried deep within my words. The envy of knowing a view like it were a friend. Of knowing the route home like muscle memory. Of having a place you could miss. Gravel road memories and "usuals" at local diners.

"I'm jealous you get to live here." I break the silence with an easy joke that I deeply mean. "There are few places prettier than this."

I try to not look over at him, but in my peripheral vision, I can still see his smile.

"My dad loves this place so much, he wanted to move away," he says.

"Why would he leave?"

"He told me it feels like he's overwriting a VHS tape of happy memories here with lonely ones. He mentioned selling both houses and moving into some old fishing cabin on Lake Michigan."

Looking over, I watch his expression shift as he sips his coffee. I wonder what it would be like to love a place so much you would leave it, just to keep it being a place you loved. To prevent it from becoming polluted with sadness and grief.

I may have stayed up too many nights reading *A Christmas Carol* as a kid, but once my dad died, I felt like our house was haunted. And not that his ghost wandered the halls, slamming doors and tossing plates across the kitchen. But I felt like the ghost of what my family could have been was always there. I watched my friends' parents pray over dinner together or take walks around the neighborhood together. The ghost of my family ever achieving that creaked down the hall, reminding me I would never, in fact, have it. Reminding me that people leave, and they don't always come back. But I never really considered that people could, in fact, stay.

"I met Dollie," I say. And this brings a chuckle out of him.

"Oh yeah? What did she have to say?"

"Oh, I could never betray a bookseller's code. What one talks about with their bookseller must never be repeated." I hold my hand up like an oath. "It will be my honor to never tell."

His chuckle turns into a real laugh. "She called me after you left."

I whip my head to look at him, and he continues looking straight ahead.

"What did she say?" I press.

He shrugs. "Oh, I could never betray a bookseller's code."

Now I'm the one left shaking my head. "Fair."

"She told me this beautiful girl came in. And asked if it was true if you were just here for work. Or if it was more."

My stomach flips and I can't bring myself to let him say it isn't more. So instead, I ask, "What's Dollie's story? Is she married?"

"She was. Her husband died a while ago. I think she had a son, but they're estranged. She won't talk about it. Or him. Tanner helps her out a lot. He's looking at buying some of her land."

I'm about to ask what Tanner was saying the other day when he said that Rhett had some explaining to do, but our coffee and time have run out, and Rhett is standing, giving me his hand to help me up.

And when I let him, he pulls me straight into his chest. For a moment, neither of us moves away. We stand there with the cold wind pushing us together. Our chests breathing against each other. I finally break away because I know a moment longer would be too long for my resolve to keep strong.

"We should go," I say, and he nods. He picks up his thermos, and we walk back down the trail and toward the houses in silence. Nothing but the sounds of leaves and damp earth beneath our feet accompany us. Rhett even walks me up to the steps of the cabin. I pause there, giving him a chance to say something, anything. But he doesn't. So I turn and walk up the steps. It's not until I am at the top of the steps that he says my name.

"Once a week isn't enough," he says finally. "I think we do our best work when we are together."

Together.

Of course, I should say no. I should simply walk back up these steps and tell him I will see him in a week at the diner like we had agreed. Or, I consider, we *can*, in fact, be coworkers. We can just pick up and move along with our careers, and leave whatever tangled web we had in the past.

"Come by in an hour," I tell him. "Bring more of that coffee."

"An hour." He nods with a gratified smile and turns back toward his house.

I close the door behind me and hurry to clear off the dining table and counters. Toss another log in the fire and fluff the pillows. I crack the window for that fresh northern air and light a candle on the counter, all while telling myself I am doing it to set the writing mood. Maybe it's partly true. But after I shower and throw on some makeup, I know better.

The cabin smells of warm smoke and the pumpkin candle when Rhett announces that he's here. I turn and watch him come in the door, not bothering to. Kicking his shoes off at the door. A smile, barely there, grows on his face at the sight of this place.

"Hi," I squeak out. My stomach somersaulting at the sight of him.

"More coffee?" He holds up the thermos with a proud smile.

"God, I love you." I say the words so quickly, they don't pass through a single filter. He raises his eyebrows, and I flush the deepest shade of embarrassment. "Sorry . . . I just . . . "

"It's coffee," he finishes with a smile. "I get it. It's fine."

Fine? I want to roll my eyes, but then Rhett's eyes wander over to the bookshelf like he is looking for something.

"I've read a couple so far," I say, watching him look at the books.

"Any good ones?"

"A few Jo Atwoods. And then just my new copy of Wells Stevens again since you never gave me mine back." I pour two cups of coffee.

"Didn't I?" His eyes tease me with a smirk.

I flush at what could be confused with flirtation.

"Nope. I had to buy a new one."

He fights a smile but doesn't say anything.

Rhett picks up the full mugs and brings them over to the table. I stall when I realize I used the mug I painted with Hannah last year. That stupid thing I didn't want to make in the first place but now can't shake myself from.

"Tulips were my mom's favorite," he says, looking at the dainty flowers I painted.

Of course, I didn't paint them for his mom. I painted them because he brought them to me. Because I can't see them and not associate them with him. Even my favorite flower brings me back to him.

"You never told me your mom was Jo Atwood," I say finally, joining him at the table.

He narrows his eyes. "You didn't know?"

"How would I have known?"

"You didn't Google me?"

I shake my head. "Nope."

A smile grows. "I assumed you knew and just didn't bring it up. Everyone is always bringing it up. Most people think I'm just a product of nepotism."

"You are." I laugh into my cup, and his uneasy expression instantly breaks into laughter.

"Ready, Dorada?" he asks. "Just for that, I am going to be extra harsh today."

"You better, Atwood."

We spend the next few hours sorting through scenes, talking about themes and symbols. We jokingly argue about the grammar in a line that I didn't want to change. He tells me it has to change. I say no. He cracks a smile, caving quickly.

"You were the one who told me all your edits are just suggestions."

He bobs his head, trying to find his way out of his own statement. He can't. "That's true."

It almost feels like old time. Almost.

Once the sun sets, Rhett stretches his arms out, checks his watch, and then begins to collect his things. I tidy up my things as well, and I count this as a victory. A small win toward us being coworkers. We made it a whole afternoon with no distraction. Depending on what you define as distraction.

Rhett is at the door, lingering on the threshold like he always he used to.

"Tanner also called after you left the bookstore," he admits. And the reminder of that conversation with Tanner makes me flush with nerves.

"Now what did *he* have to say?"

"He said you played along with Dollie. Not telling her who you were. Then she found out and made you sign some stock."

I smile and nod. "She did."

"I am sure everyone in town has one by now."

"That's exactly what she told me. And she said if I signed some, then people would be willing to buy a second copy."

His smile lines crease. "Did you sign all of them?"

"Every last one."

He smiles in a way I've missed.

"Tomorrow morning? Here?" I ask—hopeful.

"Tomorrow morning. Here," he confirms.

I tell him good night, and rather than peeking in secret, I lean in the doorway and watch him walk back across the driveway and up to his porch with his hands shoved deep in his pockets. He glances back over at me, the corner of his mouth turning up into a sheepish grin. One that has me questioning everything.

25

LAST FALL

My sheer embarrassment alone about getting caught with Rhett has me scared to let him back over to my apartment. So, when he texted me that he would be leaving his place to come over soon, I told him I was already on my way to his place with coffees. By the time I get up to his apartment I don't even need to buzz in because he is leaning in his doorway, arms crossed over his chest. A smug grin on his face.

"Don't tell me you're never going to let me come over again," he says as I walk around him to get up to his apartment. My eyes flutter at the feeling of being close to him again. At the smell of him.

"Ha." I kick off my shoes and hand him his cup. "I haven't decided yet. I will never willingly see Elyse or Myranda again. I know that for sure."

All I can picture is Myranda hightailing it back to Runclave to tell him now not only was I not ready for a real career as an author, but I'm hardly a couple of months into this, and I'm already making out with my editor like a loved-up teenager.

The realization of how fragile this could be hit me this morning when Myranda sent me a meme about sleeping with your coworker. And all I know is that I can't let this jeopardize my career. And I had almost let those feelings do just that.

"Well," he says. "I'm glad you chose to see me instead."

I whip around to look at him, and the flirtation in his voice sends warmth over my body. "Let's focus. We are approaching our next deadline, and I need to have total focus on this. You know what I mean."

He nods, his little smirk finding this all too funny.

"And if you can't behave when we work together, then we can meet at coffee shops—"

"*Me*, behave?" he asks, his eyebrows nearly hit his hairline. "May I remind you which one of us was grinding on my lap last night?"

"May I remind you which one of us pulled me there and held me there?"

God, what I would give to go back and not be interrupted.

"And if you need extra work to keep busy, I'm sure you can find some projects you can be keeping busy with." I motion to his messy dining room table, with papers piled high.

He walks over and tidies them. "A couple."

"Okay, then pick one."

I sit at the opposite end of the table, which pulls a laugh from him.

"Lauren. Come on."

"Nope." I shake my head. "I'm not taking any risks."

Not this close to a deadline. And sitting next to him would likely absolve any power I still have over myself. And with his eyes dragging up and down my body, that power is already flickering.

In college, I spent a lot of my time in the library, learning the difference between summative and formative assessments, learning the different classifications of education and other things that were of no interest to me. Class after class on how to conjugate verbs, but nothing on classroom management. Classes on how to use yet another picture book to enhance a social studies lesson, but not on how to talk to parents. I spent hours poring over the study guides and books and failed quizzes—just to pack up and leave the profession behind anyway. It drained me. I was wrung out and not even left to dry.

But now I spend even more hours poring over my story lines, characters, themes, and verb usage, and I don't go home drained. I don't end my day with a numb mind and bruised heart. Even here, doing a terrible job at avoiding Rhett, I think back to that year of teaching. When I was all but begging on my knees for the kids to just sit quietly and pay attention for a few minutes so I could get through a single lesson. Now, I don't have to sit through another staff meeting that could have been an email and I don't beg for anyone's attention.

"What are you thinking about?" Rhett asks.

"Teaching," I admit. Erasing the sentence on my screen that made no sense.

"Would you ever go back? Say you realize you hate writing; would you go back to teaching?"

"Not in a million years," I answer quickly. "If writing doesn't work out, then I'm going to work at a bookstore. Or be a librarian or literally anything other than a teacher."

He shakes his head. "If your writing doesn't work out, then I will have lost faith in the book-reading community as a whole."

I shrug. "I can't afford to get my hopes up."

And I made the mistake of that, when I chose to go into teaching. Teaching wasn't a lifelong passion by any means, but suddenly I had convinced myself it was going to be an easy daytime gig that would let me write on the weekends and summers. And my hopes were up one moment, then they were six feet under after that first day of school. Two panic attacks and crying in the supply closet on my lunch left me questioning every choice I made that had landed me there.

"What would you do if you weren't editing?" I ask, desperate to get out of my head.

"I don't know. I never really thought about it. I never really knew anything different. My brother and sister were always the sure ones. I was too worried about them getting their grades in on time."

"What are they like? Your siblings."

He laughs. "Jackie is the opposite of my dad. He is all business and suits and math. He was playing 'desk job' when he was five. My dad can never sit still and has to be using his hands. Makes him a good handyman, I guess. But Jackie is love-sick the way my dad is. His girlfriend is just about the sun to him, and my dad is the same way with my mom. And Gwen is . . . " He pauses for a moment to think. "She had won homecoming queen by a landslide her senior year. That's what the announcer said too. So one minute, she is standing center field with my parents, crying while they place the crown on her head, then as soon as halftime was over, she was putting on her jersey because she was the kicker for the varsity football team. Jackie made the mistake of telling her she could never make the football team, and then, of course, she wouldn't take no for an answer."

"I could never be that brave."

"I think you're brave." Rhett flips the paper he's editing. He says it like it's a blatant fact. Indisputable. "I don't know many debut authors who would let me tear apart their work the way you let me do with yours."

"Brave and unwilling to fail are different things."

There's a momentary pause, then Rhett clears his throat. "You would love my sister."

"I would love to meet her."

I don't know if he was offering an invitation or just pointing it out, but for the rest of the day, I think about Rhett and his family. Wondering what they were like all together. His sick mother, handyman dad, stubborn sister, and love-sick brother. And how this serious, watchful man fits in with them.

Then another thought hits me. How would he fit in with *my* family? Would my mom grill him and look down on him because he is an editor and not an author himself? Would him being a best-selling editor be up her to her snuff? What would Paul think? Would he even care about Rhett's claim to fame? Would they drink a beer out back while grilling in the summer? Would he help clean up the wrapping paper after a messy Christmas morning? I can picture it, like it was already written out before me. I can see Rhett with my mom at the kitchen island, drinking their coffees black. Then fear creeps inside my brain—I'm attaching myself to something temporary. I've grown roots in this little world we currently exist in. But as time ticks and deadlines approach, it's growing toward its end. And I have no idea what that means.

"Your brain is spinning, isn't it?" Rhett says, breaking me from my thoughts.

"Huh?"

"Your mind looks busy," he says and goes to the kitchen. "You have this very concentrated face when your brain gets moving."

"You know. The deadline," I half lie and begin to shuffle my things in order.

"Why are you packing up?"

"Because it's getting dark and I have to—" I stammer, and his playful gaze freezes me.

"Lauren." He tilts his head at me; my body sways a touch. "Stay. For a little while, at least."

"No distractions. Remember?" Maybe we surpassed that after two glasses of wine.

"We are done with work for the day. We can just hang out, talk for a bit."

"*Hang out.*" I scoff. "Right. Is that what you call what Myranda and Elyse walked in on?"

If he only knew that if he asks one more time to stay, I would say yes. His desire is burning dark green in his eyes.

But he swallows hard and shakes his head. "Let me drive you home."

I could easily tell him I am fully capable of getting my own uber. Especially considering his card is still on my app. But I don't. I let him pull on a coat and follow me down.

"Once this book is done, let's talk about this," he says seriously.

I play stupid. "This?"

"You and I. Once we get your manuscript submitted, we have to acknowledge what is going on here."

"Okay—" I begin, but a voice interrupts us through the dark.

"Hey, guys!"

We turn to see Cal outside the bookstore, bringing in the chalkboard sign from the sidewalk.

"Hey, man." Rhett waves, and I try to pretend that I am happy to see Cal there when, in reality, my mind is tripping over what Rhett just said.

"Elyse is about to be home with food and drinks. Do you guys want to come watch the game?"

I don't know what game he is talking about, but as I am about to say no, Rhett is already saying yes.

"We would love to." He answers for both of us.

"Great. Swing on by when you're ready. It'll be on soon."

When Cal goes back in the store, he flips the sign to "Closed," and I whip around to Rhett.

"*We* would love to?"

He shrugs. "What? You don't want to hang out with Elyse?"

"No, I do, but she knows, and it will be awkward."

He lifts his hand and tucks my hair behind my ear with a knowing smile. His fingertips trace the tender spot he left there. "You can tell her we are just friends. Tell her it was a misunderstanding. Tell her drinking wine on someone else's couch is a just-friends thing. But then you have to tell her hickeys are just a friend thing too."

"Rhett." His name comes out in a huff, my breathing already picking up as he hovers there over me.

"I'm going to go drink a beer with our friends. And I would love for you to come too," he says before spinning away, making me want to pull him back into me and see *exactly* what he means by the last comment.

"Fine. But we *are* just friends," I lie.

He turns back around, and in a few steps his face is hovering above mine, eyes gazing down with our lips only inches apart. "You can call this whatever you want to Elyse or Cal. But don't try and tell me that we're just friends."

His eyes skate up and down by body but before either of us closes the gap, he backs away.

After that momentary lightning strike to every cell in my body, I take a step toward him.

"You're right." I set my shoulders straight like some wine-tipsy attempt at showing my resolve. "We're only coworkers."

Rhett's eyebrows skyrocket and the shit eating grin on his face tells me he doesn't bellieve me either.

"If you two aren't going to make out, can you help bring the bags in?"

I step away and see Elyse is standing next to her car, a knowing smile on her face.

"Of course we aren't." I turn from Rhett and walk straight over to Elyse. "And we would be happy to help."

"You're not a good liar," Rhett says into my ear as he pats me on the butt. I miss his touch the moment he reaches for the bags. He winks then turns to walk ahead toward the store, leaving me stunned on the sidewalk.

Elyse only shakes her head with a laugh, and I just hope the dark night disguises my flushed cheeks.

26

NOW

Rhett is knocking on my door first thing in the morning before the frost even melts from the windows. I'm sitting at the table with my knees pulled up to my chest under my oversized shirt, my hair in a lopsided bun, and my eyes are entirely focused on the steam over the cup of coffee in front of me. I dig the palms of my hands into my eyes, trying to grind out the sleep.

I assumed I would hear from Rhett later today. But now he's coming through the front door with his thermos of coffee. I thought that with us, old habits die hard. But now I think that maybe they don't die at all.

"I brought the good coffee." He lifts the thermos up to me.

"Thank God."

"You're still buying your coffee at the grocery store, aren't you?" He asks, pulling new mugs out of the cabinet. They seem small as he wraps his hands around them. Am I jealous of a damn mug?

"There is a total of like four stores in this town. Where else would I find it?"

He smiles at me over his shoulder. "You gotta go see Porter

Morton over at Morton's bar. He roasts his own coffee that he has flown in from Colombia. Nobody roasts coffee like Porter."

He pops open the fridge. "Oh." He seems surprised. "You did go to the store."

"Uh, yeah?"

He shakes his head and pours the creamer into my cup. "I thought it was just an excuse to get out of there the other day when you left the diner."

"We have a lot of work to do," I say quickly.

The corner of Rhett's mouth quirks up as he shakes his head. He seems more grounded than a year ago. Healthier. Sadder.

He carries the mugs over and sets one down in front of me and one in front of him. He then pulls out my stack of papers and his laptop, and I find myself smoothing my clothes and hair.

What Dollie said about his retirement comes back. When we work together, he isn't always working on my pages. He says he has other work. He goes between his laptop and paper and pen, editing a stack of my pages at a time. Is he back to working on other people's work too? Did Myranda force him to work with me as much as I've been forced to work with him? Suddenly, my stomach is in knots at the idea.

"My dad keeps asking about you," he says after a while. "Keeps wanting me to bring in more wood or make sure your fire is burning all right."

"I am fully capable of bringing my own wood in, thank you very much."

"I never doubted your ability to do anything," he says, and the way he says it knocks the wind right out of me. Because the words don't fit the casualness of the conversation. They're serious. *He's* serious.

"You don't have to be so nice," I say, a twinge of anger sneaking up on me. "I know you don't want to be editing my manuscript."

"You think I don't want to edit your work?" His eyes are narrowed on me now. A look of genuine confusion covers his face as it borders anger. Those damn green eyes.

"Rhett. We haven't spoken in almost a *year*. I think that is a more than fair assumption."

He looks hurt, but I don't know why. I'm the one who's hurt. I look back to my computer when his silence continues to grow.

We work quietly for a while before Rhett clears his throat and stops scribbling with his red pen. He looks up over at me, and for a moment, I consider not even looking up. Not meeting his eyes. But that has always been out of my control.

"I *asked* to work on your manuscript," he says, and my heart coils, and my stomach sinks to my knees. I search his face for the lie, but I can't find it. Not in his expression, his eyes, his hands.

"You what?" I manage to get out.

"Myranda called and told me they already had someone else lined up to edit it. So I went to Runclave in the city and asked to do it. When I saw you at the bar at Ninety-Seven's? That's why I was in the city that night."

My mind is in a sharp spiral, and I don't even know which direction. *He asked? He came to the city to ask?*

"You didn't think to mention that to me that night?" is what I am able to get out.

"Myranda promised me you would never know."

Now my heart and everything else seems to slow, completely unsure of what exactly is being admitted here.

"I wouldn't know? What are you talking about?"

He rubs the back of his neck. "When I asked to do it, I told Charles my one condition was that you would never know. That they would make up some pseudonym and we would just email back and forth. I wanted to respect what you asked of me. I wanted to respect you telling me to stay away. I was even going to type the edits so you wouldn't recognize my handwriting."

Growing up, a tangled necklace would be enough to send my anxiety into a spiral. My fingers would shake with frustration as I seemed to make the metal tangle worse. Until I was able to free the chain from itself then be hit with a flash of victory. Hope. Relief, maybe. This feels like that. The knotted mess of mysteries between us becomes a touch less tangled. And it only leaves me wanting to keep untangling. Figure it out. Figure *him* out.

"Dollie said you came out of retirement for my book. Twice." I mean for it to be a question, but it's more of a statement. An accusation, almost.

He nods.

"Why?"

He waits a beat before responding. "Because Charles called and insisted. Originally, I said no. Then Myranda showed up at my door, demanding I read it. So I looked it over, and they were right. It had the same makings of a best seller, like my mom's did. My mom's Alzheimer's had gotten worse at the time; we were looking at getting her a full-time nurse. I had quit editing because I didn't want to edit if it wasn't my mom's books, and I don't know." He shakes his head, his cheeks pink and his eyes red. "I just thought if I were to leave editing, I might as well go out editing one last book that would be so much like my mom's. It made me feel closer to her, when she herself was no longer the one occupying her body."

"So after all of that. You still left." The thought comes to me as I'm saying the words out loud. "You broke my heart by not wanting me and then you still asked to edit my work?" I ask, my voice a whisper. Not sure if it's anger, hurt, embarrassment. All three?

He nods.

"What kind of torture is that? How can you break my heart like you did and then ask to be back in my life? Why didn't you just let me move on? Like I asked." My voice raises, and suddenly I'm standing, heart thrashing. "Why couldn't you have let the other editor do a good enough job and leave me be?"

"*Because*, Lauren." His voice hits deep and strong. "Your work deserves more than just *good enough*. And I had no plans for you to ever know it was me, but you emailed me your manuscript, and I realized you knew. Then you were here in my family's cabin. It was like seeing a ghost and I—"

"You can't love me like you did, leave, and then wave it in front of my face now because you feel sorry for me."

He stands now, too, and says, directly into my eyes, "I don't feel sorry for you. I never *once* felt sorry for you. I am sorry for what I did, but I knew you would be better off without me." He packs up his things. And as he turns for the door, he spins around; his green eyes, darker now, look at me with a force that pins me to where I am standing. "I *had* to leave. It's not as simple as you think. I tried to separate you and your work. But—"

"Yet here you are," I spit out. My heart splinters at the idea of working with him and not even knowing it. And now actually working with him. I'm not sure which hurts less.

He nods. "Here I am."

"You should go." My voice comes out low and hoarse. "We can go back to using the mail slot."

I don't want to hear it anymore. He has had so many chances to own up to it. Explain it away. But he never has. He bobs his head, and turns to go, leaving the door open behind him.

I slam the door shut then collapse back into the chair, the air deflating out of my lungs. Somehow, all this time later, watching him walk out the door still hurts just as bad. But I know that once he explains himself, giving whatever terrible excuse he has will just put me back in a place to be left again, because I know I will forgive him. I just don't know if I can bring myself to do it because I've already suffered one heartbreak by his hands. A second may push my heart past resuscitation.

27

———

LAST FALL

The bookstore has been transformed into a man cave. Cal has a TV in the middle of the store, and a few of his buddies I recognize from the Kensington Club are pulling the chairs around to face it. The lights are low as Rhett, and I follow Elyse over to the counter where we set the bags.

"Can I help with anything?" Rhett offers, and Elyse looks between us with a mischievous grin.

"Go keep Cal from throwing his beer when his team loses again."

"Yes, ma'am." He salutes.

"So." She eyes me then, glancing over in Rhett's direction as he walks away, and I simply shake my head.

"Don't even," I warn. "Just friends."

A laugh erupts out of her. "Lauren, I'm not blind. I'm also not deaf. I heard and saw all that sexual tension out of the sidewalk. And at your apartment?" She tosses my hair over my shoulder and points to my neck. "It's gotten darker."

I bring my hair back over my shoulder, hiding my neck. "We're coworkers."

Elyse rolls her eyes. "Cal is my coworker and my husband, and even he isn't giving me hickeys in visible places."

"It was a heat-of-the-moment thing," I say, knowing that surely part of that statement was true. "We will get over it as soon as we finish these edits. It's like that forced-proximity thing. Of course we are going to confuse hormones with actual feelings."

"That look in his eye? Just then? That was anything but confusion. It's okay to admit it. You've got it for each other."

"What can I do?" I slap my hands on the counter and begin unloading bags of chips and pizza rolls out of the bags. "Let me be busy, or this wine is going to go straight to my head."

"Let's go heat these up." Elyse grabs the pizza rolls and waves me on. I follow her back down the hall and into the office, which is as charming as the rest of the store. There is an antique oak desk with brass pulls on the drawers, and one of those green library lamps you see in the movies sits on top. It's beautiful. And in the corner stands an outdated white-plastic stand-alone microwave. Balance. Elyse cracks the bag open and tosses it in.

"What made you want to own a bookstore?" I ask.

"Instead of lemonade stands, I would sell my old books on the sidewalk as a kid." She pulls herself up onto the desk. "I got my degree in business and then a master's in library science. Then I took out a loan I couldn't afford and opened this place."

"When did you meet Cal during all of this?"

"He was already living upstairs, came down to check in on what I was working on. And then kept coming around, so I put him to work." She shrugs. "What about you? What made you want to write?"

"My sister always read to me when I was little. Her reading to me is what made me fall in love with stories, and I wanted to make my own. But there was never an actual moment when I decided I wanted to. I just always did."

"I can read books all day long." Elyse shakes her head. "But writing one? No chance. Like, I wouldn't even know where to start."

"When you know, you know." I shrug and feel the irony of my own mouth saying words that I keep avoiding. The truth I keep evading.

We go back to the counter, popping pizza rolls and burning our tongues. Rhett comes over, grabbing two beers, opens them, and hands one to me. And without saying a single word, he slips back to the game.

Elyse cocks an eyebrow up at me. "You're blushing."

"It's the alcohol."

"Sure."

"Are Nikki or Faye coming?" I ask, and she shakes her head.

"They flaked when they found out it was for the soccer game." *Soccer, noted.* "They are trying to get into some party over on the North Side. Faye is convinced they will bump into some influencers or something."

The other team must score in the other room because all the guys groan. Cal takes the moment to join us for a beer of his own.

"Are you guys actually going to put a label on it now?" he asks me quietly.

"No," I say firmly. "I can't get distracted."

Cal shrugs. "I don't know. The way he was looking at you that night at Kensington Club, when you showed up with your sister? You both might be long past distracted. He literally told his friend to not make a move on you."

"Let's go watch the game," I suggest, my skin flushing from chest to cheeks. "It sounds exciting."

Elyse and Cal exchange a humored glance and follow me. But as I go to walk by, Rhett's hand loops into mine and pulls me in front of him.

"It doesn't count as a distraction right now because we aren't working." He says wrapping his arms around my waist and pulling me back into him. "If you want to go, give me the word. I'll sleep on my couch tonight," he says into my ear.

I elbow him gently. "Rhett, I'm not sleeping in your bed."

"Well, you can't drive home, I can't drive you, and I'd rather you not leave. There's a lock on the inside of the door if you don't trust me."

I whip my head around to face him; the twinge of pain in his voice catches in my heart. "Rhett," I whisper. "Of course I trust you." Then a question itches at my brain, one I know the answer to, but also one I want to hear him admit to out loud. "Why did you tell Tanner not to make a move on me at Kensington Club?"

"The idea of any of them trying to make a move on you before I even had a chance?" His jaw flexes. "I would have had to kill them. Including my best friend."

"What if we are already far past distracted?"

"What if we are?" he asks back, waiting on me to say it, call this what it is.

The guys and Elyse erupt in cheers for the game.

"Shots!" Cal calls out and leaps from his spot on the couch, hurrying to the counter, where he pours tequila into red Solo cups. I turn my back to Rhett again, pressing into him.

"That looks like a very bad idea," I say, but Cal is passing out the cups and everyone is throwing them back.

Another goal comes quickly, and Cal pours another heavy shot into all our cups. I am having to will myself not to turn around and face Rhett when he places his lips on the side of my head.

The game takes a sour turn, and their team, the red one, begins to lose. The shots slow, both in the net and in our cups. Everyone's excited smiles shift into long frowns. Slumping back in their seats, they watch in dismay. One of the red players kicks and misses the net.

"Ah, for fuck's sake." One of the guys throws his hands up. "The refs are going to cost us this game."

Rhett leans down and whispers in my ear, "I can't focus on this game with your ass grinding into me." His hot breath flushes my skin with goose bumps.

I should break away. The logical side of my brain is telling me to not cross another line but instead I just burrow back into him more. Then other team scores again and you can feel the hope drain from the room.

"Let's go," I whisper to Rhett.

Elyse winks as she sees us making an Irish exit out the front door.

"Water?" Rhett asks from his kitchen while I cuddle under his blanket on the couch. A wave of exhaustion has come over me.

"Please," I say.

"You know, I played varsity soccer in high school," he says. "I was pretty good too."

"Did you know who was playing in that game tonight?"

"Oh yeah." He brings me the glass. "My favorite team was playing."

"Yikes. That was probably tough to watch." My eyelids grow heavy.

"No, I liked the other team. But I couldn't tell them."

"Rhett! Go back then. You'll miss them win," I say and slide deeper into the couch. "I'll be here sleeping when you get back."

He laughs. "You're not sleeping on the couch. You'll sleep in my bed. I'll sleep on the couch."

"No." I tuck the blanket up under my chin. "Go back to the game."

"Yes. And if you think for a single second that I would rather be anywhere other than here with you, then you're out of your damn mind. Come on, babe. Up."

Maybe it's the alcohol, or the late hour, or Rhett tucking the hair behind my ear, but I let him pick me up and carry me to his room. It's dark, but I can see the bed is made like it was to be inspected. More bookshelves line the walls. His nightstand is neatly stacked with books; mine amongst them. A little tinge of embarrassment comes over me at how impersonal my own apartment is compared to this.

Rhett sets me down, pulls back the blanket and motions for me to crawl in. I don't argue, I just follow his silent orders and climb in. Pulling up the blankets, Rhett kisses my forehead, and I just melt deeper into the bed.

"Rhett." I call out to him at the door, the bed swaying beneath me.

"Yeah?"

"Earlier, about locking the door. I trust you. It's my own self-control I don't trust."

"Goodnight, Laure," he says, and I can hear the smile in his words. Then he leaves the door open a crack. I want to call out for him to come get in with me. But before I can, I fall asleep surrounded by the smell of him on his sheets.

28

NOW

The Weather Channel predicted a swell of lake-effect rainstorms to hit overnight, but I don't remember them predicting the monsoon that has rolled in. I am awoken by a crack of thunder and a flash of light so bright; I thought all the lights had been flipped on. I lie there, listening to the cabin creak with the storm, when I hear the dripping. I sit up and pull the cord of the lamp on the nightstand. It's coming from the corner of the room: water dripping down the wood paneled wall and into a growing puddle. I rush over, trying to spot a hole, but it's coming up from the attic. I wiggle the door to the attic, but it won't budge.

"Shit," I mutter and hurry downstairs and find a mop bucket in the closet and all the towels I can find to try to prevent any more damage. The bucket catches some of the drip, the towels soak up what has already leaked in. I know it won't last all night, and I don't want Jack to think I can't handle watching out for his house.

Then I remember the phone numbers on the side of the fridge. A small, lined piece of paper listing services and phone numbers to call. The auto shop, pizza, animal control, diner, and a twenty-four-seven repair number. I'm dialing the latter and praying for forgiveness for waking whoever this is up at this ungodly hour. The clock over the stove says five.

"Jack Atwood," the voice on the other line says, sounding still mostly asleep.

"Oh, Jack. It's Lauren." I drop my head into my hand, of course. "I'm so sorry for waking you up. I didn't know—"

"No apologies, kiddo. What's up?"

"There's a leak in the roof, I think, and it's coming down from the attic. It's not too bad yet, but water is coming—"

"Be there in ten," he says.

"I'm so sorry—"

"No apologies allowed." I can hear him smile. "Just throw some coffee on."

"You got it," I say. I start the coffee and attempt to shove some logs into the fireplace.

I expected Jack and his toolbox. And though I shouldn't be, I'm surprised when I see Rhett on my porch alongside his dad. Their eyebrows scrunched together the same way. Both look as if they've been pulled from their bed in the middle of the night. Well . . .

"Hey, kid," Jack says. "Rhett, you remember Lauren, right? She's the one who had breakfast with us at the diner."

Rhett and I glance at each other, and it would almost be funny if it weren't so sad that we are being introduced like strangers.

"Rhett." I nod.

"Lauren." He returns the gesture.

"You guys want some coffee?" I ask, and they both nod.

"I'll meet you up there." Jack says and grunts his way up the stairs.

I pour them each a cup, remembering from the diner that Jack likes his with more creamer than I do.

"You came." I say and hand Rhett his, and I don't miss the way our hands brush.

"You called."

"Because your dad needs help."

"Because *you* needed help, Laure," he says, threads of desperation in his voice.

We stand there, staring at each other for a moment and it should surprise me when he reaches out and tucks a loose strand of hair behind my ear. But habits are habits after all. When I don't say anything— because what can I say— he tips his head towards the stairs, and I follow him up with Jack's and I's cups.

I watch as Rhett's eyes linger around my room, and it makes my stomach twist. His dad assesses the leak in the corner while he moves over to the door near the closet, the one locked shut. He swipes his hand across the top of the frame and grabs the key, inserts it into the handle and twist to reveal a narrow set of stairs and a single lightbulb on a string. Then he returns the key and yanks the adjacent cord and stares up at the nearly vertical twist of stairs.

"I can go, if you just tell me—" I start to say, but Rhett gives me a look, then picks up the toolbox and squeezes his way up, his shoulders reaching both walls. He turns just out of sight, and we hear the *clunk* of his toolbox onto the attic floor.

"How's the writing coming along?" Jack asks, filling the silence between us.

"It's coming," I say. "The first deadline is coming up, so we—I am getting nervous."

"Do you like to write?" Jack asks, gazing around the dark, lamp-lit room.

"Yeah. I do." I smile.

"My wife loved writing, but other writers, I wonder if they actually like it or if they just do it as a job, you know?"

"I actually love it," I admit, missing how that sounded out loud. The past few months of working on this next book has been as therapeutic as it has been painful. This story idea had been bouncing around my head, a story about love and loss and continuing to love anyway. Laced throughout were my actual pain and hurt, all hidden within metaphors, characters, and descriptions of weather.

"You know, Rhett edited a novel last year. He came out of retirement and everything for it. He said it was like his mom's work. God, he was so taken by her, that author." Jack laughs. "He would come home all those weekends that fall, and that project was all he would talk about. About this brilliant girl and her book he got to help with."

"Oh, is that so?" I ask, pretending to keep the conversation going and pretending like my heart isn't pounding. Hard.

All those trips home he was coming here and telling his family about me? I chew on the inside of my cheek while I listen to Rhett rustle around upstairs.

"Yeah, but then he moved home and retired again, and doesn't talk about work anymore." He glances over to my night-stand, and I see something catch his eye.

"That's the book—" He points at *Golden Hour*. "Wait." He looks over at me, eyes wide, as he realizes who I am. "You're . . . "

I nod and his eyes widen, and he smiles. "Oh, maybe don't mention I told ya all that. It's no secret that he adores you, but you know how private he is."

Adores. Present tense. As if it's still happening.

"Dad?" Rhett calls from above. "Can you send Lauren up with a few more of those patches?"

"Sure," Jack calls back and digs through his box, getting out another package. He nods toward the staircase where the cold draft is coming from. I pull my sweater tight and head up. There is nothing more than a few boxes in the corner and now Rhett, who still takes up the entire open space.

Taken, his dad had said. *Adores*. Yet he still left and didn't come back.

"Are you okay?" he asks. And I stand there and hate myself for still loving him.

"Yeah." I toss him the package.

"I need you—" he says, and my stomach flips. "For a moment," he adds, nodding up to the angled beams overhead.

I walk over, and he points up. "That's where the leak is coming from. I filled it with this stuff, and we can put this patch on. It should hold until we put a new roof on in a year or two." I'm looking and listening, but all I can focus on is how close we are standing to each other and the sound of my heart pounding. Or maybe it's his heart. Or both.

"I need you to hold this part up for me, and I can seal it in place and then it will be set for now," he says.

He moves his body just so that he is standing directly in front of me. Our hands are up, mine holding the patch thing in place, his are smoothing it out. Rhett gives a short grunt as he moves something into place. He smells like laundry and a shower and sleep. I want to freeze this moment so we can stay right here and pretend that everything hasn't gone so wrong. Pretend that this tether between us is stronger than the heartbreak that tied to sever it.

"Okay, I think it's all set," he says.

Our arms drop, but we don't move. Our chests come together with our sharp intakes of air. I open my mouth to say something, anything, but nothing comes out. My mind is on everything but this damn leak. Rhett stares back at me, waiting for me to say it. Maybe yell at him, let my anger run over into today.

His hands come up and find their places on either side of my face; his forehead drops against mine.

"Laure," he whispers, and my whole body is moments from melting into him. Ever so briefly, our walls are non-existent. There is a clarity in his eyes and a heat in my cheeks that neither of us can hide. "I want to explain."

"Rhett? Everything okay?" Jack calls up.

His thumb stops rubbing my cheek but my heart still pounds.

"Yup, we are set. Just going to dry up and we'll be down," Rhett calls back, his eyes still locked on mine, unflinching. Unmoving. His hand keeps my face pointed at his. I place my hands over his, holding them against my cheeks for a moment longer.

But I don't trust myself to be this close to him. I drop my hands, step away and climb back down the stairs, refusing to look back. Jack is picking up his bag, a slight look of amusement when he sees me. "I'm glad he had you last year. It was the happiest we had ever seen him."

When Rhett comes down, he doesn't look at me. He keeps his eyes down and carries the used rags with him. The three of us go down into the living room, which doesn't feel much warmer than the attic did.

"Here." Rhett goes over to the fireplace and adjusts the logs, adding a new one, and suddenly the room fills with warmth. "That might help. The furnace is pretty old."

"If you ever need someone to come over and help out around here, you can give Rhett a call." Jack yawns. "I could use some alone time at the house."

"I'll keep that in mind," I lie, rubbing at the tiny scar in the palm of my hand. "Thank you, guys, for coming over so quickly. Really — I appreciate it."

"Of course, kiddo. Anytime. We will be here." Jack waves and heads for the door, Rhett lingering behind.

"Can we try again at working together?" he asks. "Just meet at the diner? We could meet later today."

I feel flutters in my belly at the pleading in his eyes.

"Okay."

He gives a curt nod and follows his dad out the door. I watch with an aching heart and think of Jack wanting to leave a place to avoid overwriting the good memories with painful ones. And I wonder if you can love a person so much that you would leave them, just to keep them being a person you loved. To not pollute them with your sadness and grief. Maybe there is truth in it. Or maybe it's just a truth the Atwood men believe in.

29

NOW

Hannah guilted me into Thanksgiving at Mom's house this year. Last year, I bailed on account of just having moved to the city, saying that I was going to spend the holiday with friends. It wasn't true; I just didn't want to face my mom, fearing that she would see through me. Though I was loving my work—and working with Rhett—I wasn't loving the city, and I couldn't face her and her be right.

This year, though, Hannah told me Winnie was begging for me to come visit and spend the weekend there too. So I packed a bag and left the cabin with a text to Jack giving him a heads-up. He wished me a happy holiday and told me he and the kids would be visiting Jo and making dinner. My curiosity wanted to stick around. See if they were going to bring her home from the nursing home for Thanksgiving. See if I could get a chance to meet *the* Jo Atwood. But I promised Hannah.

Part of me thought to let Rhett know that I was going home when we were working together yesterday. But things have been going well without getting our personal lives involved. We meet at the diner. We work. We go home. We are coworkers and we need to keep it that way.

By midafternoon, I am pulling my car onto the brick road in front of Paul and Mom's House. I park behind Hannah's beloved minivan and cross the street. The eaves on the house are as ornate as the wallpaper inside. The brass historical society plate near the door looks freshly shined.

Up the front steps, I knock to no response, so I step in—and into the chaos. Winnie is skidding around the corner, exploding with laughter with Paul close on her tail, threatening to throw her into the pond out back. Ethan is on a call in the front room, pacing and ranting about something. Part of me wants to walk over and knock some fucking sense into him. But instead, I give him a passing glare he doesn't even reciprocate.

I hang my jacket on its designated hook and step down the hallway, passing wainscoting and wallpaper and brass sconces that cost more than my rent for the month.

Loud laughter comes from the kitchen, where I find Hannah at the counter and Mom stirring a pot on the stove.

"Uh, hello?"

"Oh!" my mom exclaims. "When did you get here?"

I check my wrist, where a watch should be. "Now? This is the time you told me to get here."

"Oh, come in, come in." She waves me over. "You have to try this soup."

She digs out a spoon, shuts the drawer with her hip, and tells me to blow on it. It's good. But it also tastes like every other soup she has ever made. Hannah pats the stool next to her, and I notice she's wearing her wedding ring. It strikes me as odd and sad. That she could be treated so horribly by Ethan and so wonderfully by Tanner, and she still wears the ring given to her by Ethan.

Soon, Winnie and Paul come barreling into the kitchen. Paul rests his hands on his hips, and I can hear his labored breathing.

"Hey, kid." Paul comes over and ruffles my hair. "How's the new book coming along? Heard you're staying up in Michigan?"

"Yeah. So far, so good. We are working on edits now."

Ethan's voice raises from the front of the house. Hannah's eyes flare in fear as she swoops up Winnie. "Want to go play out back for a bit?" Her smile is forced but believable.

I quickly follow them out with our coats in hand.

"So," I say, poking Winnie's arm. "How old are you now? Twenty-four?"

She giggles. "Aunt Laurey, I'm four!"

"Oh!" I exclaim. "Thirty-four, right."

"No, just four!"

"You're not *just* four. You're four! That's a big age, don't you think? You have to use almost all your fingers on your hand to show how old you are. *And* you're in preschool. Do you love it? Your mommy tells me how smart you are."

Winnie shakes her head no. "I hate it."

"You hate it?" I look at Hannah as she zips up Winnie's coat.

"Winnie goes to the private school Ethan and his brother went to. His parents take care of it."

"I hate it," Winnie says again. "I want to see my fishy." She takes off, zipping down past the rows of out-of-season roses and dahlias.

A large green hedge borders the yard, and at its very center is a pond filled with koi fish, turtles, and frogs. Even though it's past its peak, it's still so beautiful. I did a lot of writing out here that first year of teaching. If I wasn't locked in my room, I was out here.

"She thinks everything is hers." Hannah sighs, sitting on the steps of the patio. "The tree in the front yard. The seat next to me at the dinner table. The white fish in Nan and Grampy's pond."

"She really hates school?"

"God, it's awful, Lauren. She cries every morning. She cries when I pick her up. And she was never a big crier. She has always been so content. But she says she has no friends and that her teacher is mean. I want to take her out and put her in our old school, but Ethan said it's a Forrest legacy. Generations of their family have gone to these schools, and it would be noticed if I pulled Winnie."

"Speaking of. How is Ethan?" I ask.

"Sleeping with his assistant." She sighs. "Saw the text messages on his old iPad he gave to Winnie. Her name is Maggie."

"Do you know her?"

She shakes her head. "I don't think so. I can't find any people he follows online named Maggie, so it may even be a fake name. I don't know."

"I'm surprised he's here."

"I threatened him within an inch of his life. Told him I would tell his parents about his affair and that I will move in with Mom and Paul with Winnie if he didn't show up for her."

"Why don't you?"

"What? Move in?"

"Actually, *leave* him."

She takes her hands and smooths back her hair, the dark circles under her eyes more obvious out here in the setting sun.

I take her hand in mine. "Winnie deserves to see her mom be loved and be treated well. She deserves to see her mom happy, like you were that night with Tanner."

"A single evening with a nice man doesn't give me the pass to give up on my marriage. And besides, she doesn't really get it. She thinks he's just tired because he works so hard. What if she sees *me* as the villain for leaving, while she sees him as a hard worker?"

"I wish Mom had the balls to leave dad." I stand to my feet.

"Leaving Ethan isn't a new idea either. It's been bad for years, Hannah."

"Maybe," she says finally.

"Tanner says hi, by the way."

She whips her head over to me, but Winnie comes flying back to us, tears in her eyes. "Honey, what's wrong?"

"The water is frozen! My fish is dead!"

"Baby, it's okay. They swim down to the bottom where the water won't freeze. It's how fish survive winters. They just get where they will be safe through winter."

I look over at Hannah and wonder if she caught the analogy in her own words.

"Or you can just get out of the pond," I tell her quietly.

Mom calls out for us to come in for dinner. She sits right at Paul's side. And I sit across from Hannah, who smiles over her at her daughter like she's a sunset in the flesh. The table is a heavy oak piece they had custom made. It's big and sturdy and often empty.

"Let's say grace." Paul reaches his hands out, and I watch Ethan physically recoil at the idea of holding my mom's hand before he finally caves in and accepts her hand.

"Lord, thank you for family. Thank you for our livelihoods. And your grace. Amen."

"Amen," we echo.

I sneak a peek at Ethan, his black hair freshly trimmed, his blue eyes focused entirely on the plate of food in front of him. Hannah leans over their daughter, helping her get situated.

I remember when Hannah went away to college. We never heard much about it on her trips home, which grew fewer and further apart. But one time she came home with Ethan. They were all over each other then, her legs draped over his, his hands in her lap. They would lean into each other's ears with all these secrets that would make her blush.

Now if you walked in, you wouldn't even know they knew each other, let alone were married.

"How's the house?" Paul asks either Hannah or Ethan, but both seem to be in their own little worlds.

"Huh?" Hannah looks up at us.

"The house? How is it holding up?"

"Oh." She blushes. "Sorry, yeah, it's good. The construction company came through last week for some of those touch-ups, you know. Scuffed paint, dud outlets, all of that. I showed them the basement, where they didn't even finish that storage room. It's all beams and cement floor."

"They didn't finish the storage room?" Ethan asks, seeming to suddenly become aware of our conversation or that he wasn't alone in this room. "Why didn't you tell me?"

"I did, remember? You worked late the night the inspection guy came by. They had some of their supplies just sitting in front of the door, and I had to get around it and saw there wasn't even a lightbulb in there."

He clenches his jaw. "You didn't tell me that."

"Ethan." Hannah sighs. "Let's not."

He opens his mouth to argue, as if none of us were sitting here watching this go down. But his phone rings.

"I need to take this," he snaps. The grinding of the chair legs against the floor reverberates through our bodies as he slides back and disappears into the front room. The lock clicking behind him.

The name on his screen read, "Mags."

"How's the brother-in-law, Sebastian, doing?" Paul asks. And I admire his attempt to keep things light.

"Good, I think. Last I heard, he got a promotion at the firm and was considering proposing to his girlfriend Gigi."

"Oh, how nice. Can't wait to meet her," Mom adds.

"Yeah. Us too." Hannah drinks.

We all quietly shovel food into our mouths, each silently wishing, I'm sure, that it was the pizza that Winnie had asked for. Mom fills the silence with updates on the happenings of the country club until Ethan comes back, lighter and happier. He doesn't offer anything to the conversation, and he just sits and continues eating. When we finish, Ethan's phone rings again, as if on cue, so he stands and leaves his plate on the table, disappearing to the front room. We don't acknowledge it. But the shifting eye contact around Hannah is unmissable. Paul looks at Mom, who looks at me, then I look back at Paul. Hannah just quietly takes Winnie up for a bath and bedtime.

"I can kick him out," Paul says and begins to clear the table.

"I'll make sure the door hits him on his way out," Mom quips in solidarity.

And I add, "And I'll lock it after him."

After Paul and I finish cleaning up, the three of us settle into the living room with a *Jeopardy!* rerun and glasses of wine. When the "Double Jeopardy" round finishes up, we hear Hannah come back downstairs and knock on the office door. Then we hear it open and click quietly shut behind her.

Ethan's yelling starts quickly. He accuses her of being crazy and says that it's just work calling. We can't hear her response, but he yells again about how nothing he ever does is good enough. How he makes all the money to support her and Winnie's every last whim, like dance class and the new house. He's only met by silence.

Paul stands to go step in, but we hear the door to the front room fly open, and Paul, Mom, and I freeze, not breathing. I realize the irony of Mom now sitting frozen as the screaming ensues around her. The look on her eyes makes me wonder if she is realizing the same thing.

"What am I going to tell Winnie in the morning when she sees that you left? Again?" Hannah asks.

"I don't know, *Hannah*. I don't care." He spits her name out like a bad taste in his mouth. And the sound of the front door slamming shut behind him echoes through the house.

"That motherfucker," Paul says just to us.

Hannah's footsteps finally come down the hallway, and we are greeted with her big, teary eyes.

"Hey, baby." My mom waves her over and Hannah crawls into her lap. "It doesn't have to be like this."

She nods, and my heart aches watching her. Hannah has spent my whole life taking care of me. She was the one telling me to dump shitty high school flings. To get rid of asshole friends. Shielding me from our own parents, while helping me with my science fair projects. And there isn't anything I can give her now. There's no guarding or guidance I can offer her. I feel helpless watching her heart break apart like this.

My mom whispers something into her ear, and Hannah wipes away the tears that escape again. It's then I realize that she isn't wearing her wedding ring on her hand like I had thought. It's the mother's ring I got her for Mother's Day after Winnie was born.

"Do what I never had the courage to do," Mom says, and Hannah nods again and sighs. She stands.

"I told Winnie we could have a slumber party, and she could sleep in bed with me. She's probably waiting."

"Go on." My mom sends her off like a child to bed.

"Paul." Hannah pauses before leaving the room. "Do you still have the number for that attorney you told me about?"

"Of course, kiddo. I'll give him a call; I'll take care of it."

My mom looks at Paul quizzically as Hannah heads to the front door. The sound of her locking Ethan out echoes down the hall before she heads up stairs to Winnie.

"At their wedding reception," Paul starts, his lip quivering a touch, "Ethan was at the bar. He didn't recognize me next to him,

I guess, and he told the young bartender, who was hardly legal, that he may have rushed the whole thing. That he didn't know how long it was going to last. He told her that he would give her a call when the wife threw in the towel. Hannah overheard the whole thing; she had been getting a drink for you, Lauren. He turned the opposite way, not even realizing she was there. I told her then that I had an attorney. That the moment she needed, all she needed to do was ask. It got back to his brother, Sebastian. We had to convince him not to murder his own brother at the reception."

My stomach churns, and I want to go get into my car and hunt him down. I want to break his heart the way he has broken my sister's. The way my father broke my mother's.

Paul sends off a text, and in a moment, his phone buzzes back. "The attorney is in."

"He doesn't even need details?" Mom asks.

"I have been keeping evidence all along." Paul shoves his phone away. "She may not be my blood, but you girls are all that I have. I won't make any decisions for you, but I wanted to help her out the moment she needed it."

My mom wipes a tear away, and I see the sadness for her daughter. But I also see that she, herself, realizes finally made the right choice in a man.

Now it's Hannah's turn.

As I am walking past Hannah's door, heading to bed, I hear a sound I memorized as a kid. Popping my head into her room, I listen to the all-too-familiar story. It nearly knocks the wind out of me when I hear the words in the voice I know better than my own.

"And the wild things roared their terrible roars and gnashed their terrible teeth and rolled their terrible eyes and showed their terrible claws."

I slip into the room, and Winnie scoots over to let me cuddle into bed with them. I try to hide my tears as they slip down my cheek and into Winnie's blond curls. Hannah reads to her daughter like she used to read to me; placing emphasis on the fact that when you feel out of control, it's okay to disappear into imaginary worlds for a while.

30

LAST FALL

The moment Rhett steps foot back in the city from visiting his hometown, he meets me back at my apartment under the guise of the looming deadline.

He gives a quick courtesy knock before letting himself in. It's only been a long weekend, but the sight of him makes my stomach flip like a damn pancake. He's wearing a Lac Dunes sweatshirt and backward baseball hat, and I want to crawl into his arms. His eyes look tired, but when they land on me, I see the spark in them. The corners of his mouth curve into a grin.

"Hi," he says. "I missed you."

"I missed you too."

He sets his stuff down and instantly is wrapping me in a hug. My face burrows into the spot just below his shoulder, and I inhale the scent of him and plan how I'm going to steal this sweatshirt.

"Herman said if I keep it up, he might ask you if he can make me a spare key to your place," Rhett says into my hair.

I crane my neck up to catch the glimmer of amusement in his eye. But he pulls me back and places a kiss on top of my head. "Let's hit this deadline."

For the next week, we live and breathe my manuscript. Running it over and over again. Making sure it's ready to go. We live in sweatshirts and sweatpants. He's either at my place, or I'm at his. We start by eight every morning, and we don't leave until after eight every night. Wine and coffee fill our cups interchangeably. His eyes linger on me while we work, my hands find his shoulder and back whenever I need to move around him, our knees rest against each other under the table.

His Lac Dunes sweatshirt—the one he left behind on my couch—becomes my choice of attire because it smells like him. I cling to it each night we return to our respective places and not stay the night. It makes me feel like he's still with me. That he's wrapped around me in bed.

By deadline day, he and I are standing in my kitchen with my laptop on the counter. Our glasses of wine are empty again and our hearts thudding in our chests.

"This is it," he whispers into the side of my head. His hands are on either side of me, caging me in against the counter as he presses against my back. Our bodies perfectly fitting together as he places a kiss on my shoulder then drops his chin onto it. I nod and hover the mouse over the send button. And then with a lump in my throat, I press it. A beat of silence follows, then the sound of the email shooting off then— relief.

I spin around and our arms envelope each other.

"You did it, Laure," he whispers into my hair.

I squeeze him tight, feeling small in the warmth of his arms. Then a drip on my shoulder forces my eyes up. He's looking at me with a tearful expression that exudes pride and pain. His fingers brush a stray hair behind my ear and before I can say anything, he is kissing me like the preacher said we could.

"Rhett." His tongue finds mine and my knees falter. Our tears mix on our cheeks as he pulls my mouth to his again and again.

Reaching down, he pulls my legs up around his waist and then with a free hand, he swipes the laptop away and sets me on the counter. The strength of his arms nearly knocks the wind out of me. His lips trail down my jaw to that soft spot just behind my ear.

"Is anybody planning on stopping by?" he asks gruffly.

My voice doesn't come to me, so I just shake my head no. Electricity shoots from his mouth pressed there, and his teeth nip at the skin.

My head falls back as every ounce of adrenaline courses through my body.

"Oh my God, Rhett."

"You're brilliant." He groans back before pulling away. "I am so fucking proud of you."

"Thank you. Thank you for believing in me."

"You never needed me." He laughs into my lips. "You had it in you all along."

"Take my clothes off, Rhett." I command, and he doesn't hesitate to reach for the hem of his sweatshirt that I'm wearing. I reach my arms up, letting him pull it off.

Typically, I would have been scared for a man to see my body, see the way it folds when I sit or the marks I earned from being the tallest girl in fifth grade. I'd worry about the splashes of freckles on my chest and back. I'd worry about the dimples on my butt and hips. But for the first time, not only did I not care, I also wanted him to see them, me. There isn't a single part of me that is insecure as his eyes fall to my body sitting before him.

His jaw clenches, and that stoic expression shifts into something hungrier. His green eyes melt into deep emerald pools and the look alone sends pulses through me and goose bumps across my body.

Rhett has had a front-row seat to my brain, which is far more intimate. But somehow, watching his hands comb through my pages and now doing the same through my hair, I feel a rush that I can't assign words to. The same sense of being pulled in. Of being seen. His green eyes like a dock light, calling me to him.

I take my turn to reach for his shirt, and he helps me slide it up over his head. His body is no mystery; I have studied and memorized the way it looks under a thin cotton shirt. I have traced the width of his shoulders in my mind more times than I can count. I had seen him like this when we got caught, but goddammit, I don't care if the building is burning down, I'm not going anywhere now.

My hands trail down his chest as he leans in front of me. I reach the waistband of his jeans, and I slip my fingers just under the elastic.

"Tell me you want me." He groans. "Tell me this is what you want."

"Rhett, of course I want you." My words are almost a desperate whine. "I have wanted you every moment since I met you."

He grunts at my confession, dropping his forehead into mine. Then he swoops his arms down, lifting me off the counter and carries me through the living room and to my bedroom; his lips never leaving mine.

I am all but thrown into the bed. Then he comes down on top of me, pressing himself between my legs, and God, I have never hated his jeans or my pants more. His lips find their home on my neck and on my collarbone, and my mind swims with the smell of pine trees and musk. The sensation of him hard against me floods my brain.

Rhett pulls back only an inch as his eyes frantically glance around my face, his eyes molten emeralds. The tension is thick in the air, and there's no use cutting it. Might as well drown in it. In him.

"Please," I beg, and the twitch in his jaw ignites as he beckons for me to arch my back. He reaches around me, unclasping my bra, and throws it to the side. He sucks in a breath with a slight shake of his head.

"My God, Laure." He groans.

Then a rush floods through me as our lips collide again, unable to inhale each other fast enough. My hands fumble with my pants, but his hands stop mine. "Let me. I have you."

I nod and drop back while I let his calloused fingers grip my waist before he tugs my pants down my legs. He lowers back down and presses his lips to the inside of my ankle then places more small kisses up the inside of my leg, and God, I could die right here. My heart is thrashing as heat is furiously flooding through my body. When his lips reach an inch inward, I feel my breath catch, and my hands grasp his hair.

"Oh God." The words slip out of my mouth as I feel him between my legs. And I can feel his smile against my skin.

If there was a book on my body, I could swear Rhett already has it on his nightstand. His hands are under me, pulling me up to him by my ass, and my fingers stay tangled in his hair as the heat gathers right where his mouth is.

"I need more. Please. I'm on birth control." I find my voice speaking out loud after a minute as the tension begins to become too strong. Then he's standing, unbuckling his jeans and tossing them, along with his boxers, aside.

My jaw goes slack at the sight of him standing there above me and he only chuckles before coming back down over me. His hips rests between my legs and the weight causes my head to spin into an oblivion.

"Are you sure?" He whispers.

I want to hit him for even asking. For making me beg.

"I've never been more sure," I gasp out and pull his mouth into mine. He smiles against my lips and slowly presses into me.

The feeling of him inside me knocks me entirely off my axis. And as we move together, I wonder if I will ever recover if I don't feel this again. That if this, him, is what my body needs to be centered around.

"God, you feel better than I ever dreamed." He groans into my ear with slow movements. "And I dreamed of this a lot."

His words make me light-headed. And so does the way his hand is gripping my chest as he moves and the way his lips mumble praises into my neck. Our bodies shift and move with each other like they knew what to do all along. Our hearts just waiting for our brains to catch up. I come undone and he follows quickly after and collapses next to me.

"You're perfect," he whispers, kissing my temple. "Every inch of you. Your legs, your hair, your mind." His fingers trace over my body like he's remembering each place he touched, marking it as his. "Perfect."

31

NOW

When we first moved into Paul's house, all I could think was how different it smelled from the home I grew up in. It smelled like fresh linens and coffee. Not old carpet and shut windows. Though it was better, it still wasn't home. Then, the longer I lived here, the more used to it I became. I no longer smelled the lemon cleaner and laundry. Now, laying here in bed, I smell it. I'm aware of the cleaner and detergents. For the first time in a long time, it doesn't smell like home. It doesn't smell like a low burning fire and fresh coffee. It's not the cabin.

After what feels like hours of sleepless twister, I untangle myself from Winnie, who is clinging to me like a little monkey, and slide out of the bed. She must have dragged in my bag last night before I came up, setting it up right next to hers.

And though it makes my heart flutter, I know it's time to go. If I stay much longer, I don't think Mom will be able to bite her tongue anymore. Unsaid things grow out of the floorboards when we pass our two-day trip allotment. But seeing Winnie's little bag next to mine and the clothes spilling out of it makes me sad for some reason. I don't know if it's because of her dad, or if it's the impending, life-altering things to come for them. Or just the innocence I once knew, ever so briefly.

After I carefully place a kiss on her forehead, Winnie mumbles goodbye before stretching and rolling back over to fall back asleep, her little cheek smooshed against the pillow. Hannah doesn't stir.

Creaking stairs carry me down through the early morning haze that comes in from the windows. Silent goodbyes are a lot easier on everyone. Especially for Mom. Words were never much her thing.

"Sneaking out?" Paul calls from down the hallway.

"Trying to." My hand freezes on the doorknob. I set down my bag and go to Paul, who is reading the newspaper at the kitchen island.

"Have some coffee before you go." He smiles, his reader glasses on the edge of his nose, his crow's-feet stretching from his eyes. I had been too busy noticing Mom aging to see he has too. That man who showed up in our lives with a job for Mom, now still the exact same man. Just grayed.

He has laid out mugs already. An *L* mug for me and an *H* mug for Hannah sitting, waiting. A little mug with a *W* waits, too.

"How's Michigan?" Paul asks and slides over a mug with the perfect creamer to coffee ratio.

"It's new." I admit. "Different. But it's gorgeous."

"Are you okay on money? If you need any, you know you can call me."

"Yes Paul. I know."

"Promise me, you'll call if you need anything. Money. Lawyers. You name it."

If I have learned one thing about Paul over the past ten years, I have learned he means everything he says.

"I promise."

"Aunty Laurey." A croaky little voice comes down the hallway, and I see Winnie with her messy hair and twisted-up pajamas. I haven't slept that hard since I was her age, I'm sure. Her cheeks flushed the sleepiest shade of pink.

"Good morning," I say, and she pads down the hallway and crawls into my arms with her blanket around her shoulders; her body racked with a massive yawn.

"You aren't leaving yet, are you?" Her little sleep-filled eyes look up at me.

"We would love to have you for another day," Paul says. "It's supposed to rain all day anyway. May be better to travel later tonight."

"What do you think, Win? One more day?"

She nods happily.

"Let me warm up that coffee then." Paul smiles and walks over to the coffee pot. "What about you, kiddo? Want a kid coffee?"

"Mm-hmm." She nuzzles into me.

"Kid coffee?" I ask, and Paul nods with a performative seriousness.

"Oh yes. It's our most popular drink at Grampy's coffee shop."

Winnie giggles as Paul adds the tiniest splash of coffee and a lot of chocolate milk to her little *W* mug.

"For Winifred?" he calls out and looks around the room, really giving her the coffee shop experience.

"Can I put in an order for a grown-up coffee?" Hannah says from the hallway. Her dark hair falls over her shoulders, and her arms are crossed over her chest. She wears a Detroit Lions T-shirt and shorts, and it strikes me how young she looks.

"Oh, absolutely," Paul says. "Are we talking like adding a shot-of-whiskey? Or—"

"Black coffee," Hannah says with a playful warning in her eye. "Black coffee will do."

"Same for me." Mom comes in, too, now and sits next to me at the counter.

"All right, my girls." Paul pours Mom's coffee. "What's for breakfast?"

"Pizza?" Winnie asks.

"How about breakfast food?" Hannah says, leaning on the counter across from us.

"We have pizza for breakfast all the time."

"*Winnie* Mouse pancakes?" Paul suggests.

Winnie approves, and we all are quickly assigned jobs.

Mom and I start cutting the berries. Hannah mixes up the pancakes. Paul starts getting everything set up. It's a smooth morning. It's a quiet, polite morning.

Winnie laughs as Paul dramatically flips a pancake, pretending to be surprised each time he catches it in the pan.

We all have two "Winnie" Mouse pancakes before Paul even gets to his own, which Winnie insists must also be mouse shaped. Strawberries used as her bow and blueberries for her eyes.

"When are you girls planning on heading out?" my mom asks over her coffee. "The weather is supposed to be bad today."

"Aunt Laurey said she will stay!" Winnie informs them. "We can watch movies and paint nails!"

"Do I get to pick the color this time?" Paul asks, and Winnie shakes her head no.

Soon, we have brought pillows and blankets into the living room, and Winnie has her pink sparkly nail polish and mismatched toe spreaders ready to go.

"Any good coffee shops near you in Michigan?" Mom asks after a while.

"No, but there is a diner in town—"

"What about spas?"

I catch Paul's eye roll across from me, and we both chuckle.

"Mom, they don't even have a McDonald's. Let alone a spa."

She shrugs. "What about gardens? Have you found any gardens yet? Hannah would love to go and visit the gardens."

"Not that I know of. It's a really small town. Traverse City is a bit north, and I'm sure they have some. But I just stay close to the cabin and write."

"You could have done that from here," she quips but then seems to instantly regret the sharpness in her tone. "But I'm sure the trees are pretty this time of year . . ."

Later, when the storm properly rolls in, I meet Hannah in the kitchen to refill our coffees when I find her typing out a text message. She then slams her phone onto the counter with a grunt.

"Everything okay?" I ask. And she shakes her head.

"Come on." I grab our jackets and motion for her to follow me. "Let's go sit on the porch."

The back porch is closed in, so though the thunder grumbles and rain-ice mix pelts down, we remain dry and warm enough.

"I always loved their garden. Even out of season." Hannah sighs. "I always dreamed of having my own."

"Why haven't you started one at the new house?"

She shrugs. "Ethan thought it would be too messy looking."

Another flash of light stretches across the sky, and a crack of thunder follows.

"Want to talk about the text you got?" I ask.

"It's Ethan. He sent me this long text about wanting to go to therapy again once he is back from his *breather*." She gives me the air quotes around the last word. "That he is feeling really good about us, and how excited he is to see his girls."

"Did he apologize for yesterday?"

She shakes her head. "He's with her."

"What?"

She pulls out her phone and goes to the Find My app and clicks on the one that reads, "Winnie's iPad." It's in the middle of an upscale neighborhood in Chicago.

"She left her iPad in the back of his car last night before he stormed out." She sighs. "He sent this text while he was with her."

"Is it really over?" I ask her. "Are you really going to leave."

She sucks in her cheeks and wipes away a stray tear. Then gives a quick nod of her head, and I could let out the biggest sigh of relief. I could jump up and down and kiss her. But instead, I tell her how sorry I am and wrap my arms around her, offering her the only thing I can. My love.

"I never thought I would end up like Mom did."

"You didn't end up anywhere yet. You still have the choice. Who knows? Maybe you and I and Winnie could move somewhere. Throw a dart at the map and follow it."

"I wish Ethan would just walk out first so I don't look like the bad guy."

"Mommy!" Winnie peeks her head out from the back door. "Our song is on the TV!"

Hannah blushes. So I follow Winnie in and listen as the movie plays "Smooth," by Santana and Rob Thomas. And Winnie sings along, knowing every word.

"I can explain." Hannah laughs, coming in behind me.

"I'm telling Tanner about this," I inform her quietly. "You'll have to come up. Since he's been inviting you all this time."

She crosses her arms, fighting a smile. But not fighting me on this.

32

LAST FALL

The city sounds are quiet this morning, the snow muffling the car horns and traffic. I roll over and watch Rhett through the open bedroom door. He's walking around the kitchen, pulling down mugs while the coffee brews. He's standing in only his boxers, and I take a moment to memorize this view. Maybe because of some deep premonition that this won't last. Or some instinct telling me that I would miss it. I don't know. But I hold my breath and etch the lines of his body into the back of my mind. Memorize him pouring the mugs full and carefully carrying them back to the bedroom.

"Morning, Laure." he whispers, tucking a strand of hair behind my ear.

I feel the blush creep back up my body. I sit up, clutching the blankets to my chest as if my body was some mystery now that the sun is back in the sky.

"Good morning." I take the cup from him, watching his eyes dance around my bare shoulders.

"How does it feel to be done with the book?" he asks, his morning voice low and gravelly. It makes me want to pull him right back into bed. And it makes me regret every time I sent him home each night we worked late.

A buzz comes from the floor, and Rhett ignores it.

"I don't even know. I'm waiting for Runclave to call back and tell me it was all a big joke."

"That book"—Rhett shakes his head and leans to place a kiss on my temple— "was anything but a joke."

I whisper a thank-you as his phone buzzes again. He grumbles and sets his mug down on the nightstand before digging the phone out of his pants pocket on the floor. When he presses the screen, his face shifts into something almost expressionless.

His expressions have been slow, steady, with watchful eyes that had a million thoughts running through them like leaves in creeks. He always rubs his neck, touches his hair. He expresses his thoughts in little gestures and strong hands. But now, sitting on the edge of what I—as of this morning—considered his side of the bed, he doesn't say anything. Not with his voice, his arms, nor his eyes. Rhett stands, dresses, then shoves his phone in his pocket.

"Is everything okay?" I ask, and his eyes dart to me like he forgot I was there.

"Oh, yeah. Sorry. It's nothing." He leans over and kisses me; it feels almost forced.

"I have to go. I'll call you," he says, his voice unsteady. He pulls back, and his eyes search mine. I don't know what for, but the sadness in his eyes is obvious. I want to pull him back into bed, beg him to stay. But soon he is up and leaving, and I must be mistaken to see tears in his eyes as he goes.

I'm left in bed, unmoved from where he found me just moments ago. Wondering what the hell just happened. My coffee is in my hands, and his is still steaming on the nightstand.

⌇

Two days stretch by before I get an answer to my texts and calls.

"I can't stay on," he says quickly when I answer his call. "I just wanted to tell you good morning. Again, I'm so sorry I left like I did I just..."

Panicked, I finish for him in my mind.

We danced the line for too long, then when we finally got around to how we really felt, it was too late. It must have scared him and he ran.

I choke back the tears I didn't want him to know I've cried at the embarrassment of being so sad. "Why *did* you leave?"

He sighs. "Lauren—"

"What? Are we just supposed to talk and ask how the other is without acknowledging the fact that you quite literally ran out on me?"

He doesn't say anything.

"You know what?" I say, "Sure. Fine. No distractions, right?" I hang up on him and chuck my phone against the wall, knowing I won't get my safety deposit back with the dent it left behind. It narrowly missed the picture frames on the wall. One of them is the photo of us at Ninety-Seven's when Elyse and Cal faked our engagement. But we weren't looking at Elyse when she took the photo. We were looking at each other. There was love there; I just can't figure out where he lost his, because mine is drowning me.

As December passes in snowfall and bitter cold, those unanswered phone calls fade into the occasional text message. A *Hi* here and a *Good night* there. Part of me hopes that he just up and left the city all together. That I don't need to be nervous about running into him when making a coffee run.

Yet I check the tables along the walls for glimpses of him anyway.

Elyse calls to check in when I miss another book club meeting, and she says she saw Rhett that morning. He popped into the store looking the worse for wear. It confirms my worst fear: he is here, and he hasn't left the city. Just me. He is still within a close drive and has made no effort other than a lousy "Hope you're okay" text.

All I can wonder is whether he still gets gas from the gas station where I get my pizza And I've never been the wiser.

ONE MORNING, or midafternoon, my phone dings. It's an email forwarded from Myranda.

MYRANDA,

Please let Lauren know the book has been approved and sent to the printer. She should have an early print soon.

Thanks,

Rhett.

MY THROAT TIGHTENS as the tears begin to burn. It felt over when Elyse said he was still here, but now there is no denying it. Our words being siphoned through my agent? I chuck my phone across the apartment, and it smashes against the wall again. This time, a splintering sound follows as it crashes down to the floor, creating a twin dent next to the last one. I've lost him so many little times over these few weeks, so why does the final absence cut so deeply

"What's going on?"

I spin and see Hannah in the doorway. Words don't come to me; I just stare at her.

"Sorry," she says, looking behind her. "The door was unlocked. I knocked . . . I wanted to surprise you for the day. Celebrate you being done with your first book."

I can't get out any words.

"Lauren, honey, what happened?" Her face changes from confusion to concern as she comes in, shedding her coat and shoes.

"He left," I choke out, realizing the tears have started falling. Or really, they haven't stopped since he left. "It's over."

"Your book? Did you lose your book deal?"

I choke out an unfunny laugh. "No. Him. Rhett. We're over."

"Oh, Lauren." Her voice cracks my final wall, and then she's hugging me while I cry into her shoulder, like I knew I would once it ended. When the excitement was over and the only thing that kept us together came to an end. "What happened?"

I shrug. "I don't know. I submitted my book, we slept together, and then in the morning, he left. He brought me coffee in bed, then he was gone."

"He didn't say why?"

"No."

"Let's get out of here." She pulls back. "No more giving him any space in your brain. If he can't explain himself, then he doesn't deserve your heartache."

God, I wish I could believe that.

"Come on. We are going to paint some pottery."

This causes a laugh to sputter out of my mouth. *"What?"*

"You heard me. It's where I took Winnie when her dad missed her dance recital. She loved it."

"I'm not going to go paint—"

"It isn't an option. We are getting out of this shitty little apartment. And away from the idea of him."

An hour later, we are sitting across from each other at a paint covered wooden table, painting mugs like children at a birthday party. A mom and her daughter are painting piggy banks across the room, and the teenage girl working here is on her phone, unbothered by the lack of customers.

"What are you going to paint?" Hannah asks, and she shuffles through the bottles of paint she selected.

"I don't know . . ."

"Something springy. Something to get us through winter," she says, and I think of the quote at the beginning of *Honeycomb*.

"Though we bury ourselves in the dirt now, come spring, we will have roots in what once covered us, and a view from much higher up."

Tulips it will be. The ones you plant in the fall that bloom in the spring. The ones he brought me. The ones he planted in the fall within my heart and never stuck around to see bloom in the spring. So when I shatter it against the wall in a few weeks, it will save me some money on a therapy visit.

Hannah fills the time with telling me about Winnie and her dance classes, nightmares, and disdain for any food other than pizza.

"A single dad at Winnie's dance school sent me flowers. He got my address from the costume order form and had a dozen roses delivered to the house. And I didn't even care if Ethan saw them. I didn't care if it was going to make him angry. But it didn't. He saw them and didn't even ask about the man's phone number inside."

"Did you call him?" I ask, amused at the image.

Her face twists. "You know what my first thought was when they were delivered?"

"What?"

"That I hate roses and I wonder what Tanner would say if he saw them."

I choke on a laugh. And she narrows her eyes on me.

"He would have been the one to deliver them himself," I tell her.

A smile grows on her lips. "That's probably true."

I add another little, pink-tinted flower on the handle, imagining it shattered on the floor already.

"You know what you should do? You should throw a book release party on New Year's Eve." Hannah's eyes widen with the idea. "It will help get your mind off things!"

"I'll only have the early prints in then, and I don't know who I would invite—"

"Well, me. Your book club, right? They would come. And your agent, and maybe Mom and Paul would come in for it! It would be so fun. Winnie would love to come visit you."

"Maybe," I say noncommittally. It could be nice to be around the people who haven't walked out. But also, having a book release party and not having him there would feel wrong.

We finish painting our mugs, and the teenage girl at the counter says they will be ready in a week. Then, Hannah insists on hot dogs at a shady corner shop that sells food on rollers and off-brand soda by the can. After eating at the squeaky stools, we head back to the apartment, where Hannah helps me clean without me even asking. She just quietly kicks off her shoes and begins tidying the mess I couldn't bring myself to clean. She talks about a good place to hang a sign for my book. Where to set up the drinks. All these years later, and she still is being a mom when I need one most.

"Did I ever tell you about what Ethan's brother Sebastian said to me at our engagement party?" she asks as she scrubs off a dish.

"I don't think so."

"He pulled me aside after all the speeches and asked if I was sure about what I was doing. If marriage was really what I wanted. I think he knew that Ethan was just like his dad, and I think he knew I hadn't seen that side of him yet." She sets the dish aside and starts the next. "He knew, and he tried to talk me out of it."

"Do you wish you would have done it any differently?" I ask her and sit across from her at the counter. And this makes her pause, considering. "Marry Sebastian instead?"

She laughs and shakes her head. "I would go through every moment of it again if it meant I got Winnie. It's worth it for her. Besides, I never saw Sebastian like that. Big lumberjacks aren't my type. He was always a brother to me."

After a while, Hannah places a kiss on my cheek before returning to her family in the suburbs, leaving me to plan my book release and New Year's Eve party on my own. However, I find myself excited. This party, a little glimmer of hope. The idea of having Elyse and the other girls around, my mom and Paul coming to see the little life I made for myself here. The proof would be undeniable that I have made it. You couldn't refute the fact that despite everything, I had come out the other end with a damn good book.

On the couch that night, I ordered myself a nice dress and a big poster of my book.

I spent the next couple of days inviting everyone over for New Year's Eve and to dress up. I shopped for snacks, champagne, and tacky decorations. And for a few nights, I didn't cry myself to sleep.

There would be good moments after him. Even if they start out with a forced attempt at making them.

33
<hr>

NOW

The sight of the "Welcome to Michigan" sign settles me instantly. Despite the tension with Rhett on the other side, this place has already creeped into my bones, and I can't imagine the pain it's going to cause when this is over. Where that sign welcomed me back, the "Now Entering Green Branch" sign is my green light at the end of the dock. Like it's just been waiting on me to arrive. The sleet storm just a few hours south in in Illinois, translated into a full-on snowstorm up here. The orange and brown trees are covered in a soft blanket of snow.

Suddenly starving, I drive straight to the diner. I make it three steps inside, see who's at the counter, then take three steps back toward the door. Before I can make it thought, Mayben catches me and waves me down. Damn it.

Tanner and Rhett turn to face me and my stomach flips. Tanner smiles then gives a quick glance over to Rhett, who isn't smiling. His eyes are narrow on me as his jaw clenches. Is he disappointed to see me? Is my heart racing?

"Come on in." Mayben pats the spot at the counter in-between Rhett and Tanner.

I steal myself an ounce of bravery and take the seat.

"How was your trip home?" she asks, sliding over a glass of water.

"Great." I smile but wonder how she knew. Did Jack tell her? Did Rhett?

"How was Hannah?" Tanner asks. He's fighting a grin as he sips his drink.

"She was all right," I tell him. And wonder how much longer I will have to be the liaison between them. "Her and Winnie were dancing to your karaoke song."

He smirks as a wicked blush hits his cheeks.

"Here, Lauren." Mayben has shifted the boxes into the cooler and picks up a slice of pie for me. "You have to try Willa Morton's pie."

"Isn't Morton's that country bar on the side of town?" I ask and pick up one of the forks Mayben has laid out. "Where everyone gets coffee from around here?"

"The finest run-down institution this side of the Mackinac Bridge." Tanner says.

After one bite, I learn they're right. There may be no better pie than Willa Morton's pie.

Mayben gets a single bite before Tanner takes the fork and steals a bite too.

"Honestly, I would give my left kidney to learn how to make this." Mayben snatches the fork back. "But Willa doesn't share the recipe."

"She's been teaching Gwen," Rhett finally says.

Now the other two fall silent. "She's teaching Gwen the most protected recipe in the Midwest?" Tanner asks and looks over at Rhett. "Maybe I should have kissed her back all those years ago. Who knew she would have been my key to getting this recipe?"

My eyebrows hit my hairline.

"No, not really," He stammers. "I mean, yes, she kissed me, but I don't mean I *should* have— I just love this pie—"

"Oh, shut up." Mayben shakes her head and thumps him upside the head. "We all know you are madly in love with Hannah. She's all we have heard about for the past year. At this point, I think you're going to take her last name if she'll ever marry you."

"I'm working on it," he grumbles with a smirk.

I fight a laugh and excuse myself to the restroom while they fight over the rest of the pie.

"Besides, you're one to talk, Mayb." Tanner says quietly as I'm walking away. "You'll be an Atwood soon enough. Or maybe he can take your last name. Rhett, what do you think?"

My feet are cemented into the ground. *What did he just say?*

Spinning around, I see Rhett is shaking his head with a bashful smile, Mayben is blushing and oh my God. That's why Tanner told me to talk to Rhett. He was trying to warn me. It's the truth Rhett has started to tell me so many times, he just hasn't been able to admit it out loud to me.

Rhett's really *is* with Mayben.

That's why he's been trying to talk this whole time too. I don't even make it to the bathroom. Instead, I turn and dip straight out of the restaurant and to my car, ignoring the confused looks on all their faces. I drive right back to the cabin, slamming and locking the door shut behind me.

34

LAST WINTER

I stand with my back against the wall at my party, drinking Rhett's favorite wine in a new dress. Elvis is playing on the record player, and the decorations glitter in the low lamplight. I cleaned the kitchen and tidied the living room all day today. I took care of the mess that the lack of motivation has left me over the past month. I even got some balloons and strung a couple of streamers over the windows, just like Hannah suggested. Snacks in the kitchen are on the nicest plates I could find in the cupboards. Champagne is on ice and ready for the midnight countdown.

Hannah texted this morning that she couldn't make it. She said Winnie was up sick all night, and Ethan wasn't around to stay home with her. My mom and Paul texted, saying they were happy for me but had forgotten about previous plans they couldn't break at the country club.

The party started at eight.

At eight thirty, Elyse texted that she and Cal were with her parents for New Year's Eve and couldn't make it like they originally thought they would, but she promised she would make it up to me.

At nine, Faye and Nikki called and said they got invited to an exclusive party downtown that they were going to go to, but I was welcome to join them if they were still out after my party.

Ten came, and Myranda texted that she had to catch a flight to LA to do some networking last minute. Which left the few girls from the office she invited to cancel too.

And now it's nearing midnight, and the person I shouldn't have sent an invitation to, isn't here either. And his absence hurts the most.

It crosses my mind to skip my own party. To grab an Uber to some shitty bar nearby and disappear into a crowd so huge that I will be completely alone. To get drunk with every other lonely person there and stumble back after closing the place down with some regrettable tourist who would be honored just to be chosen. Yet here I am, showing up for myself when nobody else has. Heartbroken that I wasn't chosen.

Every passing minute puts a tiny crack in my heart. Nobody is coming. The embarrassment makes me start cleaning up when the countdown to the New Year grows closer.

My little launch party, my attempt to celebrate my book, is echoing my success to an empty room. And the cake on the counter with twenty-five unlit candles sits untouched.

Quickly, I begin to shovel the silly decorations I bought into a garbage bag while tears drip embarrassingly from my cheeks onto the pile of mail at the top of the garbage can. But before I can dump the cake in, candles and all, an envelope with a red stamp catches my eye. I dig it out and see Rhett's name scribbled across the front. I wrote it in red ink when I sent him the invitation to this party. I don't even remember getting this back. It's stamped "Return to Sender."

I drop it back in, and I shove the cake in on top of it.

Chugging down the glass of wine, I talk myself out of throwing the glass across my apartment. I put the food into baggies and shove them in the fridge because I can't afford to just throw it all away. I am angrily wiping the tears away when a knock at the door startles me.

I should be imagining Hannah there or hoping to see Elyse. Even expecting Myranda to surprise me with balloons or a bottle of champagne. But I don't. I think of the one person I want here, and through the peephole, I see the bloodshot green eyes I have been waiting on.

When I swing open the door, Rhett is standing there, with windblown hair, flushed cheeks, and a sniffling nose. His chest is racked with heavy breaths, and his mind seems busy. Dark.

Almost a month has passed between waking up together and now. The look in his eyes that morning, what I mistook then as love, is there still. Or maybe it *is* love. But just some broken version of it.

"I hate your wine," I snap when he doesn't say anything. "I fucking *hate* it."

"I love you." His voice is steady and low, and it hits me like a fist straight into my lower gut.

"How dare you," I whisper, my feet barely keeping me upright. It takes every ounce of my strength to not throw myself into his arms and breathe him back into my lungs. He lowers his head to meet my eyes.

"I love you. I can't stay, but I love you. I will *always* love you," he chokes out, tears beginning to escape his eyes and roll down his cheeks. "I'm leaving, but I love you, and I need you to know that."

"I hate you," I lie. "I hate you. How dare you show up here and say that."

His eyes flick around the room and then back to me.

"That's okay. That's good." He says it like he has some desperate desire for my rejection. "You should hate me. I deserve nothing from you but your hate."

"You don't get to say that. Knowing damn well I don't hate you. I'm not the one choosing this." I choke on my tears and find myself taking my palms and pushing his chest. "You don't get to show up here, telling me you love me and promising to leave. It's not fair. It's not fair that you won't let me love you back."

"God, Lauren—" Rhett grasps my hands and holds them to his chest.

"Look at my life, Rhett. Look around. My apartment is empty. This was a party. A fucking party, and you weren't here. Neither is anyone else, but *you* weren't here. And that's what killed me. You didn't come. I even got ready for tonight. I put on a new dress and felt pretty. How stupid is that?" I spit out the word *pretty*, because it isn't enough. Being pretty or feeling pretty. It was never going to be enough. He's running, and I'm fighting.

"Lauren, you're so beautiful. I can't . . . I want to stay, but I'm a mess. I can't be what you need. I'll only hurt you in the end—"

"Be fucking honest with me!" I yell and yank my hands away, wanting him to fight back. But I know he won't. He's never going to. I push him again, but I'm the one who almost goes backward. He catches me, but I yank away because I will just seep into his grasp. I can hardly see him through my tear-blurred eyes. "For once, be *honest* with me. Stop this dance like we can't say what we're thinking. Don't pretend we haven't been falling in love all this time."

Rhett drags the back of his hand under his nose. "Lauren, I know we have been falling in love. And that's why I have to leave. You deserve something easier than what I can give you. I will love you for every second for the rest of my life. But I can't ever ask you to love me back. I won't let you. I will never ask you to forgive me. But you will thank me one day that I spared you. Please know this isn't your fault."

"Ten . . . nine . . . eight . . . seven . . ." the TV calls out behind me.

"But I will ask you to know that I love you. That's why I'm leaving." He grabs my face between his hands as I cry, and I'm angry that I can't see him through my tears. I want one last look at him. Because I know it's the end. I know this is our implosion. No matter how many times I blink, I can't seem to clear the tears.

"Six . . . five . . . four . . ."

This is our end. There is nothing more. There is no fighting.

"Three . . . two . . . one . . ."

He never even gave me the chance to fight.

"*Happy New Year!*" the TV voices call out.

"I love you," he whispers one more time, and places a kiss on the side of my head. "Happy Birthday."

Then like a ghost, he's gone. I stand in the doorway, my chest aching from another sob.

"I love you too," I admit as the stairwell door begins to close after him. This time I do break the wineglass. I take it by its delicate stem and smash it against the steel door. The red drops spill down like blood. It looks like I threw my heart after him, but the shut door caught it instead.

I am suddenly stunned by the reality that he has left me here like everyone else has. Now I'm crying in the hallway, drunkenly cleaning up the broken glass and wine on my hands and knees. I know now that my birthday will never be the same. I know it as soon as I shovel the glass into my hand, and it slices across my palm, leaving real blood on the ground now too.

My heart breaks knowing that even my birthday isn't safe from people not loving me enough to stay.

35

———

NOW

I am switching over the laundry, replaying yesterday in my head over and over again.

You'll be an Atwood sooner or later.

I wonder exactly how things went so horribly wrong in a year. Never did I think that I would have a front-row seat to watching Rhett move on. I don't call Hannah and tell her yet. Because saying it out loud would make it too real.

The laundry dumps out of my basket into the washer, and my phone begins buzzing in my pocket.

"Hello?" I press the phone between my ear and shoulder and add detergent.

"Lauren?" Myranda's voice shakes. I stand straight and grasp the phone.

"Yeah?" Cold chills lace my skin.

"Hey. Okay. So don't shoot the messenger but . . . " She trails off.

"Myranda, what is it?" My hands have frozen, and icy chills shoot up my neck.

"Charles isn't loving your manuscript so far. He said it's too sad and serious."

"And? What are you saying?" I ask through gritted teeth, my heart sinking deeper into my belly.

"I'm saying he might pull the plug. Might. He said you need to turn it around and make it lighter or it's done. I overheard him talking with the finance team, and he mentioned possibly cutting you off. You have time still but—"

"He can't," I say, knowing full well he can. "He can't, Myranda. My first book debuted on the best-sellers list. Granted, not very high, but you even told me how impressive that is for a debut. Surely you guys have more faith in me than this."

"*I* do," she says. "I swear, I believe in you and this manuscript. But Runclave runs a business. He knew you were able to create a really great contemporary romance. But he doesn't think your readers will want such a shift in mood so early on."

"So what if he drops me?" I ask.

Myranda hesitates, then lets out a breath. "Let me worry about that. For now, you keep working on this manuscript, and I'll worry about Runclave. You have a few weeks until your deadline still."

"Are you telling me to take my book and make it a cheesy romance? Because I would rather burn the manuscript than do that to it."

"No. I will never tell you how to write a book or to change your story. I'm just telling you what Runclave is saying. If you believe in your story, then prove it to him."

Prove it.

I hang up and try to steady my breathing. How can I write the most vulnerable and real story that I can, and still be turned away? How is this not better than my first? Before my brain and heart check in with each other, my feet are carrying me out the front door, into the snow, and across the driveway before my feet begin to slow at what I'm seeing.

Mayben is standing on Rhett's front porch. She has her hand on his arm as he smiles softly down at her. After last night, hearing what Tanner said, I knew it. But seeing it? It's another blow to my crumbling.

He moved back home to what he knew. To her. He showed up and gave me his big dramatic exit speech a year ago before coming home to her.

I can feel the creeping corners of embarrassment blur my vision as Mayben catches my eyes and nudges Rhett. He turns to see me and dares to smile but then he must read my face and quickly drops the smile. A pickup truck grumbles up the driveway, and Tanner gets out with his baseball hat on and grease stains, well, everywhere.

"You started the party without me?" He claps and rubs his hands together.

Before anyone can respond, I am turning. Leaving. My feet stinging as the snow seeps into my shoes. I don't make it very far before Rhett catches up and grabs me by my arm, spinning me around.

"Laure, wait," he pleads.

I yank my arm from his hand and push him away. "Don't call me that. You don't get to call me that anymore."

"Lauren, talk to me. Tell me what's actually going on." He steps closer. "We've been avoiding it long enough."

"It's nothing. It's fine. You're allowed to move on. I'm not mad," I lie. How foolish I was to have hope that somehow, we would figure our shit out.

"Yes, you are." His already deep voice drops an octave. His words— a challenge. "You *are* mad. Tell me why you're mad. Say it out loud." His voice is a challenge.

"Because I love you," I spit out quietly and push him again. "I *still* fucking love you. And I shouldn't. I should hate you, but I can't, and Runclave might be dropping my book, and I'm more upset at the idea of you loving someone else than I am at the idea of being dropped. If you're dating Mayben and you're happy, then fine. But if by some miracle, Tanner and Hannah ever get together, I will support my sister, but don't expect me to sit by and watch you love someone else."

Determination is replaced by confusion as he narrows his eyebrows. "Wait, what? Runclave might *drop* you?"

I swipe my hand across my cheek, removing the tears before they freeze. That's what he got out of all of that?

"He said it's too serious. Too sad. That what I wrote wasn't the love story he wanted. That's what's funny, though, isn't it? It's not the love story I wanted either. This is what I get from writing about real heartbreak. Writing about *you*." My finger is pressed into his chest. I am so tired of pushing him. Begging for him to fight back. I drop my hand and start to turn from him. But he grabs my arm, turning us so he stands between me and the cabin.

"Lauren, I am not—"

"Hey, kiddo! You're back!" Jack calls out as he steps out from the house. But Rhett doesn't drop my arm. I bite the inside of my cheek to keep my lip from trembling. "We're having dinner for the twins' birthday, Come on by!"

"I can't." I will my voice not to crack. "I'm heading home."

Rhett's face contorts in confusion. "Home? What do you mean?"

"Your rental isn't up for another month," Jack adds.

"I have to get back early. You know, meetings and things." I lie through my fucking teeth while Rhett stands, refusing to move. He's trying to read me, like he always has. I just wish he had better comprehension skills.

"Well, then that's even more of a reason to come for dinner. Please, I insist." Jack smiles sweetly.

The side door opens again, and this time, out walks a tall,

thin guy with deep-set eyes and a wide jaw. His build is narrower than Rhett's, but the expression on his face is still all Atwood.

"How much pasta do we need for dinner?" he calls out, but his voice trails off at the sight of us all.

"A lot," Jack calls up to him. "We have Tanner and Lauren joinin' us. Lauren, this is my other son, Jack. We call him Jackie. Jackie, this is Lauren Dorada. She's renting out the cabin next door."

Realization hits Jackie like a brick. "Oh. *Oh!*" While my chest heaves with heavy breaths, he nods like this is all very exciting. "Gwen and I have been putting bets on when Rhett would finally bring you home to meet the family. He's been in love with you for long enough."

"Fuck's sake," Rhett grumbles, dragging a hand down his face.

And Mayben laughs nervously. "Babe, chill out."

In a moment, I realize Mayben isn't, in fact, talking to Rhett. She's talking to Jackie.

36

NOW

Words simply spin through my mind as I watch Jackie wrap his arm around Mayben's waist and plant a kiss on her lips.

My eyes dart back to Rhett as he watches me understand what's going on. And realize what's *not* going on. They continue their conversation while Rhett, with his hand on my arm, pulls me closer to him.

"Mayben is dating my brother."

I shake my head. "But you two were just—"

"We were waiting on Tanner to get here. It's the twins' birthday, and he needs help bringing in the beer cooler."

"I don't understand. Your dad said you two dated—"

"We did. But it was high school. I set her up with Jackie after I moved away to school."

Jackie skips down the steps to us. "Nice to finally meet you, Lauren." He shakes my hand, then claps Rhett on the shoulder. "Come on. Help me get the cooler out of Tan's car."

The two brothers bring the massive cooler up the steps, and Mayben opens the door so they can shuffle it inside, with Storm at their feet. Then it's just Jack, Tanner, and me in the driveway.

"He's crazy about you." Jack pats my shoulder. "He hasn't stopped talking about you since the moment he met you. When that agent of yours called that she was setting you up here, I knew it would work out eventually." He winks and heads up the porch.

"You knew?" My jaw is somewhere near the ground when Jack simply winks and heads inside.

Then I turn to Tanner. "When you said I needed to talk to him, then said that thing about Mayben becoming an Atwood—"

"I wanted you to talk to him because he's in love with you, and he is shit at communicating. He just needs some encouragement. And the future Atwood thing? Jackie is looking at rings for Mayben. They've been talking about getting engaged for months now. Jackie even asked our dad for his blessing a few weeks ago and he spilled it to her." He rests his hand on my shoulder in a way I imagine a brother would. "Come on. Jackie is a great cook."

Stepping over the threshold into Rhett's childhood home is like stepping into a personal museum. An homage to the Atwood family. A pile of shoes by the door, coats tossed over the stair railing. A hutch lined with books, including mine among his mother's; even *Honeycomb* sits on the shelf. Laughter and loud stories echo down the hallway lined with photos. I kick off my shoes and shed my jacket and add them to the others.

Jackie and Rhett set the cooler near the back door. The crow's-feet crinkling by both brothers' eyes squeezes at my heart. Gwen, I presume, pops her eyes up to me and puts her hands on her hips. She is all of five feet tall with dark-brown curls that frame her face. She has those Atwood green eyes and full lips. She's beautiful. As if this family could produce an ugly child.

"Is this . . . " Gwen's smile grows as she looks between Rhett and me.

Rhett steps over, placing a hand on my lower back. "Gwen, this is Lauren. Lauren, this is my little sister, Gwen."

"Little, my ass." She laughs and hurries over to me and wraps her arms around me in a hug.

"I can't even believe you're real," she says, squeezing my face with her hands. "Rhett was right. You're gorgeous. Let's get you a drink. Mayben, you too. Any girl that one of my brothers is in love with deserves a drink. Maybe two. Especially you, Lauren. You deserve an extra for all Rhett's brooding."

"Keep my counters clean, please." Jackie warns his sister. "A chef is at work here."

"Which do you prefer?" Gwen holds up two bottles to us, a white and a red, ignoring him entirely. "I am also a bartender. I can make however strong of a drink that you need."

I ask for the white; Mayben wants the red.

I look over my shoulder and spot Rhett watching me closely. The questions piling up in my head.

"You have to tell me everything," Gwen says to me, pouring heavily. "How did he get you out here? Did he pull that Stevens charm?"

"Stevens?" I ask.

"Mom's maiden name. We always joke that any charm that we have is just from Mom's side of the family. My dad is as charming as a bent-out-of-shape canoe. Sometimes I wonder if I got all the charm in the genetic pool."

"Uh, I didn't know he was here. My agent set this trip up for me. It wasn't until your dad sent him over to bring some wood in that I realized what was going on."

"No fucking way." Gwen's jaw drops. "You're kidding. You really had no idea?"

I nod. "None, I was pissed."

A brush of confusion crosses over her face, but she pours

herself a glass of whiskey and leans against the counter. "But you stayed, right? You didn't see him and take off."

"Oh." I laugh. "I tried to. But my sister talked me into staying."

"Oh! The one Tanner is in love with?" Gwen asks with a mischievous glint in her eye.

I nod. "The very one."

"Lauren," Mayben says, softly touching my arm. "I am so sorry that you thought there was something going on between me and Rhett. I assumed he told you I was dating his brother. I, of course, should have known better. Communication was never his strong suit. But we should totally double date."

"Oh, we aren't dating. That ended. We are just coworkers," I tell them.

"I don't confess my love to my coworkers in their driveway very often." She laughs.

"Well, Rhett is very—" *What is Rhett?*

"Complicated?" they say together, like they'd been waiting for someone to see it too.

We laugh when the boys make their way over, getting their beers from the cooler. Rhett comes in and leans against the counter across from me, watching me carefully as he sips his beer.

"Rhett Wells." Gwen sighs. "You're a tricky bastard."

Wells?

"What did you say your mom's maiden name was?" I ask, and like some magic password, it makes Rhett's jaw clench and eyes close. Then he blinks them open and looks at me like he knows exactly why my brain is spinning for once and where this spiral will end.

"Stevens." He answers for her.

I stand and go back down the hallway. Rhett's footsteps trailing behind me as I walk to the booklined hutch by the front door. My book next to Jo Atwood's books. But there, mixed in among the others, is *Honeycomb*.

By Wells Stevens.

I flip open the book and turn to the back. There is no picture. Just a blurb about the author.

Wells Stevens was born with a love of stories and editing them. This is his debut novel. Stevens lives between Chicago and North-western Michigan. Every bit of his career he owes to his mother.

"Lauren." Rhett's voice behind me is deep and gruff. My eyes flutter closed.

"Why wouldn't you tell me?" I force the words out; each one feels like it's wrapped in sandpaper. Another lie by omission.

"Because you loved it."

I turn slowly to face him, looking from the book in my hands up to his face. There's always been stories in his eyes. I just didn't know he ever got them to paper.

"Rhett, this is my favorite book. I keep it on my nightstand. You watched me carry it around. You still have my original copy with my annotations. How could you not tell me it was *yours*?"

He takes a step toward me as I take another step back.

"I didn't want me writing it, to ruin it for you. The mystery of it."

A wave of pride crashes against the shore of hurt. How could we have sat side by side for as long as we have, and this information was never brought up? And more importantly, how did I not figure it out sooner? Him writing a book isn't surprising. If anything I want to kiss him, I'm so proud. But him keeping it from me is what's knocking the wind from my lungs.

"I need to show you something else." He nods toward the stairs.

Fight-or-flight has me ready to go. To leave this man I truly know nothing about and go back home and pretend this never happened. Take this past year and some odd months and count them all as a loss. But...

My heart wants to know. It needs to know. So, I nod my head into some sort of order and follow him up the stairs and into a doorway at the end of the hall. The floor creaks beneath our feet as we enter a dark room.

Rhett turns on a lamp to reveal a bed covered in an old green quilt. It sits across from a tidy desk that faces out the window. There are small tidy stacks of newspapers, books. Nothing like my growing unorganized stacks back at the cabin. My feet carry me around the small space, my hand running along the footboard of the bed.

I can feel the way his eyes follow me around. I turn around and find him holding two books in his hands. The first is the proof of my book. After the party invite came back as a "Return to sender," I gave Myranda this copy to get it to him.

I take it and flip it open. The inside cover is covered in my handwriting; some words blurred from the tears I cried when I wrote it.

R—

I don't think I will ever understand what happened between us. How we went from coworkers to whatever we were and then to nothing. I will never understand how I ended up working with one of the greatest editors and having him believe in me more than anyone ever has. Then finding myself falling hopelessly in love with your passion, your work, and you. I don't think I will ever understand why you left, and I don't think I will ever be able to write you out of my heart. You told me, that night, you wouldn't ask me to love you, but you asked that I knew you loved me. And maybe that's what this book was about all along. About loving someone, despite every hesitation, pause, question, and moment of doubt. Having all those things and still loving them anyway. I will never ask you to explain it to me, why you left. But I will ask you to never let me love you again. If we ever see each other again, I ask that you walk away. Keep your back to me and never tell me you saw me. Never call, or come by, or tell me you love me again. Because I'm not strong enough to walk away, but most of all, I'm not strong enough to watch you walk away again. I think I would come completely undone. Everything that has happened, well, that's between us.

 —L

THE PAIN I felt when I wrote it comes back like a fucking anchor in my chest. It sinks, low and heavy.

Then he hands me the next book. One I don't recognize.

White Wine, by Wells Stevens.

"This is what I worked on last year. When I wasn't working on your edits, I was writing this. It's supposed to come out at the beginning of next year. Open it."

My fingers shake as I open the cover, knowing exactly where he wants me to look. I flip to the dedication.

For the one who helped me fall back in love. With wine, with carryout, with editing. Your love outranks all other accolades.

A tear drops onto the page, and I look up to see the tears in his own eyes.

"Flip to the back," he whispers.

I do, and there is a small bookmark placed between the pages. But it isn't a bookmark. It's a memorial card they pass out at funerals. In the center is a woman smiling with deep crow's-feet lines framing deep-green eyes.

IN LOVING memory of

 Joanna "Jo" Atwood

February 24, 1957 – December 31, 2023

Born in Elizabeth, New Jersey, Joanna Atwood, née Stevens, passed away surrounded by family in Green Branch, Michigan, on the evening of December thirty-first, two-thousand twenty-three. After a few long months of decline, our beloved Jo is now at peace. She leaves behind her beloved husband, Jack Rhett Atwood, and her greatest works of art, her children: Rhett Wells Atwood, Jack "Jackie" Stevens Atwood, and Gwendolyn Joanna Atwood.

In lieu of flowers, the Atwood family asks for donations to be made to Alzheimer's research. The formal obituary can be found in the *Traverse City Times*, written by her son and long-time editor, Rhett Atwood.

MY EYES FALL BACK to the day she died. Last year. New Year's Eve of last year. My party. My birthday. I think Rhett is saying my name, but all I can hear is my heart thrashing in my chest, the blood pumping in my ears.

"Oh my God." I gasp, the back of my hand held to my mouth to hold back a sob.

"Laure," I hear again.

When I meet his eyes, I realize I am sitting on the edge of his bed, and he is kneeling before me. Hands on the sides of my thighs. The intimacy of it pulls me right out of my head.

"Your mom. That's why you left. She was sick and then died. That's why . . . but you were at my apartment that night. I don't understand? Your dad said you were going to visit her for Thanksgiving. I thought he meant at a nursing home."

"Dinner's ready!" Jack calls up the stairs, but Rhett and I don't move. I'm holding the little card with his mother's face that so much resembles his own. His lips quiver at the sight of it.

"Her grave." Tears slip down his cheeks. "On Thanksgiving,

we visited her grave. Lauren, I had to leave. I will explain every-thing later, but I swear to you, I didn't want to leave. I know you wrote those words; you asked me to never explain. But please. Let me."

"Come on!" Gwen yells up. "I would come up, but I'm afraid you're having make-up sex, and I don't want to be scarred for the rest of my life."

"We're coming down now," Rhett calls back to her. Then to me, he whispers, "Will you stay? Please? Then after I explain, you can leave if you want. But please let me explain. Everything."

I can't find words, because there aren't any. Instead, I simply nod.

37

NOW

The Atwood family dinner table is small and rickety, and we are all crammed in, elbow to elbow, with fold-up chairs pulled up from the basement. Despite the full room, the absence of Rhett's mom is suddenly palpable. The empty chair silently left in her honor hits me in a place of grief I've never known. Jack mentioned moving to the cabin before they had to put her in a nursing home. I believed she was still there, the Alzheimer's rendering her a shell of what she used to be, and Rhett just didn't want to talk about it. But she was gone. This entire time.

"Well, nobody told me that in Detroit if you're going north and accidentally take the exit toward Canada, then you can't turn around. You have to literally *leave* the country and tell them on the other side you made the wrong turn," Gwen says over a bottle of beer like it were a campfire flashlight. "So, we end up in Canada, explaining to the pissy border agent how we were *trying* to get to the music festival in downtown Detroit, but we made a wrong turn. Then they asked why we were coming from the south when we were originally coming from up north. So we had to tell them that Taylor and his big head took, like, five wrong turns. But then the damn drug smelling dog perked his ears at our car, so they made us pull off to the side, and searched our car. Which would have been fine until they found Rodney's weed under the back seat. Then we were all detained in their little offices, and I had to flirt our way out of getting locked up. Me, Padma, Rodney, and Taylor still call ourselves Canadian outlaws."

Jack shakes his head. "I'm so glad I didn't know about this at the time."

"Where was Patrick during all of this?" Tanner asks.

"Being chickenshit at home, I'm sure," Rhett quips.

"Patrick"—Jackie leans over the table toward me— "was Gwen's high school sweetheart who ended up breaking things off like a dickhea—"

"Okay, let's not," Gwen chirps and sips her drink.

"They were voted most likely to get married their senior year." Jackie leans back and throws his arm around Mayben's shoulders, then tips his head at his sister. "Imagine that."

She flips him off.

Mayben settles under Jackie's arm, then gives him a quick shove with her elbow. "Oh, stop teasing her."

I glance at Rhett to see if it bothers him to watch his own high school sweetheart with his younger brother. But he isn't looking at them. He reaches under the table, places a hand on my thigh, and squeezes it. My broken heart has a pulse again. Though it's thready, it's there. I fold my hand over his and take in the smiling faces around the table. I have no idea what's next, but for the next couple of hours, I will live in this happy little bubble. Because there's hope in it.

"It's not as bad as when she almost got arrested for breaking into the high school pool," Rhett says, and Jack's head shoots up, shocked.

"*What?*"

"I get a call one night from the same Taylor Hamilton. He was leaving a late football practice and saw the cops putting her in cuffs. So I went to save her ass, but when I got there, she and Rodney's dad, Sheriff Ruhlig, were shooting the breeze. Talking about Rodney's shit grades."

Gwen is smiling like it's still just as funny now as it was then. She then begins telling her side of the story, and she is a flame of energy that everyone gravitates toward. Everyone leans in an inch to hear whatever she is going to say next. All but Rhett, who is sitting back, smiling at his sister and at his family. With his hand clasped to my leg, I feel like I might float away if he were to let go. And I'm not ready for that. Not yet.

Once we finish eating, Jackie and I end up doing the dishes, Rhett goes to help Gwen set up a card game, and Mayben and Jack are packing up leftovers. The whole family chips in.

"Rhett is an egg," Jackie says as he hands me another plate to dry.

"Huh?" I ask, peeling my eyes away from watching Rhett and his sister laugh together, his eyes finding mine every few moments.

"Rhett. He's an egg. He's got this hard, smooth surface, but he's soft inside. He's like our mom."

I slide the plate into the cabinet Jackie directed me towards.

"I know you turned him away, but if you—"

"Turned *him* away?" I ask turning my attention back to him. "What are you talking about?"

"When he came to the city to see you last year. Didn't you turn him away?"

I set the rag down to see if he's teasing me. Or joking. Or what. But he's not.

"He came to say goodbye," I tell him. "He showed up and told me he loved me, but it was over. Then he left."

Jackie clenches his jaw then looks beyond me. "That motherfucker."

"Did you guys think *I* was the one who turned him down?"

He nodded. "Yeah. Dad sent him after you. But we were a bit distracted when it happened, so we didn't question it when he came back crying and not talking. We assumed you turned him down."

Once we finish cleaning up the kitchen, Gwen calls us into the living room for the card game. Hanging on every inch of available wall in the living room are framed photos. Brace-faced Jackie and pigtailed Gwen on what looks like a first day of school. Serious Rhett on his mom's lap on a beach. *Lac Dunes* is scribbled in the bottom corner. Another of whom I can only imagine to be Gwen standing with her legs poking into the sand, her head of curls tilted to the side as she squints up happily at whoever is taking the picture, and a gangly, dark-haired boy I don't recognize smiling next to her. There's one of the whole family in front of the White House with big, crooked smiles.

The walls are a mosaic of who they are. This complicated man was once a serious little boy, who cracked tiny smirks in photos in front of the Canadian skyline in Detroit or mini golfing with his siblings, holding their clubs over their heads in juvenile triumph. I spot another of Rhett from a few years ago maybe; he and his mom are on the porch of this house, drinking white wine.

"He used to drink white wine with her," Jack says, nodding toward the picture. "The rest of us liked red, but he would drink white with her. He stopped drinking it when she took a turn for the worse. He hates red wine, no matter how stubborn he is to admit it. He likes to punish himself, I think. In a lot of ways."

I glance over at Rhett and see him deep in a discussion on the phone.

"Are you gonna stay for a little longer?" Jack asks. "We're getting ready to start the game."

"Sure." I tell him and go to Rhett.

He sits with his arm along the back of a large chair and nods for me to sit in the empty spot next to him. As I sit, I swap my glass of white for his red. He hesitates for a moment, but he takes a sip, and his free hand finds mine. Gwen pauses a moment when she sees the glass in his hands. She just smiles and looks at me with that mischievous look only an Atwood can give, then turns to the cards in her hands. Everyone I gathered around the coffee table, some of us on the couch, others on the floor.

Jackie wins the first two rounds, Mayben wins the third, Storm gets a hold of a couple cards and chews them up and Gwen wins the last. And soon, we all have had a splash too much to drink. All but Rhett, who is still slowly sipping the glass I had given him earlier. We bail on cards when Jack gets out a cake he made from the fridge. He carries it to the counter with a nervous pride in his rosy cheeks.

Happy Birthday, Jackie and Gwennie is written in his messy handwriting on the lumpy and poorly frosted surface—the furthest thing from a beautiful cake. But Gwen smiles from ear to ear as she sits at the counter.

"Don't forget to take a picture with it!" Mayben says, and the Atwood family freezes. The air has been sucked out of the room. "Here, I'll take it. You guys get in."

After a brief pause, they all shuffle up to the counter, arms thrown around each other, and smile in front of the messy cake.

"Okay, now just the twins," Mayben instructs.

"Their mom always took pictures of them in front of their cakes. Without fail. It's a tradition. In a photo album somewhere, there is every picture with their cakes right at this counter." Tanner says.

You'll be an Atwood soon enough, he had said. Now that takes on a whole new meaning. But it isn't entirely true. Because she already is one. With or without a ring.

After cake, they pass around gifts. Tickets to a Detroit Tigers game for Jackie. A pair of bright-emerald-green earrings for Gwen that perfectly reflect her eyes. There's not a drop of loneliness in this room.

Once the excitement dies down, we settle in, watching the Lion's win another football game so I decide to make my exit. My brain is still spinning, and I just need to go somewhere quiet. Begin to comprehend everything I've learned tonight.

"I'm heading out," I whisper to Rhett while the movie *Twister* plays in the background.

"I'll walk you home," he says.

"It's okay." I squeeze his hand. "We can talk tomorrow. Stay with your family."

He looks back to his family and waves. "I'm walking Lauren back. Don't wait up for me."

His brother and sister elbow each other with laughing smiles, and Rhett helps me slip my coat back on. The whole room echoes a "Goodnight" as we slip out the door.

As our feet crunch through the silent snowfall up to the front door of my cabin, the weight of that book, that dedication, that date, all begins to pile up. The unanswered questions, and even the answered ones, twist in my head.

"I'll start the fire," Rhett says once we're inside. I pour us two glasses of my favorite white wine and find a spot on the couch; watching him shuffle the wood around in the fire. When it's to his liking, he rejoins me on the couch.

"Where do I begin?" he asks.

"The beginning," I say. "Tell me everything."

38

RHETT

I was a quiet kid. I had a habit of turning into myself, shutting down when things got hard. Talking about painful things was so debilitating that I avoided any and all mention of anything uncomfortable. And I had thought this was something I had outgrown, but whenever I went home for the weekends to visit my mom and dad, I could feel myself slipping back into that frozen fear. When I went home, I never knew what I was walking into.

Mom had been diagnosed with Alzheimer's a few years before. It started with her seeming more forgetful. She was forgetting her medication or when she last ate. Mismatching her clothes. Forgetting doctors' appointments.

But then it became bigger lapses in her memory. Forgetting the way to the same grocery store we have always gone to, or getting lost on a walk around the neighborhood she has lived in for nearly thirty years. When I came back to town, she would always greet me with her big smile, a pat on the back, but then ask me the same questions she asked me on the visit before. It was paralyzing to watch.

Dad called me in August after I'd been away a while,

saying Mom wasn't doing well. I walked in the front door, and the woman standing there looked nothing like my mom. She was the shadow of who my mom once was. It had been a month or maybe two since I had been back, but in that moment, this frail, blank-eyed woman standing before me, looking at me with my own green eyes . . . it felt like years had passed.

"Hi, Mom," I said quietly, afraid if I spoke too loudly, it would set something off.

She cocked her head to the side slightly, flinching at my words. Her movements were quick and jerky. Her hands were unsteady, and her eyes flickered about.

"Sir?" she called over her shoulder. "There's a man here. I think he's trying to sell something."

I nearly doubled over at that sentence. Those words, each a stab into my abdomen. Into my heart. My dad—whom, I realized, she called "sir"—came around the corner.

"Jo, honey, this is Rhett. Do you remember Rhett?"

She stared at me for a beat too long. Her eyes frantically searched my face for some bit of familiarity. But it didn't come. She shook her head.

"He's your son. *Our* son."

My mom whipped her head back to my dad.

"No!" she yelled. The sudden outburst threw the house of kilter with the force of her frail voice. "No! You're my nurse— that's what you said!"

"Let's get you some tea. You love tea."

"I know that." She spat the words out, and my dad walked her into the living room, setting her up in the recliner. He placed a kid's cup with a straw in front of her, and I knew I shouldn't stare, but my heart was racing like it's finding a way out, to fall at my mother's feet. For her to see me.

"What do you want?" she snapped again, and I recoiled.

"Nothing. Can I help *you* with anything? Can I get you something?"

"My blanket," she directed, and pointed toward an ugly orange crumpled blanket on the floor. I picked it up and placed it over her lap, then returned to my spot on the couch. I watched her as she sipped her tea and dozed off. I don't even know how much time passed as I stared at the woman in the chair, the woman with none of my mother's warmth or wit. None of her charm or deep-rooted kindness.

A while later, she blinked her eyes open.

"Rhett, sweetie—" she croaked. "When did you get into town? Come give me a kiss."

I couldn't get my feet under me fast enough. "Hey, Ma, I just walked in while you were sleeping."

She smiled a half smile. I kissed the side of her head and held her hand.

"Can you ask your dad to make us some spaghetti?"

"Of course," I promised her and squeezed her hand, holding onto every ounce of her I could before she drifted back away.

"And Rhett?" her voice croaked out.

"Yeah, Ma?"

"Will you be the one to write my obituary? I wouldn't trust, or want, anyone else to do it."

"Mom, no. You don't need me to do that. You'll turn the corner. You'll get better." I pleaded with her. Or maybe I was pleading to God. Neither ended up listening.

Mom gave me a knowing look. "Rhett. Please. Promise me you will." Tears began to stream from her watery eyes, and my insides twisted.

"Mom. I can't—"

"Honey." She squeezed my hand. "*Please.*"

My heart ripped as I nodded. Agreeing to the one thing I wish I had never been asked to do.

After she fell back asleep, Dad and I sat at the counter, talking about the last few months. How bad it had gotten, so suddenly. The anger, the violence, the screaming. He wasn't sure if he could do it on his own. And when I offered to move home, he said no. That Mom wouldn't want that. Jackie had just moved in with Mayben. Gwen was living near her job at Morton's Bar. She would want us to keep living our lives.

Just as I was about to crawl into bed that night, Runclave called me. I had fully retired from editing at that point. Once my mom stopped writing, I only worked on a few other projects but found it was too painful to edit other people's work if it wasn't my mom's. I was writing myself, too, so I called it quits on the editing.

I was able to make a decent name for myself already with my writing without my mom's name to get me there. But it still stung as I was moving on and my mom was frozen in time. But when I answered Runclave's call, I hoped for news on my deal for my second book. Instead, he told me about this debut author and how he wanted me to take a look at her work.

"Charles, please. Not to be that guy, but I really don't give a shit. I am done editing. I'm working on my own—"

"Just read it, as a favor. For giving you that book deal and working on this next one, please."

"Go fuck yourself, Runclave. I said no." I hung up.

He called again and I let it go to voicemail.

Mom spent the rest of the weekend sleeping off and on in her chair. That brief peek behind the curtains of her clouded memory had been only that—brief. I cried the whole way back to the city.

I hadn't even gotten my shoes off yet when Myranda Grant, of all people, began pounding on my door. I had seen her around Runclave's offices over the last couple of years. And I had heard the whispers and talk about them. Age difference and all. His wedding ring seemed to play no role in the rumors either.

"It's really fucking good, Rhett. She writes just like your mom did," she yelled through the door.

Did.

It was a punch to the gut. There I was, coming back to the city like a coward while my mom was deteriorating in Michigan, slowly. And now they were dangling this in front of me like it would make me feel better. And it only hurt. Made my mom feel replaceable. Reminded me that because of this illness, her career was over.

I opened the door to tell her off, tell her I was not reading a goddamn manuscript of some wannabe. But Myranda stood there, a pile of papers in her hands. "Rhett, you are the only one who can make this manuscript what it's capable of being. Only you. It's good, but you can make it *really* fucking good."

Goddammit. I took the papers from her.

"I have a meeting with her in a couple weeks. If you accept, I want you to start right away, and then I want you to be there to meet her," she said.

I closed the door on her, tossed the pages onto the couch, poured myself a glass of red wine to choke down, and prepared to read the first twenty pages and then promptly throw it away.

That night, I devoured the entire thing in a single sitting. By the end I was crying. I cried because of the characters. Because of this girl's writing. Because of my mom. I cried because Myranda was right. She *did* write like my mom. And it nearly killed me.

Before even laying eyes on her, I was fascinated by her. And I was nervous as hell before meeting her. So at that first meeting, to distract myself, I brought the morning's newspaper to study some obituaries. I had no idea where to start. So, I took my red pen to them to figure out how to write something worthy of my mom.

Then I saw her before she saw me.

Lauren Dorada.

She was this almost-red-headed wave with deep-brown eyes. She scanned around the room for a moment, chewing on her cheek, her forehead wrinkled in deep thought, and I lost my breath. She was beautiful. Ridiculously fucking beautiful.

Though she was hidden behind her jeans and sweater, I could see the pull of her curves and rounded hips. She looked soft, safe. Any real thought flew out of my mind when she spotted me. I forced myself to swallow, but I couldn't look away. Her face carried a million emotions, shifting so quickly I didn't have a chance to read a single thought. And suddenly I found myself wanting to. I wanted to overanalyze every shift of her eyebrows and lips. I just wanted to look at her. Study her. Write her.

Reading a manuscript always felt like reading a diary, whether it was my mom's or someone else's. The raw, broken pieces of a person scattered among the pages like ashes to the sea. Pieces of them within the names and descriptions.

I felt like I knew her, and we hadn't even met.

But there was no way I was ever going to ever cross that line. In an instant, I told my heart to stop pounding in my chest and get straight to it. That's what she wanted. At least that's what Runclave said in the voicemail he left after I hung up on him. The one where he went on to describe the project and her like I hadn't just told him to fuck off.

"She doesn't say much. She's kind of stoic. She's either quiet or straight to the point. Never both. Like you. I think her gears are spinning, and she isn't messing around. So don't try to bull-shit her."

She doesn't want me to bullshit her or give her flowery nonsense. She wanted to make this manuscript a book. And still tired after reading it again in its entirety the night before, I promised myself I wouldn't let this damn beating heart get in the way of what she really wanted. And from what I read, I knew she deserved more than a passing infatuation to distract her.

I knew, just in that single meeting, that Lauren Dorada was going to be the reason my life would never look like it once it did. She was going to change everything for me.

Then a few days later, I was at the bookstore below my apartment—the one my neighbor Cal and his wife, Elyse, own—and I heard her. Lauren. Her voice cut through the air like a damn storm siren. I peered around the corner and saw her browsing books. Her cheek was tucked between her teeth as her eyes darted around the shelf. A book clung to her chest as she searched. But not just any book. *My* book. She was here for Elyse's little wine club that daylights as a book club. And she had *my* book in her arms. Against her chest.

But then I was brought back by her calling her editor "arrogant" to the other women. She was talking about me, and I didn't even care that she was insulting me. I was overwhelmed at the idea of her just holding my book in her hand and me being on her mind. I knew then, fully, that I was a goner.

I was about to slip out without her seeing me, because I knew she would be embarrassed if she knew I heard her. But then she turned the corner and ran square into me. My hand flew to her arm to steady her. Or that's the excuse I gave myself. I laughed as the realization hit her that I overheard her call me arrogant. She was flushed, and it was the hottest thing I'd ever seen and heard. Because it was true and she knew it.

I didn't have an ounce of control over myself when suggesting we work together in person after that. I hadn't stopped thinking about her since we met, and all I knew was that I needed to keep being around her. Whatever that meant.

Soon we were spending our time at coffee shops together. I would catch her eyes lingering on me, and she would catch me staring too. She always ran her hand through her hair, flipping it around while deep in thought. She chewed her nails down to stubs when the edits got a little more complicated.

She was always sizing me up, watching and looking at me for answers deeper than the ones I was giving. And I was constantly on the edge of just telling her that the book she loved, the one she always had with her, was *my* book. But somehow, that felt like exposing the secret of Santa, and I couldn't bring myself to do it just yet.

I owed Cal for putting my book up on the front table at his shop and recommending it to everyone who came in the doors, so I promised to get him and some buddies into the Kensington Club. But my best friend was in town for the week, so I decided to just call ahead so they could all go in without me. Tanner was more of a dusty-country-bar kind of guy anyway. I only kept the damn membership because my mom loved this place, and it was where she celebrated when she got the news that she was cancer free. I wanted to keep the membership active for when she got better.

But then, Cal called and needed me to add a few names to the list. The book-club girls. And Lauren's name was on the list. So I changed my plans and dragged Tanner along.

"Who is that?" Tanner asked later when Lauren stepped onto the rooftop, his jaw nearly on the ground.

"Don't you dare," I warned him.

He whipped his head to me, eyes wide with a shit-eating grin.

"That's the girl? The author? Isn't it?" Tanner asked.

"She's hot."

The words came out of one of Cal's friend's mouths, so I gave the asshat a single look, and he immediately cowered away.

The word *hot* felt out of place on her. She existed among words so much grander. None of which, however, would ever do her justice. She stood there, taking in the scene, chewing on her lip. A tight black dress and hair in waves that I wanted to tangle my fingers in. Lauren Dorada was the brightest fucking star on this rooftop. And she didn't even know it.

I hardly even noticed when a dark-haired woman stepped from behind Lauren. The only reason I did was because Tanner choked on his beer at the sight of her.

By the end of the night, Lauren's body was pressed against mine in a smoky karaoke bar, and I had to talk myself out of kissing her right then. She looked up at me with those doe eyes. There were worlds behind them, and I wanted nothing more than to visit each one.

And just when I was ready to throw caution to the wind and taste her lips like I had wanted to since I saw her in the coffee shop, her sister swooped in and dragged her away.

"Oh my God," Tanner shook his head. "We're going to marry sisters. Aren't we?"

Damn it, we sure as hell were if I had anything to do with it.

While I was getting swept up in this girl and her story, Mom was getting sicker. My weekends were spent helping spoon-feed her in between her screaming fits. She no longer knew who we were or why we were at her house. But Dave and Christie next door were selling their summer cabin, and we jumped on it. Mom would stay at our house with a full-time nurse, and then Dad and I would stay at the cabin and fix it up a little bit, with the intention of renting it out to make a little extra cash.

But as things were spiraling at home, the city would call me back, and I would be staring at Lauren over a candlelit dinner, pretending we were engaged and pretending that our kiss didn't just completely change me. I was sick to my stomach over my feelings for her and wanting nothing more than to let her in.

But her focus, her drive—she never took a day off. When we texted after a long day of working, it would be nearly midnight, and she was still working. And I knew in my gut that the last thing she needed was my family to weigh her down. Slow her down.

Then Dad had to transfer mom to a memory care facility over in Marnmouth and I felt like everything was slipping through my fingers. So, I bottled it up and bottled her up and did a bad job at talking myself out of being in love with her. Especially when she'd sunk into my side with tears while I read her the same book I read my younger sister on nights Mom and Dad were at a doctor's appointment and I had to put her to bed. Gwen loved the idea of being in control, reigning over the monsters in her life, while Lauren loved the idea of an escape into a fictional world.

Then after months of work, and endless bottles of wine and pots of coffee, Lauren finished the book. We were in her apartment, and she looked at me with those eyes. It made me want to devour her and wrap her in my arms and keep her safe all at the same time. I wanted to let her in. To open my chest and offer her my heart. Which would have been only a formality, because it already belonged to her.

Our arms clung to each other as I pressed my lips against her head. I wanted to know her body the way I intimately knew her mind. No. Wanted isn't the right word. I *needed* to. And standing in the lamp light of her kitchen on a cold Chicago night, I had this feeling that it would work out for us. I could see it. I could see her coming to my hometown. Meeting my mom and dad. Sitting at our family dining table. I saw forever.

We stripped our clothes layer by layer until she was pulling me inside her. We were tangled together desperately, and it felt like I finally did one thing right in my life. Our tongues and lips and legs and hands all intrinsically found their places with the other's. She moaned my name below me that night, and I could have died happy. She begged and I provided until we melted together into the sheets beneath us.

I was ready to ask her to marry me right then. I had the ring in my pocket. My mom had thrown it off the previous weekend and hit me in the chest with it, telling me she liked her other nurse better. Dad, with tears in his eyes, told me to keep it. It belonged to whatever woman I would love. He said Mom had told him that in one of her few lucid moments. But that fear crept back in. The fear that Lauren deserved more than what I had for her right now.

In the morning, I made us coffee and brought it to her in bed. Her back was lit by soft streaks of sunshine. Those little red bumps on her arms and the muss of her red hair over the pillow begged me to crawl back to her. And in an instant, I realized I wanted to spend every morning like this. For the rest of my life.

She sat up and pulled the blanket up to cover herself like I hadn't had my mouth on every inch of her skin just hours ago. And like I wasn't about to do it again the moment we got some caffeine into our systems. I was ready to tell her everything when my buzzing phone cut through our loved-up haze.

I was ready to throw it out the window when I finally caved and looked at it. But then I saw the ten missed calls from Jackie and Gwen and my dad. Every hope plummeted to the bottom floor with that single message.

It's time. We had to bring mom home. Decisions need to be made, read a text from my dad.

I swiped my tears away as I packed my things, apologizing quietly as I kissed her one last time. Knowing I just needed to go because a proper goodbye would prompt her to follow me to what was waiting for me on the other side of this drive home. I promised to call her because it was the only ounce of hope I could offer. But in reality, sparing her from all this was the best I could offer.

When I got home, Dad, Gwen, Jackie, and Mayben were drinking coffee at the kitchen table. They looked older. The gray in Dad's hair had doubled. Jackie was gaunt and Gwen, puffy-eyed. I had never seen Mayben look sad a day in her life, and now she sat next to Jackie, as broken as we were. They told me Mom was upstairs resting; she'd had a really bad fit that morning at the nursing home, and it ended in a seizure. Dad said the doctors at the hospital talked about some proteins that build up in the brains of patients with Alzheimer's and can cause seizures and this seizure did a number on her.

"Then she should be back at the hospital!" I yelled. "Why is she here? She should be getting treatment!"

I'll never forget the tearstained looks on each of their faces. They were so tired. And Dad's shake of his head was answer enough.

"We tried," Mayben said when nobody else could. "They said to just make her comfortable."

The days ticked by while we hovered in this desolate limbo before the end finally came. Mom grew more lethargic, unable to get up from her bed, staring at walls for hours on end. She hadn't been herself for a long time. But now she wasn't anybody anymore. A weathered shell of a person.

We mourned her before we lost her. My brother, sister and I on either side of her, telling our memories about running around the Chicago Zoo as children, standing in the bird house. Gwen loved it best because Jackie was afraid of birds. We laughed together through our tears as we told Mom's closed eyes how he still was. Jackie reminded her of my fear of elevator that was born on one of our trips to Chicago as kids. When we got stuck in one at her publisher's office for all of twelve minutes.

At night, when I finally checked my phone, I saw I missed a couple of texts and a missed call from Lauren. But I couldn't call. Because if I did, I couldn't lie to her about what was going on here. I would have to say it out loud, and I couldn't do that. I couldn't speak about watching my mom's body forget how to work. Watching her eyes forget to blink and her body shut down was something I couldn't put into words, no matter how many times I tried. I wrote message after message for Lauren, trying to explain. Every time she texted or called, I found myself drowning in the explanation of where I went. I even resorted to filtering our communication through Myranda. And I knew it would break her heart. But it would keep her heart safer in the end. Because I knew my mom wasn't going to survive this. And I wasn't sure if I was going to either.

Those days, I kept finding myself on my parents' bedroom floor next to their bed as Mom slept. The same place I brought my blanket and pillow to when I was young. When the storms were big, and I felt small. It's funny how the storms had only gotten bigger, and I only felt smaller.

And I wept. Like a child, I wept for my mom. For the singular life we had and the immeasurable moments that still run on a loop in my mind. Like riding bikes down the gravel roads, with her cheering me on as she ran on behind. Her homemade spaghetti that I have tried to recreate for years but have never gotten quite right. Or those days she was elbow-deep in novel edits, and she still found time for a movie night. Jackie would sit on the floor in front of the TV, Gwen on Dad's lap, and I always knew my spot was under Mom's arm, watching her write rather than watching the movie. That ugly orange blanket always stretched across our laps and a mason jar of tulips nearby.

"Rhett," Mom's voice croaked out one evening. "Tell me about her."

"What?" I rushed to her side and grabbed her hand.

"The girl," she said. "The one you keep going back to the city for."

I laughed despite myself. "Her name is Lauren, and she's—" What was she? What words would do her justice? So, I tell her.

"You love her." Mom says when I finish.

I nodded. The tears clouding my eyes.

"Give it to her." Though the words were weak, I knew what she meant. The gift I gave her years ago. "It belongs to the girl my son adores."

"Mom—"

"Thank you." Her voice was hoarse, and there was a glint of knowing in her eye. I leaned in to hear her voice, and she kissed me on the side of the head like she always had growing up. Her love was shaped in kisses on my head and time spent together.

I called out for my dad, and in an instant, he was there. Mom lifted her hand and touched it to his cheek. He held his hand against hers for a moment before pulling away to kiss it, his eyes lingering on the lines of her palm. Their love line still had time to go.

Gwen and Jackie came rushing, too, and for a moment, just a moment, my mom was back. She remembered us. She remembered how to smile; she remembered how to blink and to sniffle. She even knew to wipe the tears that fell from my eyes as I clung to her hand like a goddamn child. For a moment, we had her before we fully lost her.

She died that evening, holding our hands. And together, our new family of four cried all the tears we had been holding onto for the past five years while she declined and grew worse and worse. We sat around in numb silence while the coroner came and left. While Dad made the phone calls to cousins and aunts and uncles.

I had spent months reading obituary after obituary so I could get it right for her and do my mother an ounce of justice in words. But there, at her bedside, I knew it wasn't going to happen. No words in this world were going to amount to a fraction of what my mother is.

Was. What my mother was.

"December thirty-first," my dad whispered. "Today was the day I asked her to marry me."

"December thirty-first," I whispered, begging my mind to remember why this day rang important in my mind. Then it hit me like a freight train. "Lauren."

"What?" my dad asked. "Lauren? The girl you've been working with?"

"It's her birthday. Today's Lauren's birthday."

"Go," my dad said with a look of determination on his grief-ladened face. "Go get her. It's what your mom wanted. She hoped you would have been brave enough to go after her."

"I'll drive you," Gwen offered, and a few hours later, my little sister, the one I bailed out so many times, was dropping me off in front of Herman, Lauren's doorman, who looked at me with only a fraction of the disapproval I deserved.

"Can you ring up to her?" I begged and dug through my pockets, but I had already emptied them to him over the past few months. "Please. I don't have any cash—"

"Go," he said, opening the door. "You deserve to see the heartbreak you caused."

I ground my teeth and went running up the stairs. I stood there for five minutes before finally knocking. Talking myself in and out of what I was about to do.

The door swung open. Lauren stood there, hair pulled up away from her face, earrings dangling just above her heaving shoulders, eyes narrowed and red. She looked beautiful. Sad. There was that echo of sadness that had grown up with her, but this was different. This was angrier.

"I hate your wine." She spat the words out at me. "I fucking *hate* it."

"I love you," I said, and she recoiled like I was afraid she would. Words we both knew were true, but it was too late now.

"How dare you," she whispered, that righteous anger dripping off each word.

"I love you. I can't stay, but I love you. I will *always* love you." I choked out the words. None of which I had rehearsed on the drive down. I had spent hours silently planning the perfect goodbye, and this wasn't how I expected it to go. "I'm leaving, but I love you, and I need you to know that."

"I hate you." She took in a ragged breath and said the words with her whole body, yet they came out weak, untrue. "I hate you. How dare you show up here and say that."

I looked over her shoulder. She had cleaned up; the photo gallery was filled with actual pictures. Pictures of her book club. Pictures of us. There were bottles of wine on the counter, red and white. A stack of books on the coffee table. Copies of her book.

But my eyes fell back to her. She was wearing a black dress that hugged every inch of her body like it was spun and sewn together for her and her only. The rounds of her hips and belly . . . and, God, I fucking hated myself more in that moment than I ever have.

"That's okay. That's good," I insisted, though the words were traitorous on my tongue. "You should hate me. I deserve nothing from you but your hate."

"You don't get to say that." Her voice was a low grumble. "Knowing damn well I don't hate you. I'm not the one choosing this." She chokes on her tears and pushes my chest. "You don't get to show up here, telling me you love me and promising to leave. It's not fair. It's not fair that you won't let me love you back."

"God, Lauren—" I grabbed her hands as they pressed into my chest. Desperate to hold her. Desperate to give her better than this.

"Look at my life, Rhett. Look around. My apartment is empty. This was a party. A fucking party, and you weren't here. And that's what killed me. You didn't come. I even got ready for tonight. I put on a new dress and felt pretty. How stupid is that?"

The words came out ragged. Cold.

"Lauren, you're so beautiful. I can't . . . I want to stay, but I'm a mess. I can't be what you need or deserve. I'll only hurt you in the end—"

"Be fucking honest with me!" she yelled. She yanked her hands from mine, and I missed them instantly. But she reconnected them again with another shove. One I was sure she thought was hard. Wanting me to fight back. I could see that rage in her eyes, the one she stifled. The rage she had translated into passion that she kept buried within every inch of her.

She pushed me hard enough that she lost her own balance and almost fell backward. I caught her, but she pulled away from me with such force that it made me freeze. Tears were streaming down both our faces at that point. "For once, be *honest* with me. Stop this dance like we can't say what we're thinking. Don't pretend we haven't been falling in love all this time."

The fucking countdown into the New Year blared in the background. I wiped the tears from my eyes to see her better.

I spilled into a speech that I prayed would help her understand that it wasn't her fault. That I was just too broken. I grabbed her face in my hands, and I told her that I was leaving because I loved her.

"I love you," I whispered and kissed the side of her head. "Happy Birthday."

Then, before I could change my mind, I turned back toward the stairs. She sobbed behind me, and it took every fiber of my being to keep myself walking. I told myself that if I didn't walk away now, I would only crush us both down the road if I didn't make it out of this heartbreak.

"I love you too," I heard her say as the stair door closed behind me. I almost turned around and went back to her. But a wineglass crashes against the door. The sound echoed through the stairwell, and I wish I had stayed long enough to be its target. I deserved it. I still do. I always will.

I thought that I was sparing her down the road. Sparing her possible years of me questioning my role in this world if my mom wasn't in it. I wanted her to know that it wasn't her fault that I left. That it was entirely mine. And that I loved her.

Yet here I was, running away like her dad. So maybe she would learn to hate me like she hated him. And as long as she didn't blame herself, then it was okay. I'd take her hate if she didn't blame herself.

But I did keep her copy of *Honeycomb*. I would look at it when I couldn't sleep which was most nights. I studied the notes she made. The doodles and scribbles lacing each page. Even the dried tears on the pages. It was all I had left of her.

Myranda had found my address back in Michigan and sent me the proof of Lauren's book. I was left sitting on my bedroom floor, my back against the door, reading and rereading her tearstained handwriting, telling me to never let her love me again. Her scathing words had hurt me worse than I ever imagined, but they were still not even a fraction of what I deserved. I read them over and over as a self-inflicted prison sentence.

Months later, Myranda texted me that they were going with a new editor for Lauren's next book. I had expected this, but when I looked the guy up, I learned he was some intern with a horrible portfolio and minimal experience at all with fiction work. So a couple of hours after that text, I was standing in Runclave's office, all but begging on my knees to be put on her project.

"I'll take on a fake name, a fake email. You can't let that shitty editor touch her work. You know it deserves better," I told him. "I'll do it for free. I don't need the money."

"Fine. That's fine," Charles said with a sigh. "Whatever sells more books."

That night, I went to Ninety-Seven's and thought about kissing Lauren the first time a few tables over. So, when she walked in with her book club, it felt as if I had summoned her with my broken heart. She looked so fucking beautiful. The rain had dampened her hair, but her eyes were still that bright golden brown under the chandelier's glow. And right then, I knew, for a goddamn fact that my life would never amount to an ounce of anything worth measuring if this girl wasn't in it.

I also knew I should have left. Of course I *should* have, but I couldn't bring myself to just yet, because after the day's meeting with Runclave, I had very little reason to come back to the city again. And I wanted to cling to that moment, even in secret, for a little longer. I wanted nothing more than to be in the same room as Lauren Dorada one more time.

But then she sat next to me, and I could tell she had no idea I was there. Knowing my feet should have had me halfway out the door already, I offered her one last bit of kindness. I ordered her a glass of wine, dropped the cash, and began to leave. But her voice—God, it cut through the air, and it was directed at me. Like a storm siren, even all these months later. And if I was one thing, I was irrevocably and unconditionally in love with Lauren Dorada, and my attention fully belonged to her.

I reminded her of what she asked of me. Of what she wrote

in the cover of the proof she got to me. She asked me to not let her love me. And I tried to do the right thing. I tried to walk away, but she was looking at me with those big brown eyes. The ones that felt like home, even after all this time.

"Laure." I croaked out, my own voice not trusting me to be strong enough to walk away.

"Please," she pleaded softly. "Wait. Stay."

So.

I stayed.

39

───────

NOW

I t's long past midnight when Rhett finishes telling me everything. It's like his heart is sitting between us on the couch. The tears have dried, but my head hurts, and my eyes are puffy. So many thoughts are spinning through my head. It's like a top that can't find its balance. All this time, he was going through more than I could even imagine. And I cursed him from a city he no longer lived in. My anger feels less fitting as he explains the dark place he was in while losing his mom.

I reach down and fold his hand in mine. It had been absently trailing the seam on my pants as he unloaded years of pain.

"I wish you felt like you could have told me then. I wish I could have done more to help." I say into the silence, and he looks at me with a new shade of pain in his eyes.

"Laure, I knew if I told you, you would have. But I couldn't risk distracting you with everything. That's why I turned in on myself. This was all on me. I wish I could go back and tell you. I'm in therapy now. She helps me talk about things, asking people what they're thinking, not just assuming and bottling it up. Before, I was so convinced that if I talked about it, talked about my mom, I would spiral and wouldn't be able to get out of the spiral. So I just turned inward and wouldn't let anyone in. It was Mayben who encouraged me to go to therapy. That's what we were talking about that day at the diner when you walked up. She asked how it was going; she was telling me she was really proud of me, because she got Jackie to go, too, and it made a huge difference for him." The words tumble out of him.

"Why now? Why tell me all of this now?"

"I was in such a dark place when she died. Admitting it to you meant that it was real. I didn't talk about it for *months*. Then you showed up here, and I saw you in my family's cabin. And for the first time, I thought maybe I had been given a second chance. But then you were so upset when you saw me here; I could see it all over your face. And I didn't want to drag it all back up if you didn't want to hear it, and it's still so hard to talk about. But, Lauren, if I could go back and do it differently, I would. I wouldn't have walked away. I wouldn't have let you tell me to stay away. I would have, and I should have, stayed and told you what was going on. I truly thought, that night I showed up to your apartment, that I was doing you a favor. I didn't know how I was going to survive the next few months or years of my life without my mom."

I place my hand to his cheek and use my thumb to wipe away a tear. "And there is nothing going on between you and Mayben?"

The corner of his mouth quirks up, and a small chuckle comes from him.

"We dated for a few years in high school. But she was Jackie's best friend first and had been since they were in kindergarten. I assumed that if he wanted to date her, he would have. It wasn't until I was graduating that that I saw the way Jackie looked at her and I realized I never looked at her like that. He loved her— he was just chickenshit. So I stole his phone and texted her from it, asking her out. The rest is history. She's more my sister than Gwen is most days— I swear to you."

It clicks suddenly that I was never going to not let him back into my heart. Because I never fully let him out. And over the past year, instead of writing him out of my heart, like I thought I had been doing, I only wrote him deeper into it.

"I didn't know you were jealous of Mayben until you said that in the driveway about watching me love someone else. I thought you were just mad at me still. I swear, there is no one else. There never will be," he says. "Lauren, It's only you."

My restraint snaps, and I pull his face to mine and press my lips against his.

And like no time has passed, his hands find their places on my body, his tongue finds mine, and we pick up where we left off. We let our bodies catch up, our lips make up for lost time, and our fingertips explain how much we missed each other. And just before we jump off the deep end, I pull away but leave our foreheads resting together.

"It's late," I whisper, "if you want to go home ..."

Rhett shakes his head. "I told them not to wait up."

"But they're all going to know."

He pulls away farther now, looking at me with those dark, curious eyes. "Know what, Laure?"

My mouth opens to speak, but the words dry up, heat puddled in my stomach.

He lowers his eyes. Challenging me. "Tell me, Lauren. What will they know?"

"That you're going to take me to bed. They're going to talk."

"Let 'em," he says, standing. "Besides, I just got you back."

He takes the blanket off the couch and throws it to the floor. We shuffle the trunk out of the way and grab every pillow and blanket we can find—from my bed, the spare bed, the closet, inside the trunk—until the floor in front of the fireplace is covered. Rhett motions toward the blankets and says, "Sit."

I look up at him with surprise at the command in his voice. But I don't question him. I do as he says while he goes over to the door, where his coat hangs on the hook. He reaches into the pocket and pulls out a long, thin box wrapped with a green bow, then brings it over to me.

"What is this?" I take it from him.

"A late birthday gift."

"Rhett, my birthday isn't until the end of the month."

He nods toward the package. "I have a gift for you then, too, but I had this for you last year. Before my mom died."

"Rhett." My voice comes out like a warning. "You didn't need to—"

"I wanted to. And I should have."

I slip the bow off the velvet box. Clicking it open, I am momentarily stunned at what I am looking at. It's a long, thin gold necklace with a single deep-blue gem at the bottom. Even in its simplicity, it seems like a well-loved piece. My hands shake as I run a finger along the gold chain. It looks and feels like a golden thread.

"It belonged to my mom. I bought it for her when I was eighteen. I had saved up some of my checks from editing her books, and I bought her a necklace with the stone for the month her first novel was published, which was December. And then you came along." He chuckles with wet eyes as he stares at the necklace too. "And your first book was published in December. You were born in December. And I just don't think it should belong to anyone else other than you. My mom told me so."

My eyes flash up to his. "What do you mean, she told you so?"

"There were these moments that last month with her when she was lucid. More herself and she asked about you. So, I told her all about you and how brilliant you are. I told her that I came out of retirement because your work reminded me of hers and that you like white wine like she did. How you watch me when you think I'm not paying attention and that your birthday is New Year's Eve and how it suits you. I even told her how you put more cream in your coffee than dad does and that I learned to love Elvis because it's what was on your record player when we danced, and my mom loved Elvis too. She told me that this belonged to you. The girl my son adores."

Adores. Present tense. As if it's still happening.

All my words are stuck in my heart, and I just stare at the glisten in his eyes. Love. Present tense. Like it's still happening.

"Here." Rhett motions to take the necklace. "Let me."

I turn and hold my hair out of the way as he loops the necklace around my neck. Once he connects it together, he places his lips against the clasp.

I turn to face him, and he has a softness in his eyes that makes me wrap my arms around his neck and pull his lips into mine.

"You need to promise me one thing," I say between the kisses.

"Anything." He sighs into my mouth.

"Be honest with me. Even if it's not the easy thing, just be honest."

"Can we start now?" he asks and wraps his hand down below me, pulling me into his lap.

Electricity flashes through my body where his fingertips touch me. I nod as he pulls me down against his lap, and I can feel how badly he wants me.

"I haven't been able to write a single word since things ended between us. But since you showed back up again, I haven't been able to stop. Editing your work makes me a better writer. You make me better." His voice is gravels as his teeth find my earlobe.

I peel myself from him, and he watches me with a careful eye.

"I'm not changing my book. Just so you know," I tell him suddenly, making sure we are on the same page. "I'll make sure it's good, and I'll spend the next month working my ass off, but Runclave can kiss my ass if he thinks I am going to change it for him."

"I would have never let you change it anyway," he says but his eyes are traveling up and down my body. I let out a shaky breath and let him pull me back to him. I shush the fear and the creeping thoughts of what comes after this. Of where we will be left in a month when I have nowhere to go and he isn't leaving here. I silence it all because right now, there's hope, and I let him pull my body under his while we take our time with each other.

"We have the whole night ahead of us," he says, slipping my sweater off over my head.

Rhett's mouth remembers its way around my body like it no time has passed. He places every kiss and bite right in a place that makes my hips roll.

Soon we are both naked, and he has me back on his lap. This time, the feeling of his want below me isn't hidden beneath any fabric, and with his quick guidance, I feel every inch of him. The rushing sensation makes my head drop right onto his shoulder as the painful pleasure racks through my body.

"Oh my God." I whimper into his shoulder as his hands guide my hips back and forth on his lap.

"This," he groans into my chest, "is my favorite place to be."

And I know damn well that he doesn't mean this town or this cabin.

It's not until a few rounds later, and with the blankets and pillows in no sensible order, that we finally fall asleep. And I have hope, even if it's just for now.

40

NOW

I wake to the quiet crackle of the embers still glowing in the fireplace. Rhett is sound asleep next to me with his chest exposed as it rises and lowers with deep breaths. I lean over and kiss his shoulder, making him stir just slightly.

I search the room for clothes, unsure of where we tossed them last night and settle on his shirt with nothing underneath. Stepping carefully over the creaking floorboards, I grab the brown bag of coffee beans from Porter Morton that was left on my doorstep the other day. The receipt attached had Rhett's name on it.

Once it's ready, I pour two cups for us. Rhett props himself up on his elbow, watching me come back to him.

"That looks good on you." He nods toward his shirt and leans over to kiss me before taking the mug. "God, I've dreamed about this so many times."

"What?" I narrow my eyebrows at him. "Having a naked girl in your shirt deliver you coffee in the morning?"

He shakes his head with a deep grin. "No. Having *you* naked in my shirt and bringing me coffee in the morning." He wraps his hand around my ankle like he just needed an excuse to touch me.

"I never knew I needed you shirtless in front of a fire this badly," I tell him.

He kisses my leg. "I'm sorry we missed out on so much time."

"We will have to make up for it once this manuscript is turned in."

"I almost forgot." He groans.

"Forgot what? That we couldn't just walk around naked for the next month?"

He shoots me a look like that is still an option.

"Don't even think about it." I run my hand through his messy hair.

"Let's stay home today."

My heart flutters at his words. Home. Not *my* home. Or *his* home.

I dig my roots into this moment, never wanting to grow out of it. Mornings with him, here. Drinking coffee with him here.

Home.

"I need a shower." I untangle my legs from his arms and set my coffee on the side table.

As I climb the stairs, I know he can see up the shirt, but I don't try to hide. I look back over my shoulder to find him scrambling up from the ground. Peeling the shirt off, I toss it to the bottom of the steps, where it lands at his feet. He curses under his breath and in an instant is running up after me, skipping steps.

"I actually need to shower." I laugh as I dip into the bathroom.

"Stay here," he says, following me in.

"In the bathroom?"

"No. I mean in Michigan. This cabin. Stay. Don't go back to the city."

"Rhett—"

"Or if you don't want to stay at the cabin, there are apartments in town. Dollie rents out the apartment over the bookstore downtown—"

"Rhett, I—" I can't even finish my sentence because a greater question hangs there, and I wonder. Can I move myself into his already established life and still feel at home? What if he changes his mind once I'm here?

"Okay, say I do." I slip into the shower. "Say I stay. Then what?"

"What do you mean?"

"I move here. Are you going to get tired of being with me all the time? Then where would I go?"

"Whoa," he swipes the shower curtain open. My few tears may be hidden by the shower, but he knows better. "Laure, what are you talking about?"

"I'm afraid you'll get tired of me, and losing you twice would hurt too bad."

Rhett doesn't hesitate to step into the shower with me fully clothed. His hands come to my cheeks and force me to meet his eyes. "Lauren, I swear to you, if you chose this, I'm not walking away. I will go down fighting. Therapy, counseling, a priest, an exorcist . . . babe, whatever it takes. I'm all in."

"Okay." I breathe and try to let my heart believe him.

41

———

NOW

When I get out of the shower, Rhett is waiting in my bed, reading a curled-back copy of *Honeycomb*.

"Is that . . ." My voice trails off as I reach over and snatch the book from his hands. With a few page flips, I see my scribbles in the inside cover. "This is *my* copy!"

"I had it on the shelf downstairs." He smirks. "I knew I still had it. I brought it with me when we moved in here. I must have missed it when we moved back into the main house."

I look at my notes, and I see little scrawled words beneath them in Rhett's handwriting.

"Did you respond to my comments too?"

He leans over and takes the book back. "Well, yeah. I didn't plan on it. But . . . " He flips around and goes to a more R-rated scene that I'd underlined a substantial amount of.

"I liked your notes here," he says. And I snatch the book back. He had scribbled that he, too, would like to try out this scene.

"You're blushing." Rhett leans up on his elbow, eyes dragging up and down my body.

"I am not." I pull the book out of his reach and toss it away. "My shower was hot."

His cheeks round with a smile. "We could make it hotter—"

"Rhett." I dip from his grasp just as he tries to reach for my towel.

"Lauren." He groans and swiftly is on his feet and pinning me against the wall. His need presses into me, melting my joints.

"Oh God."

"Drop the towel, Lauren," he commands in a low voice. The rush of his breath on my neck makes my head drop back against the door. And I do as I'm told.

An hour later, Rhett is asking me to come help bring more wood inside. But with one step out on the front deck, I see the minivan I would recognize anywhere.

"What's going on?" I ask, stepping down to the driveway.

Laughing comes from inside Rhett's house, and I don't even knock. I step inside and see Rhett's sister and my sister arm-wrestling at the coffee table in the living room, and I blink, thinking it must be a backward dream or hallucination.

"Hold on, Lauren." Hannah grunts. "I totally have this."

Gwen is struggling when Hannah swiftly knocks her arm over and erupts in victory.

"I'm telling you— these baby-carrying arms are stronger than people realize."

"Uh, hi?" I say, and Hannah jumps over to hug me.

"Hi!" She squeezes me tight. "Surprise! Rhett texted me yesterday and told me about all that shit Charles is trying to pull. I'm here for moral support. Winnie is with Mom and Paul for the weekend, so I am all yours."

Then she pulls back and points at a photo on the wall.

"Him." She points to the picture I saw the other day of a child-aged Gwen at Lac Beach with a tall, curly haired boy next to her. "This picture looks familiar."

Then the front door swings open, and we spin to find Tanner coming in and shrugging off his jacket.

"Hey, y'all," he announces.

His eyes move across the room, before snapping back to Hannah. She straightens in her spot and Rhett steps over and squeezes my hand, acknowledging that he saw it too.

I sneak a look at Jack, who has such a contented smile on his face while he pets Storm's head. All his children in the same house. His kids, the Auclair kids, and even my sister and me. It's a full house, and he looks to be on the verge of happy tears.

"Long time, no see," Tanner says to Hannah as he slowly approaches her. He shoves his hat into his back pocket and rests his hands on his hips as he stares at her with a smile Hannah deserves.

"It has been a long time."

"Can I get you a beer?" Tanner asks, "Or are we still getting our own drinks?"

"How about I get you one?"

A red flush creeps up his neck as he nods towards the kitchen, letting Hannah lead the way.

"Is it over with her husband?" Rhett asks me quietly.

"She called the attorney," I smile after them.

Gwen shuffles her cards, and just as we begin to deal them out, my phone buzzes in my pocket. It's a text from Myranda.

I am so sorry. The email will have details. Call me with questions.

My stomach drops, and my heart follows suit. My anxiety and intuition sometimes mix, and I can't untangle the two. But right now, I know exactly what this email is going to say. Clicking through my phone, I pull up my email. The buzz of conversation dulls to background noise as the sound of my heart thrashing echoes in my head.

"Lauren? What's wrong?" I think Rhett asks, but I click on the email from a generic Runclave email address.

Dear Lauren Dorada,

Though we found some success with your debut, we have found your second manuscript you are offering us is not the subject matter we are looking for, nor is it what we originally signed you for. Furthermore, due to your unwillingness to change said subject matter, we at Runclave Publishing have decided to not accept any further work from you at this time. In the future, if you find yourself more willing to join our team as a collaborative and moldable partner, we would be willing to listen through your agent, but at this time, you are no longer contracted by our publishing house.

Good luck in your future endeavors.

C. Runclave and Associates

I don't remember leaving the house; I don't remember running across the driveway. But I am on my couch back in the cabin, watching the fire crackle in front of me with a blanket over my shoulders. Rhett is pacing. Hannah is cleaning up the mess of pillows and blankets we didn't bother to clean up earlier. She smiles but doesn't say a thing.

It's over. I'm over. Rhett mentions something about packing up and driving to Chicago, leaving Hannah with me, while he ups and storms the Runclave offices himself.

"He didn't even give me a chance to prove it. I had a deadline. I was supposed to have more time. Myranda even said I had time," I say weakly.

"I'll call Myranda—" Rhett begins to say, but I shake my head and pull the blanket tighter around me.

"It's no use. He has her wrapped around his finger. Her allegiance is to him. It always has been."

"Obedience is more like it." Hannah shakes her head.

"It's over," I say, implying the book, but my fear that it's greater than that settles deep into my bones. If I don't have a career in writing, then I'll have to go back to teaching. And soon, the dominoes begin to fall in my mind. And they end with me having to go back home.

"What about self-publishing? Can you do that?" Hannah asks.

"I could. But I wouldn't make a living off of it. Not to start, at least."

If I watch Rhett any closer, I think I would see steam come off his head. His stoic face is a flurry of anger.

"I can't believe he would do this." Rhett shakes his head. "I know he's a shitty person, but this is low."

The three of us sit quiet for a moment longer before Hannah chimes in. "What's next? We can't change what's already been done, but we can figure out what's next, right?"

I shrug. "What's next would be finishing this book for it to sit on a shelf back at Mom and Paul's house while I stare at the bedroom ceiling, questioning where things went wrong."

Rhett's eyes shoot up to me. "Your *parents'* shelf?"

"I can't stay here, Rhett. Not without a job. I can't just slip into a teaching job here and—"

"Hey, hey, hey." He turns to me. "You're jumping way ahead of yourself. We can still find another agent, and they could help you find another publisher—"

"What publisher wants the baggage of all of this. It gets difficult."

"Of course it will be difficult." Hannah grabs my hands in

hers. "Leaving Ethan is going to be difficult. Getting full custody of Winnie is going to be difficult. Finding a new home will be difficult, but it's worth it. Your career is worth it. Isn't it? I mean you quit teaching, upped your life and relocated to the city for it. What's stopping you now? This is worth investing into, Lauren. Don't let Charles Runclave tell you otherwise."

I squeeze her hands back and blow out a long breath. When I left teaching and came to the city, I had nothing to lose. I left a shitty job and walked into my dream job. But now, I have everything to lose. This cabin. This job. Rhett.

Rhett comes over and kneels next to me. "First thing in the morning, we are going to start finishing this book and then find another agent or publisher to pick it up."

"And until then?" I ask.

Hannah leans over and picks up my phone. "We are going to block Myranda's number and eat shitty food and watch anything that isn't children's TV shows. The worst has happened. It's only up from here."

"I'll go get some food from the house plated up," Rhett says quickly. "I'll be right back."

Once Rhett leaves, Hannah nudges me. "I like him."

"Me too," I admit.

"Were you serious about moving out here?"

I hike my shoulders up and let them drop. "I thought I could be. But without a job, I don't know how I can stay."

"Well, you encouraged me to be brave enough to leave Ethan. Now I am going to encourage you to be brave enough to stay and figure it out."

Moments later, Rhett is back with two plates full of food then is walking right back out again.

"Are you not staying?" Hannah asks him before I even have the chance.

"Sister time." He smiles. "Call me if you need me." He steps over and kisses my head. "We will get started first thing tomorrow. We will finish up this manuscript and get this figured out. I'll be back before bed."

"I officially filed for divorce," Hannah says when we are alone again. "I served him the papers before I came up."

My eyes snap to hers. "What?"

"I called Paul's attorney; I filed and served Ethan with the papers. And I am petitioning for full custody."

"Do you think he's going to fight?"

She smiles a smile only a mother could. "I'd like to see him try."

42

NOW

The sun beams in while Rhett and I work at the kitchen table. Hannah has decided to make breakfast and coffee and stay for another day, at least. She tells me it's on my behalf, but I have other theories.

"I moved back in with Mom and Paul," she says, dropping more toast in the toaster.

"How has Mom been?" I ask gently, gauging what my life might be like in just a couple of weeks.

"Fine, actually. She's still Mom. But Winnie loves being there. She and Paul are two peas in a pod."

My phone buzzes next to me, and I pick it up. There's a text from Tanner.

Nice seeing you yesterday and not just hearing your voice over the phone. I'm taking you up on that coffee you promised me.

I flip the phone over and realize that it's not my phone. It's Hannah's.

"Hannah." I hold it up to her. She blushes like a schoolgirl and types a quick response before shoving the phone into her pocket, smiling.

"You guys are good, right?" She asks suddenly. "I can go into town for a bit?"

I shake my head and bite my tongue. But she sees my smile, kisses my head, and is out the door.

"What's that about?" Rhett asks.

"She's getting coffee with Tanner."

Rhett's eyebrows shoot up. "It's about time."

"It really is."

I look at him over the kitchen table and the steaming cups of coffee between us. He talks about different agents he could contact. His mom's agent, though retired, may have some connections. He also talks about some publishers we could call. And though his hope is palpable, I can't find it myself. Every part of me feels like this is the end. His excitement is only met with my hesitation. The same glimmer of hope I felt yesterday was gone by the time I woke up. It felt too good to let myself believe that I could stay. My body is restless with the anxiety of it all.

By lunchtime, we have a spreadsheet of options, and Hannah comes back with a giddy look on her face.

"How was Tanner?" Rhett asks without looking up, a playful smirk on his lips.

"Good." Hannah smiles. She drops some carryout bags on the counter. "Really good."

I decide to take a break, and against my better judgment, I check my email. And when I do, I see twelve emails from Myranda. I have half a mind to delete them, but my curiosity gets the better of me. I open the most recent email. She said she was on her way, first thing this morning. I'm doing the math in my head when I see a car pull up in the driveway.

"No shit." I shake my head and stand; Rhett's eyes follow me as I open the front door.

"What do you want?" I call out, ready to send her away.

"No. What do *you* want?" She lifts up a stack of envelopes in her hand. "I wouldn't be a very good agent if I didn't have other offers lined up in case Charles lost his goddamn mind, now, would I?" She approaches the steps. "As your friend, I am so, so sorry. But as your agent? This is the best thing that has happened to your career."

I'm still confused by seeing her here, but I step aside and let her walk past me and inside. She drops down the stack of envelopes on the table.

"Look at them." Myranda points at the stack.

I pick a few up off the top. Anne Birch Publishing. Hawthorne Publishing. Sibley and Horan Publishing.

Bird and Darce Publishing House, Los Angeles.

"Is this—" I begin, and she smiles.

"Open it," Myranda says.

I carefully pry it open with shaking hands.

Dearest Myranda Grant and Lauren Dorada,

Thank you for reaching out. We were thrilled to be hearing from you regarding your next novel. We are sorry to hear of the unfortunate handling by your previous publisher, but in the end, we believe this is a step in the right direction. We would love to fly you both out and discuss a deal much fairer and to Ms. Dorada regarding her works. We are big fans of your work and look forward to a possible partnership.

Will look to hear from you soon,

Heather Bird

Bird and Darce Publishing House

Los Angeles, California

. . .

My eyes are filled with tears when I look up at the eager faces looking back at me. "How?"

"Runclave's wife left him six months ago," Myranda says. "It was bad. I think he iced her out too long this time, and she bailed. So he's been losing it. He's been drinking and cutting off deals every chance he gets. He's self-sabotaging. I've been looking at other options since last winter. It's why I missed your New Year's Eve party. I was in California meeting with some publishers in person to get them on board. I've started hearing back over this summer, but they all wanted a full manuscript before talking numbers, so I wanted to wait and see all your options before presenting them to you. You have your choice. You said you wanted more money on your next contract. Well, girl, you got it."

"What if Runclave didn't cut me off?" I ask.

"I was planning on coming to you next week anyway. I had a flight booked and everything. Charles just forced my hand, and here I am, having to drive farther than I have driven in years."

I look through the envelopes again. The disbelief has rendered me speechless. Motionless.

"We'll give you a minute," Hannah says and pulls Myranda out to the front deck.

Rhett picks up the envelopes, too, and looks through the Bird and Darce offer. Then he looks up at me.

"Lauren . . . you could go anywhere. You could go to California; they could get you a big-time editor. This is huge for you. Or you could go to New York. You won't have to settle here."

I notice his emphasis, intentional or not, on *here.* Like it was some backup option I never wanted in the first place. And suddenly these papers feel meaningless. He thinks I'm gone, that I have my ticket out and that I'm leaving him.

When in reality, what's in my hands is my ticket home.

"Rhett. If they are that interested in my work, then they will let me keep my editor, and I'll stay here," I say. "If it's not you editing my books, then I'm not interested in any of these offers anyway. This. You. Was never settling for me. I just never thought I could ever actually obtain it."

"You're leaving the city and the chance of bumping into some important people in LA for a cabin in northern Michigan?"

"Of course I'm leaving for Michigan." I laugh.

In a single step, Rhett has me wrapped in his arms, his face buried in my neck. In my hands is the offer of a lifetime. Around me is a place that has woven itself into my heart and a place I will never be the same because of. But in my arms is the love of a lifetime.

People leave for all kinds of reasons. They leave out of fear, they leave out of cowardice, or they leave out of bravery, or out of love. But then they also arrive. Sometimes to something less, but also, sometimes, to something more.

So much more.

43

FIVE MONTHS LATER

Spring came in softly with continuous rain that we didn't shake until May. Rhett and I have stayed locked inside the cabin, working on the next manuscripts to send off to Bird and Darce. And now, on the first properly warm day, Rhett has dragged me up to the lookout spot with the bribe of a thermos of coffee and a view of the tulips. The ones he and his dad planted in the fall for his mom.

I've been living in Green Branch for almost nine months now. Rhett moved into the cabin when we got back from signing each of our own book deals with Bird and Darce in California. And we hit the ground running. Spending our days at the table or the diner, working until we couldn't keep our eyes open anymore.

"You know I love you, right?" Rhett leans over, as we sit in what we now consider our spot. Watching the green return to the tree-lined horizon, he pulls my legs over his lap. His fingers press into my thigh like he's holding me from floating away.

I peek over at him, and his cheeks are flushed. "Of course I know that. I love you too."

"I mean, I love you in a way that everything else seems so

secondary. You know? I love editing your work. I love writing. But loving you?" He shakes his head and clenches his jaw. "Loving you is the very best thing I get to do. And I'm not perfect at it. I still struggle talking about hard things, but Lauren, I want to spend the rest of my life trying to be worthy of your love."

I squeeze his hand as I gaze into his nervous eyes, my heart thumping faster and faster. "What are you saying?"

"I'm *asking* . . ." He reaches for the thermos from the basket and hands it to me.

The moment I take it, I realize there is no coffee in it.

He tilts his head towards it. "Open it."

I twist off the lid and tip a little velvet box out into my hand.

"Rhett." My breath is drawn from my lungs as I stare at it.

"Laure." He takes the box and flicks it open to reveal a thin gold band with a green emerald at its center. "I want none of this life if it's not with you. Will you *please* marry me?"

My arms are around his neck, and I'm crying before he can place the ring on my hand.

"Is that a yes?" he asks into my hair.

I lean back to meet his eyes. He wipes my tears as I wipe his. "*Yes*. Of course it's a yes."

He takes his mom's ring out of the box and places it on my finger with shaking hands.

"So," he kisses the top of my head. "Want to head to the diner?"

"Where else would we celebrate?" I kiss him again and know that beyond a shadow of a doubt I have ended up where happy endings begin.

But when we pull up in front of the diner, I see the crowd through the windows.

"Rhett." My voice is full of warning as I lean back into his passenger seat.

He squeezes my hand, then comes around to my door, swinging it open.

"Come on." He smiles so sweetly. "Mayben and Gwen insisted. We both know I can't control the women in my life."

I laugh at the truth, slide out of the truck, and let him place his hand on my lower back and kiss my head.

When we step inside the diner, the crowd of people all yell their congratulations. The Atwoods. The Auclairs. Dollie. And I feel that familiar burning sensation behind my nose as I fight my wavering bottom lip.

"We all really hoped you were going to say yes," Rhett says into my ear before kissing my temple.

At one point in my life, there was nothing lonelier than staff meetings, or concerts, or big, full rooms. There was nothing that made me feel more insignificant than crowds and big family dinners. But now, as I look at this packed room with balloons and streamers and glittering decorations, I realize that since stepping foot in this town, I have felt nothing isolating or lonely about it. I guess to be loved is to be known. And to be loved is to be seen in the busiest place you know.

EPILOGUE | ONE MONTH LATER

June has come, and I can't shake this stomach bug. Rhett and I drove down to Illinois for the final hearing for Hannah and Ethan's divorce last week, and now we're back again for Winnie's Spring dance recital tonight. The entire drive down the last week, I was nauseous. I kept my eyes on the horizon, the window cracked, and my body still. This time, so far, has been just as bad. Halfway here, Rhett pulled off to a gas station, where he bought me a ginger ale. The drink that he swore was his mother's cure-all for any sickness. He even jokingly threw a pregnancy test on the counter, at which I rolled my eyes because, of course, I've been on birth control.

My attention is pulled away from the nausea now as we stand in the lobby of my old high school where Winnie's recital is being held. We are waiting on Hannah to bring us the tickets when a tall, golden-haired man walks in the front doors with a bouquet of flowers in hand.

"Tanner?" I ask incredulously.

"Paul said it was okay that I came," he insists as he approaches, then shakes Paul's hand and then my mom's.

"You were able to get work off?" Rhett asks. "I wasn't sure if you'd make it in time."

"You knew?" Now I direct my question at Rhett, who is smacking Tanner on the arm.

"We knew you would ruin the surprise." Mom smirks, then tips her head toward the hall.

We turn and watch as Hannah comes through the crowd, her hair in loose waves and tucked behind her ears. The moment she lays her dark eyes on Tanner, her strong strides slow. But the look on her face says it all.

It's been six months since she filed for divorce form Ethan, and she's been playing it safe as the proceedings went forward. She didn't want to give him or his family any leverage over her. She didn't travel with Winnie; she wasn't out dating like Ethan was. She played it safe and strong. And it paid off. Because now, she has her daughter, her freedom, and a look on her face that she only has when Tanner Auclair is in the room.

As she approaches, it's clear. Hannah can play it safe and try to fight these feelings all she wants, but the way her entire demeanor softens, I have a feeling there will be no real fight at all. Tanner hasn't backed down yet and after the recital when he gives Winnie the flowers he picked for her, I have a pretty damn good feeling he isn't going to.

Rhett and I drive back home instead of staying the night because I want nothing more than to crawl into my bed and wait for this nausea to pass. But twenty-four hours later, I am calling my big sister crying, with a manuscript to write, a wedding to plan, and two dark-red lines on a pink plastic test.

ACKNOWLEDGMENTS

This book wouldn't have been possible, first and foremost, without my parents. They have rallied me on for years and years as I wrote and rewrote versions of this story and other stories. They have believed in me incessantly, and I couldn't be more thankful to them for that.

Thank you to my dear family and friends — Morgan, Allie, Ashley, and Sarah — who got rough copies of this story and cheered me on. Your encouragement helped me believe that this venture was worth pursuing. So, thank you. Thank you for taking the time to read my work and be honest with me.

Thank you to my editors, Carly Catt of Catt Editing and Morgan Tylutki.

Thank you to Austin Drake of Bottle Cap Creative for creating the cover of my dreams. The moment I saw your work, I knew my cover needed you, and boy, was I right. You captured a moment in time, and I will forever be thankful for your art.

Darcie. Oh, my golden girl, the hours you have spent at my side while I wrote obsessively can't be counted. You are, quite literally, the best thing that happened to me. Hence why I released this book on your birthday. I wanted my two babies to be born on the same day.

To you, the reader. Thanks for tanking a chance on my book and coming on this little adventure with me.

And finally, to myself. Because I worked my ass off on this story, and though it isn't perfect, it's mine, and I'm damn proud of it.

And to younger me. You took the time to fill notebooks, and when that didn't cut it, spent all your money on a four-hundred-dollar laptop in high school to write faster. You believed in us even then.

To Lauren and Rhett, love ya both.

Can't wait for everyone to spend a summer in Green Branch with me soon... I'll save you a seat on the front porch near the clothesline.

Talk soon,
Allison

ABOUT THE AUTHOR

Allison is lover of stories, fall, her dog, and her home state of Michigan. She lives for anything cozy. Throw blankets, candles, bonfires, and lamp light. She doesn't remember a time when she wasn't a reader. So, writing and creating stories was just an evolution of that. She wants nothing more than to get lost in a world that's not her own for a while and she hopes she can deliver that to others.

If she is not writing, she is reading, in the hot tub, or with her dog, and usually a combination of all three with a Diet Coke and lime. Find Allison on social media. @allisonlderosia on Instagram and allisonderosia.com to sign up for her newsletter.